DEATH ON CACHE LAKE

Dan Woll
John W. Lyon

LEGAL INFORMATION

ISBN: 1937391043
ISBN-13: 978-1-937391-04-1
eISBN: 978-1-937391-05-8

Edited, designed, printed and distributed by Romeii, LLC.
eBook conversion and distribution by Romeii, LLC.
Visit our website at ebooks.romeii.com

In Memory of
John W. Lyon

ACKNOWLEDGMENTS

This story began a long time ago. I wrote a vignette about a murder in the north woods. I sent it to a friend, John Lyon, to see what he thought. Much later he returned it, wrapped in a novel. That was a quarter century ago. We kicked it around and re-worked it. In the late 1990s, I shared it with more friends, Tom Conway, Sandy Hermundson, Gerry Hill, Pam Katner, Darlene Mikla, Pete Nusbaum, and Darcy Veach. They were kind enough to read it and smile, albeit wanly. It was not very good. The plot was cliché and the story was too cute by half. It sat.

A few years ago, I was thinking about college, unrest in the sixties, why it all happened the way it did and questions that are still unanswered. I realized I could make up answers in a novel. Out went the old storyline, in went a plot reveal with historical roots, and we kept the good stuff about trucks and rock climbing and trains and the north woods. We've taken great liberties to make a story. This is a work of fiction.

As the new story took root, I was encouraged by these key readers—in alphabetical order: Samantha Bluhm, Missy Brown, El Capitan climbing partner Al Czecholinski, Soul Brother Ed Dobry, Rick Eloranta, Mike Grisham, Sandy Grisham, Jenn Johnson, Shelly Johnson, Linda Larsen, Dave Larson, Diwaine Larson, Jeanne Larson, Jenny Marietta, Paul Marietta, Jim Marnie, Gerry Mikla, Chris Rivard, Kim Robel, Jim Peterson, Beth Shockey-Woll, Jenny Updike, and Kris Ylikopsa, Also thanks to Gerry Hill and Dee Simpson for inspiration and the best dog ever, Mickey, who makes an appearance in Chapter 31.

If I left you out, great apologies. I dedicate the book to my mother and father, my wife Beth, and our children, Jenny, Katie, and Shelley. (John wrote the naughty parts, guys).

The book would have never become a reality without the expertise of Jeff Redmon and Redmonlaw, Romeii Publishing and Steve Delmont, the excellent editing of Melissa Gilman, and the breathtaking cover photography of Kim Robel. I concur with co-author John who offers a nod to a hard-headed superintendent from our past whose wisdom ran deeper than most realize.

I've been knocked down in life so many times that I've lost count other than so far I've gotten up one more time than I hit the deck. I was unable to do it alone. In summary, this book is a paean to those who never give up on their family and friends and who are always there to help. Theirs is a blessed power that binds the universe together more strongly than gravity.

—*Dan Woll*

DEDICATION

Co-author John Lyon wrote the following dedication shortly before he died. I read it aloud at his funeral—DW

I would like to acknowledge Denman Kramer, a WWII vet who built runways in the South Pacific and later became Superintendent of the Hydroelectric Dam at Prairie du Sac on the Lower Wisconsin River. When asked about finding dynamite attached to one of the large transformers feeding the Badger Ordinance area, early in 1970 he said, "That's one night's sleep I'll never get back."

There is another superintendent to acknowledge, Jerry Jones, for wisdom from long ago and far away.

I would like to mention my dad who died several years ago and almost never said no to our sometimes crazy projects. However, he did say no motorcycles, which is why we both have them now. My mom now lives in Muskego at a health care facility about 10 miles from the family farm where some of this fiction may have taken place. Bless all who have been caregivers at Tudor Oaks.

Hello to fishing buddies Jerry Rosso, Tom Conway, Dan Woll, Bobbie Hanko, my brother Jim, Bob and Mickey Pauss, Marshall, Ganzerow, and others including the Shuppe Brothers, the Stoughton group and The Sauk Lanes fishing guys for Canada and Lake Michigan trips and my cousins, Tom, Howard, Mark, Kris (Greg), and the younger fifteen or so, and cousins-in-laws. Bill Henning and Jim Pfaff provided inspiration for important parts of the story. If I left you out I didn't mean to, call me and let me know.

I want to thank the Sauk Prairie H.S. Music Department teachers Karen & Sue, parents, and students who allowed me to join them these past years. You have no idea how much you all have helped me, and the Sauk Prairie Lions who continue to do good deeds in quiet ways.

In many ways this book is for my wife who has now passed away, my three children, Matthew, Sara and Carrie who made me grow up, become a better person, and turn my hair gray in the process.

John Lyon
P.S. Dan wrote the naughty parts.

CONTENTS

DAN WOLL and JOHN W. LYON

Chapter 1
The Summit of El Capitan

Yosemite Park, California
The Future

The summit of El Capitan in winter is one of the loneliest places on earth.

Almost a mile above the canyon floor, a lone skier gingerly sidestepped his way toward the sheer precipice. When he was close enough to see the Merced River thousands of feet below, he stopped and stood motionless in this chapel of alpine peace. He took a deep breath, carefully turned and herringboned back up the sloping summit plateau to the climbers' tree 100 yards back from the lip of the greatest climbing wall in North America.

John had been to this tree over 40 years before, when climbing the immense vertical face of El Cap was still a big deal. At that time, only a handful of climbers, the best in the world, had found their way up that vertical desert. He had followed the hikers' trail ten miles up the rugged backside slopes and forests to wait at the top and see if his friend, Caleb, would join the ranks of the few who had conquered El Capitan's fearsome Salathe Wall.

Caleb and his Swedish climbing partner had been on the wall for almost seven days when John reached the top. John remembered standing alone, waiting and thinking about how he had advised his friend to bring more than four days of water. Caleb never was one to listen. With only two years of climbing under his belt, all on small crags in Wisconsin, Caleb was under-prepared. His friends knew it, and found ways to decline his entreaties to partner with him on an ascent of the Salathe Wall. No matter, he headed out on his red Norton 850 Commando motorcycle with nothing but a rope, a sleeping bag, and a willingness to die trying. John followed him in his old GMC pickup.

In Yosemite, they met a Swede who barely spoke English. The foreigner had come to America to escape the demons that were assaulting his brilliant mind, by climbing the most famous rock wall in the world. There would be no time to think about demons, or self, only the immense overhanging granite wall. The Swede shared no common language, only the will to climb and survive. John had been their support. For the first three days, he watched with binoculars from a camp he had set up in the valley floor near the icy Merced River.

Now, standing on top of the fearsome summit, in two feet of snow, John recalled the 100 degree temperature that had assaulted his friends after their water had run out. In his mind's eye, time rewound and he was 21 years old, looking through the telephoto lens as Caleb fell and pulled out a piton while surmounting the giant roof. The climber's scream echoed over the valley floor from a thousand feet above as he rocketed out and came to halt 70 feet below his last anchor. Held by one trembling piton, Caleb and his partner pendulmed back and forth on either end of their 165 foot climbing rope like cuckoo clock weights. Finally, they stopped... and began climbing again. John knew then they were going to make it. He broke camp and started hiking up to meet them.

That was a long time ago.

He looked at the old pine tree, draped with dozens of ruined climbing shoes. It was a tradition, that at the top, triumphant climbers would take off their shoes, ruined by the razor sharp crystal granite of El Cap and tie them in the tree. Caleb and Bjorn had done that when there were only a few shoes in the tree. John wondered if theirs were still up there.

John retrieved his pack and took out a thick leather notebook. His mittens hampered him. He removed them, took out a pen and opened the journal to the last pages. Standing in the pink alpenglow of early winter afternoon, he painstakingly added a few sentences, then looked up with tears streaking his cheek, and closed the book. John reached in the pack one more time for a small waterproof filing box and a heavy duty black garbage bag. He wrapped the manuscript in the bag, put it in the box, and locked it with a small brass colored Yale padlock.

There was a length of red climber's rope slung around his shoulder. It was old, faded and frayed, left over from Caleb's climbing days. John tossed one end over a branch and then joined it to the other end with the grapevine knot that Caleb and the climbers had taught him. Finally, he reached in his pocket and pulled out the forty-year-old carabiner snap link that had held his friend's fall so long ago. John used the carabiner to clip the handle of the box to the loop of rope hanging from the old skeletal pine tree. Stepping back, he watched his work rock back and forth in the fading sunlight.

He turned back into the tracks he had made coming and going to the lip. He poled. Slowly at first, gravity did its work and accelerated him toward the edge. Thousands of miles of mountain skiing experience overrode any hesitation he might have felt. Standing straight and relaxed, he rocketed toward the abyss. When he reached the edge, he bent his knees and exploded outward into the crimson sunset and arctic air, 4,000 feet above the Merced Valley.

DAN WOLL and JOHN W. LYON

Chapter 2
The Night It Stuck

The Blue Hills, Wisconsin
December 11, 1968

You never think about it at the time, but you look back years later and you can pick out the moment a friendship stuck. For Caleb and me, the friendship stuck the night the Pontiac did.

The gold Pontiac Bonneville's wide track tires rolled and slipped on the drifting downhill path through the birch and maple forest. White pulpy snow plopped and slid down the windshield. The wipers worked as a team until they stalled on a heavy clump in the corner. A Wisconsin full moon on that frigid night made headlights redundant. Caleb pointed the car through the opening in the trees, leaning so far forward that his chin almost rested on top of the steering wheel.

We were on an unplowed road that a log skidder had tracked. Now it was snowing again and quickly covering up the tracks. I wished we had taken Highway 8 to Ward instead of trying to save precious bar time by looking for the shortcut over the Blue Hills. Jim Mertah had told us to take the first left at the top of the hill, warning us not to mistake it for any of the numerous logging roads that snaked off through the woods.

As soon as we turned off, I knew we had gone wrong. Caleb tried to back up. The car's tires gained traction for a second, and we jumped violently to the side. I suggested that we quit while we were ahead and walk back to the road and then down to the nearest farm. He answered by jamming the Hurst shifter into reverse, then rocking forward and over a rut toward a steep downhill section. Caleb accelerated in order to jerk the Bonneville out of a skid as we slid down the logging road. Gravity took care of the rest. A few minutes of downhill sliding later, I wished I had been more forceful in pointing out the consequences of planting oneself at the bottom of a trail-less valley in December.

I tried again, "Caleb, I don't think we should go any further."

Caleb replied, "Relax, John. This road has got to come out somewhere. It wouldn't just stop. We're in a little deeper snow now and it's just covering it up."

Big flakes loaded the glass. The gold car, Caleb's pride and joy, slid one final time. I felt the rear end drop and then lurch off. We had found the ditch. Caleb reached over and stabbed the AM radio switch, depriving us of the chorus from Tommy James and the Shondells' "Hanky Panky."

Caleb looked at me. "Shit."

I shook my head and said, "Well put. Get your boots on. We're going for a hike." I zipped my jacket and pushed the low-slung door open against the snowbank. I had worn my hunting boots to the grade school basketball game because it was already snowing when I put the kids on the bus. I even coached in them that night. Caleb looked at his black low top Chuck Taylors.

"We're not walking. I'll push. You drive." Fifteen minutes later, his pants and sneakers were sopped with cold snow melt, and his sweatshirt was soaked from his efforts. The car looked the same. Without saying a word he turned and trudged into the woods. Great. More pathfinding. Trees reached over the roadway, eerily silhouetted by the full moon. By the time I caught up with him, he had wandered in a small circle and come out back on the path down the hill. He was not in a mood to talk. I was pissed, but not too pissed to point out that he was going further into the woods. The wind picked up. New snow was piled up four inches thick on freshly cut stumps by the time we came to a small clearing. The trail spread out in different directions like fingers on a hand. It was time for the speech.

"Caleb, we shouldn't keep going further. This is not a road. It is a dead end. There is no help down here. You are on a goddamn logging trail!"

He snapped back, "Screw that! I'm telling you John, this trail goes somewhere. I'm going."

I felt hot. I was on the verge of strangling him. "Listen to me. How far do you think you're going to go into the woods?"

He turned and gave me Groucho Marx, "Halfway. Then I'll be going out."

My anger dissipated like summer rain clouds blown out by a south wind. I bent over, hands on knees, incapacitated by the absurdity of Caleb in the woods. "What in the hell did Wisconsin ever do to deserve you?"

"All right, all right!" Caleb said. "I'm wrong. So what do you recommend?"

The storm was abating. I studied the crisp black sky and watched my breath float toward the clouds, rapidly moving across the lonely whiteness of the full moon.

"OK. It's the middle of the winter. We're in the middle of a storm, and we're in the middle of the woods. The trail ends here, or maybe right over there by that… Good Lord!"

I squinted through the snowflakes and focused on the gray white ghost of a log skidder. I ran toward it. "It's a log skidder! A John Deere!" I moved closer and put my hand out and felt the huge tire chains.

Caleb was grasping for a concept. His New Jersey upbringing was in remission but unlikely to ever be permanently cured. "What's a log skidder?"

I ignored him and scrambled between the tires and up to the seat. I brushed off the snow and sat down. It was four-wheel drive, had a cable winch, and the same controls as my dad's 3020 John Deere back on the farm. Years ago, I'd plowed hundreds of acres with that trusty green and yellow sweetheart of a tractor.

Caleb sensed a plan coming together. "What can you do with it?"

His voice seemed to be coming from far below me. The wind swirled the snow around the tires of the huge machine. I fumbled for a light switch, found it and pulled. Nothing. The farmer part of my mind kicked in. Of course there were no lights. They'd all be busted off or burned out, just like some old farm tractor that had seen rough use. The hell with lights. The moon would do.

The jingle of chains told me that Caleb was climbing up. "Get down for a minute until I figure this thing out. I don't want you to get tangled up."

"Good idea. But don't go anywhere without me."

"All right." I felt for the starter control. If it was an industrial version it might have a key switch. Not this one. It was just the good old button. When I pushed it, a few chugging noises joined the wind. It was a diesel like Dad's. I hoped it wasn't a cold-blooded rascal that wouldn't fire in the low temperature. I tried again. She started to purr. It had a hand throttle and a foot feed. I tapped it and made it snort a little. Next the hydraulics. They were in a familiar location. I felt comfortable as the front blade lifted at my command. I checked the transmission and shouted over the roar of the huge machine, "I'm going to try low reverse!" It was just like the farm tractor I'd run, although the hinged middle made the steering feel different.

"Let's go! Climb on board!"

Caleb clambered up and off we went. I smiled but drove slowly. We were probably unstoppable, but I did not want to chance a run-in with a huge boulder or monster tree stump. I kept to what I could make out of the trail, and in about a quarter mile we found the Bonneville. When we got there we conferred before Caleb jumped down. I lowered the skidder's blade and matched it to the front bumper of the Bonneville. Caleb started the car, put it in reverse, and signaled with his lights. I moved forward in low and pushed that sucker all the way back up the hill to the plowed blacktop of Bluff Road.

"OK, I'll buzz this thing back down the hill. You wait here. It'll only take a few minutes." I was the picture of early twenties hubris sitting in the dented roll bar cage of the old skidder. Caleb stood by the tires which put him at eye level with my boots.

"No way. I want to drive this baby." He hopped up and left the Pontiac idling on the road with its parking lights lit. I turned the skidder around and aimed it down the hill and put it in park. We changed places. I showed him the throttle and the shift selector. Caleb put it in gear, keeping it in low idle for the first few minutes and then he drove that old beauty down the hill. There were a few bumps and close calls but soon, he had a basic command of operating a John Deere. He could not know the notoriety he would achieve the next time he put this skill to use, but that dark time was far in the future.

We chugged and jingled down fresh tracks glistening from the moon light which filtered through the trees. It felt good to extract ourselves from a monumental mess with no help. That's always the way it was with us. We would get to the bar in plenty of time for Jim Mertah's birthday party. As I hung on to the cab, I felt the power of the old machine throb up my arms all the way to my shoulders. I looked at Caleb in the falling snow. I could see him grinning. I grinned back and felt the snow touch my tongue and teeth. We parked the John Deere on the treaded depressions exactly where the big wheels had rested a half hour earlier. We killed the engine and looked up at chiaroscuro patterns made by branches against the timeless sky.

Caleb said, "Give me a couple of bucks." He grabbed my offering and matched them with a couple of his own.

"Where we gonna put these?"

"Under the seat."

I reached down and lifted the cushion that covered a rectangular enclosed area revealing a tool kit and extra oil. I tucked the folded bills between a vise grip and some links of chain.

"We're outta here!"

I agreed. "There's a party waiting. They're not going to believe this." We hiked up the trail—a diehard pathfinder from New Jersey and the farm kid mechanic.

"What a story! Two guys. Middle of the woods. Middle of the night. A snowstorm…"

We never did tell the story. Until now. I'm the only one left to tell it and what came afterwards all those years ago, and how we rewrote American history.

By the time we got to the 81-Z Club a fight had broken out. Caleb waded into the middle of it, trying to break it up, and ended up partying with a logger who complimented him on his ability to take a punch. Later on he won ten dollars when they bet him he couldn't eat a pound of raw liver. I wandered around and tried to curry favors with the few available women unlucky enough to find themselves in the 81-Z.

By 4:00 a.m. the town grader had gone through, and Caleb ushered me back to the Bonneville. He didn't say much on the way back to Winchester, although he did hum along with Hank Williams as the early morning AM radio signal crackled through the valley. When he let me out at my cheap apartment across from the river, he gave me a dopey grin and said, "Two guys! Middle of the woods. Middle of the night. A snowstorm…"

I knew we were going to be friends for a long time.

DAN WOLL and JOHN W. LYON

Chapter 3
Black Water

Eagle Chain of Lakes, Ontario, Canada
October 23, 1970

I knew it wasn't good when I heard the first loud report from the ice. It was unmistakable over the rumble of the aging GMC truck engine. The old rubber tires slipped, pulling the tail end of the truck to the right every time I accelerated. It was hard enough keeping on course over the frozen wilderness lake without the distraction of the cracking noises. The explosive cracks and snaps of breaking ice aggravated the fear coursing from the pit of my stomach to my Adam's apple. As I searched the ice ahead, I hoped the fissure was splitting behind and away from the slow moving black and green 1942 General Motors farm truck. I flashed back to my Dad's advice when he first saw my restored truck. He said to me, "John, that truck's going to be worth a lot of money some day. I hope you take care of it."

Sorry Dad.

The Eagle Chain of Lakes is over 150 miles long. The West Arm where I had eased the old truck off the Canadian Pacific rails was desolate except for the one resort outpost located seventeen miles from town. My goal was to beat the pink and charcoal sunset to Cabin #2 at the falls beneath Buzzard Lake. I had almost done that when winter's icy fingers snapped.

13

Not too many years before in happier times I fished these waters with my friend Caleb. Now my future seemed as bleak as the weather. Through the first swirls of snow in the gray afternoon, I spotted one of the few landmarks I remembered, The Three Bears, a matched set of boulders about the size of Volkswagens silhouetted against perennially green cedar trees. They were a local landmark marking the entrance to a small channel and a bay of the same name. They also mark where I lost my truck.

The wisps of snow had turned to a lace tablecloth shaking in the sky. My visibility was reduced but it did not matter. The crack was under the truck. The sudden drop of the wheels to water was arrested by the old bumper springs catching on the lip of the ice. In true General Motors fashion, the jolt was carried directly up the steering column to the wheel, knocking the wind out of me and killing the old six cylinder engine. The weight of the rear axle generated more cracks in the ice.

For a moment I could not breathe. I hadn't had the wind knocked out of me since I fell through the hay chute when I was twelve years old. My recovery time had not improved. I had to move, but I needed air. I was afraid of the black water showing through the yawning fissures in the ice. My lungs caught and I sucked in icy cold air. The old truck sat temporarily on its running boards as deep booming noises came from beneath it. I shoved the door partway open. Wet snow rushed in the cab and plastered my face. I gulped more air in panicked, shallow breaths. I was momentarily aware that the gray sky was getting darker. Water was at the running board. My wind was coming back with each sucking gasp.

I reached behind the seat and pulled out one of the two cased rifles while I started to swing on to the old running board. The momentum from the turn of my body sent the rifle skating out on the ice about 25 feet away. I hoped it was the . 30-.30 but there was no time to check.

I leaned uphill toward the jumble of boxes on the seat. I grabbed the closest one and spun it out on the ice after the rifle. My lurching around was hastening the downward adjustments of the truck. The dark red knapsack was still within reach. As I tensed to jump clear, I grabbed its black shoulder strap. My footing gave way on the slanted running board. Nine times out of ten I would have fallen flat on my ass, but a surge of adrenaline powered my arms as I pushed off the door and clawed and scrambled across the disintegrating ice. I felt the cold, sinewy hands of fear twist my intestines.

Two years earlier Bob Beamon had set a long jump record in the Mexico City Olympics that would last for 23 years. My booted broad jump across the icy black water would have made him proud. The landing, not so much. The ice and cold numbed the pain in my mouth. I looked at the blood spattered on the ice and snow and flashed back to an old high school football saying. Bloody Chiclets. However, upon further review, all my teeth were still there behind a laceration that ordinarily would have justified stitches. The rest of me was fine as long as I did not look back at the hole which had swallowed up my truck and belongings.

Dark freezing water bubbled in the gray cast of a Canadian evening. Snow mixed with foam. The wind picked up and burned my ears. The hole would be refrozen soon the way the temperature was dropping. It was a terrible way to hide my truck. I had planned on parking it up from the shore line, then cutting branches with the axe that was in the back. It was gone and there was nothing to be done about it.

The rifle was on the verge of sliding in the water at the edge of a crack. The back half of the case was wet. I gingerly stretched out, pinched the tip of the case and pulled it to me. I scrambled on all fours to the box and the bag. Gaining confidence, I tiptoed and then ran to the small island and collapsed under an ancient black spruce. I looked back at the black, boiling hole. The truck had been my pride and joy ever since Caleb and I bought it. I reminisced for a lonely, gray, snow-filled moment.

Only the brakes and drive shaft had needed mechanical work. In fact the drive shaft was why the GMC was in good shape. My insurance man told us the story when he signed up the truck. The old farmer who bought the truck new so many years before had driven it into the barn to unload feed. The extension shaft that GM used only on the long box version snapped when one side of the rear axle dropped through a missing floor plank and bound up on a beam below. He probably felt the first pains of the heart attack hauling the feed out of the back of the stranded truck to the grain bin.

After his first ambulance ride, the old gent moved to the nursing home. Twelve years later he died. The 42 GMC stayed in the barn. The estate was settled and the farmer's no good nephew took over the place along with his entire motorcycle club. The truck sat waiting in the barn buried under layers of hay, pigeon shit, and luckily an old sheet of canvas.

The nephew's first crop failure caused the sale of the truck. Hail damaged the marijuana leaves right down to the stalks. Caleb and I thought we needed a truck to haul our motorcycles around. Caleb had a Honda at that time and I had a Bridgestone basket case that broke down regularly. Before we bought the 1942 GMC truck my Bridgestone spent an entire winter in my bedroom, on a table made from a door and two sawhorses. It always needed something. We had to have a way to take the bikes to the motorcycle shop to have them refixed after we fixed them. For $75 the truck was ours. To move the beloved 42 out of the barn, we jacked up the rear axle, planked across the holes in the barn floor, and towed her home.

There would be no jacking up from the hole this time. My mind drifted like the snow. "Cold as ice…numb as ice…that's not nice…" I shook off the frozen stupor that was enveloping me and scanned the rapidly darkening icescape that was the West Arm of Eagle Lake. I had to get to the island and make a fire to dry my boots and generate heat which might see me through the night alive.

This was all because of a blank postcard.

Chapter 4
The Blank Postcard

Winchester, Wisconsin
October 20, 1970

Caleb used to talk about writing a story that would become a screenplay. I gave him a hard time. My practical farm kid side did not see much Hollywood potential on Winchester's main drag, Water Street. But stories do have to start. And so did my haircut. My superintendent had gone past subtle hints when he took me aside to give the Ducks In a Row Talk. The hair wasn't all of it. I was told, "Straighten out your life. Shape up and get your ducks in a row. Take a week. See a counselor. Don't leave town on your own." Then he held out his pink meaty hand for my truck keys. Those were the uneasy days when management teams like the Hortonville, Wisconsin school board could and did fire entire teaching staffs. Taking my personal truck keys away from me, a long-haired, hippie teacher was a breeze, given the arsenal of power administration wielded before the Wisconsin teachers' union woke up and flexed its muscles.

I turned over the keys to my black half ton Chevy pickup reluctantly. In recent years, it had been my wood hauler. My boss, the superintendent of schools, was serious. His stern round face, sharp blue eyes and aggressive stance confirmed the gravity of the situation. Word travels fast in a small town. He didn't even comment about me smashing up my new olive green Firebird and losing my driver's license.

Giving me the last chance was his personal condolence. Clean up my act or say good-bye. It did not matter to him that the school board had more to do with my present state of affairs than most folks knew.

It started as a quiet, small town affair, to the extent that is ever possible in a place like Winchester. I attended meetings, went fishing and hunting up north, and tinkered with model trains. My wife, Carolyn, took up running and became a deacon in church. She was discrete. I was stupid. The car accident she and her male companion died in answered three big questions that had been juicing coffee shop gossip behind my back:

Who?

Why?

When would it end?

Answers:

Jay Karp, School Board President.

Built and acting like one great stud.

It ended right then and there.

Jay was driving when they died. Apparently they were coming back from the golf course. Halfway home he crossed an ancient county bridge, and swerved into the guard rail so hard that one of the pilings collapsed. She was killed instantly on impact. He lingered for a day, but loss of blood and a skull fracture from rocketing into the windshield frame did him in. The whispered musings of the boys in the county shop and sheriff's department implied that there had been some form of hanky-panky leading up to the crash. The deputy's report left it vague.

Several hazy weeks and cases of Canadian Club whiskey later, I decided to follow my superintendent's advice and seek therapy. I turned to the best expert I knew. Ron the Barber. Or as Caleb once playfully penned on a check, "Ron the Butcher." Ronny cashed it.

When I went in for my first consult, the shop was early morning quiet. I heard the small fan riffling the pages of Ron's local Lion's Club calendar behind the quiet conversation of a few regulars. Early is always the best time to go to the old porcelain and glass barber shop. Whoever is there gets in on the coffee hand. The cards are dealt face up and the worst hand buys, unless it is Tuesday, senior citizen day. That's when the high hand buys. Old Harold from Ace Hardware would never play on Tuesdays.

Ronnie once told me that Harold thought I was responsible for the backward card game. The old man was quoted as saying, "That's a bunch of bull. We never had a radical game like that in the old days. Ever since they hired that goddamn

Johnny and that other long haired outside agitator teacher from New Jersey, things have gone to pot—if you know what I mean." Big Wink. But the rest of the gang enjoyed the change of pace. Harold avoided the issue by coming in on Tuesdays at noon, skipping the backward card game, but still catching the rehash of the day's top gossip, which lately was featuring me, John, the guy with the dead young wife and a whole bunch of questions and no answers.

Despite being, "that goddamn Johnny," I took my seat in the gray steel, leather-backed barber chair and listened. Ron pumped the foot pedal, raising me up several inches. Meanwhile, Bob, an old WW II vet, expounded on his view of civil unrest. "...those hippie faggot guys who are afraid to fight in a war for freedom in Viet Nam. Look in the paper. These four guys blew up the Army Math Research Center just down the road in Madison two months ago and they haven't been caught. What is wrong with our police, what about the FBI, the Border Patrol? And can you believe it? It says this one bomber, this Leo Burt, was even on the University crew team. I hope they catch'em."

The coffee hand was breaking up and the players filed out for doughnuts, and more coffee and gossip, at Jill's Bar and Grill. I heard a few mumbled, "How are ya's?" and lifted up my head. Some of the players looked away as they walked out. Their averted eyes made my face heat up with embarrassment.

I sat in the chair but didn't look in the mirror. I dreaded what I might see beyond the blue comb jar and the shave cream machine. Ron and I were alone in the shop. Ron's partner, Lester, had wandered off with the card players. He was sweet on Jill who owned the bar next door. In the mornings Jill served coffee. Lester's coffee breaks could take 45 minutes to an hour on a slow day.

"So, how's it going Johnny?" Ron said as he whipped the fresh apron around my neck. Pausing, he focused on my condition, pulled out an aspirin bottle, handed me a half-full Coke and ordered, "Take four of these. Now shove your head under the sink so I can wash it. You'll feel great in no time."

Ron is also an optimist. I drank, swallowed, and shoved, then poured out my troubles. Being the barber in a small town means you're the central stem in the gossip grape vine. He had heard it all from various sources but was considerate enough not to tell me the details I didn't already know. I still didn't look in the mirror.

When we got to the hair and beard cutting part, Ron took over the conversation. One false move might cost me an ear or something. AIDS was decades away so Ron still finished his haircuts with a razor shave.

"I know it's been rough on you. That part of your life is over though. Only you...your memory makes you go back." He worked in the oil. "...don't do anything hastily. Take a trip and get out of town for a few days. Flush your system. Then go back to what you do best. Teach. Johnny, the community still believes in you." He concluded his Swing Back to Life speech with some lightning brush strokes and a flourish of the towel.

There might have been more, but Lester came back with the self-satisfied grin of a man who has been favored by the sweetheart of Water Street.

"Here's a steeryofoam cup of coffee from Jill for ya, Ron." Ron swished the remains of my beard down the sink. He looked at me and knew I had had enough advice. He changed the subject.

"You weren't the fella to send this postcard as a joke were you?"

He was pointing behind the waiting chair to the Trip Board as he called it. On it were cards from all the guys when they went on vacation. I started when I recognized the three monolithic granite shapes framed by spruce trees on the shore of a Canadian lake. The Three Bears. I crawled out of the black leather chair, shedding pesky hairs from the apron. I pulled away the tack that held the picture postcard. There was no message on the back, but the picture on the front was meant for me. On the shoreline behind the Three Bears, a man who wore the signature Duluth Pack of a serious canoer was lifting an old Grumman over his head. The caption said, "Canoe Portage, Buckhorn Lodge."

Buckhorn Lodge Cabin #2. "Never had so many traveled so far to catch so few." "A great place to hide out but not to fish." Those had been our slogans for the trip. Caleb and I had both agreed at the time that it was our most pathetic fishing trip ever.

I turned over the postcard and saw the cancelled Canadian Queen Elizabeth stamp and the hand printed address.

Winchester Barbershop

Water Street, Winchester, Wisconsin

USA

I could make out September in the smudged postmark but not a date. I recognized the handwriting in the address. Caleb knew I would. I often embarrassed him when we worked together by comparing his penmanship to that of a third-grader showing off cursive before it had been learned thoroughly. I had heard that Caleb was in trouble and that unbelievably, the trouble was a murder charge somewhere in Canada. This card did not look like it came from a prison. I could only conclude that he was on the run, at least when it was mailed.

I sat slowly back in the barber chair.

"Do you get something out of that?" Ron eyed me suspiciously.

Dazed, I did not respond. I noticed a smudge of brown on the card. I thought absently of dried blood. I looked up quickly and stared at the mirror. The gray pallor of my shaved face was rapidly being flushed pink with a warm excitement. For the first time in a long while I wanted to see tomorrow.

I didn't know that my newfound will to live would be put to the test later that night.

DAN WOLL and JOHN W. LYON

Chapter 5
Message in a Bottle or Six

Winchester, Wisconsin
October 20, 1970

The village cops eventually figured out that I had headed north to find Caleb, but I was long gone by then. That night I hiked over to old Mrs. Kensey's where I rented storage. With my emergency bucket of tools I butchered the lock and crept into the damp garage. I stumbled around shielding the flashlight beam until I found an outlet to plug in the charger. As the battery charged, I studied the map I had put in the bucket.

The single taillight and headlights still worked after some fiddling. The radiator was full and the brakes seemed solid. I poured a little gas from the dented, dirty red lawn mower can in the corner into the carburetor. This primed the old beauty for what was to become her final ride to glory. She fired on the first touch of the foot starter button, then coughed to a stop. Not bad for an old truck that had been stored since Caleb left town two years ago.

I set the choke and tried again. This time its steady throb pulsed out the garage door into the night. I eased out on to Water Street and headed up Highway 8 and parts north. It was well past midnight when I stopped at my place. I pulled in the back vacant lot and loaded what belongings I had managed to throw together since the morning's epiphany. It was a sorry collection...a moldy sleeping bag, some

23

camping equipment, a little food, two rifles and an old leather satchel containing jeans and a T-shirt.

North of Eau Claire, I reviewed what I now knew about Caleb's and my situation. I knew that the cops were looking for me for reasons even they did not understand. Somehow, an FBI agent was involved and I was a person of interest. I knew they wanted to question Caleb about bodies that some late season fisherman found in Quetico Provincial Park, north of Ely, Minnesota and the American border, and that I was Caleb's best friend. That's what they told me when they had caught up with me earlier that evening in Winchester and questioned me.

It had not been hard finding me. I was in a bar.

Bill Kelly, one of the county deputies, as well as the overworked, single parent of one of my students, found me when he went off duty. He told me what was up over his first beer. It was my fourth or fifth but who counts? Not me. Not then. As the conversation continued, the postcard began to make a little sense.

We were in Jill's new tavern in town. Being the newest place in town, it wasn't bad. Much oak woodwork and a soft touch on the lighting made a difference. Plus it had a bowling alley and a dance floor. People went there to eat a quick lunch or spend a relaxing evening gossiping about the school district and their local church. Or me. The beer signs behind the bar were subdued. Caleb and I had always been partial to the old revolving Hamm's beer signs with the canoe circling endlessly around the waterfall campsite, but this was tavern nouveau. It would have to do and it did. You could say it had small town class. Ladies approved of their restrooms.

Out of uniform and in casual clothes, the dark-haired cop looked like a vacationing defensive end—from Ireland. It had been a year since his wife died of cancer, and he was just beginning to show an interest in the fairer sex again. With his cold blue eyes and jet black hair, he left a trail of broken hearts all over the county. Unfortunately, he was too dumb to capitalize on it. Think Cyrano de Bergerac with a lower IQ and a .44 magnum. Billy, as the old men, former teachers, and widows knew him, pulled up a stool next to me.

"Hey John, what's up?" he said as he clasped a big hand around the back of my neck and gave it a shake that was both friendly and threatening at the same time. I was still in good standing with the law at that point. He was impressive even out of his deputy's uniform. His bench press muscles flexed beneath the lightweight polo shirt and blue polyester slacks. Realizing that I was expanding my self-pity list, I called over Jill, the barkeep that night.

"Two tall ones, please."

Jill was a tall, muscular, auburn-haired girl, wearing a pastel green blouse and a shorts outfit which attracted big time stares from the softball players at the pool table. She looked at my nearly empty beer glass and Billy's shoulders from across the bar. She looked directly into his Irish blue eyes. She did not want to acknowledge shaggy me. Being part owner, she had standards. I was borderline.

Their eyes met for an instant. I remembered what it once felt like to have time stop like that and wondered if I would ever again share that moment with another. Then she hustled off down to the end of the bar to catch the orders of the softball guys.

Billy let out his breath, "God, I'd like to spend just one night with her."

"Why don't you?"

"What?"

"Can't you tell? She likes you."

"Right. I'm a cop. I only got that because of my Dad. She may be a poor farm kid, but she's smart. One of the profs at the Tech school told me she should be at Madison."

"You telling me you're chicken, right?"

"Listen. Change of subject. You hear from your buddy Caleb?"

"Why?"

He interrupted himself to look across the bar as the frosty glasses were placed in front of us. "Thanks Jill. I like your outfit."

She bit her lip, smiled furtively, and turned back to her business. He blushed.

"I haven't seen him in a year I guess," I said.

He feigned disinterest, "Really? When?" He was rolling circles on the bar using moisture from the cool beer glass. "You should have let the Department know." Forearm muscles rippled lazily.

"It was summer. Before you guys were looking. He wanted me to go on one of those marathon portaging trips of his. I couldn't make it. You know how he is."

Billy made a face. Even bench press Billy called in sick for Caleb's canoe trips. Once was enough. The first year Caleb came to town, he talked Billy into running the ledges on the Brule River during flood stage. Billy's macho pride cost him a compound fracture of his right arm and a splintered thousand dollar Wenonah canoe. Caleb hauled him to a hospital in Superior. Then he offered fifty dollars to a high school kid he found smoking dope in the parking lot to go back and try it again. They not only succeeded, they portaged back and did it twice more. The fourth time they wrecked canoe number two, and Caleb got to try out mouth to mouth resuscitation on the high school kid. Billy rubbed his right forearm thoughtfully, winced, and came back from an unpleasant daydream.

Billy leaned back from the bar. His moves were cat-like. A large cat.

"Yeah, I guess I do know how he is."

The juke box was playing Hank Williams. I once conned Caleb into accompanying me on "I'm So Lonesome I Could Cry" when I was courting Carolyn. He liked to harmonize right over that minor chord. I drank faster and began to slide into a familiar groove.

Billy leaned closer.

"John, I got something to show you. I'm not supposed to say anything, but your friend is in big trouble."

He reached over to his jacket draped over the bar stool next to him and pulled a news clipping out of his pocket. "Read this."

Apparent Murder Victim Found by Fishermen

Nakotah Rapids, Ontario—A spokesperson for the Ontario Provincial Police disclosed that the body of an adult male was discovered in a remote area of the Quetico Provincial Park earlier this week. The badly decomposed and brutalized body, believed to be that of fishing guide, Jacques "Lucky" LaJeunesse was found by a fisherman on a canoe trip to the northeastern quadrant of the park.

The body was identified at headquarters last week by Mrs. LaJeunesse through the articles of clothing, a family rosary, and other equipment found in the area. Also missing from the same area of the park are Gerry Roper and Caleb Pratt, teachers in the Ely, Minnesota Public School System. Witnesses in Nakotah Rapids say they had seen the two men recently but could not establish a specific date. They are being sought for questioning in the LaJeunesse incident.

An anonymous officer said that officials also believe that LaJeunesse had a client with him but there are no details available on the unknown client's whereabouts. It is believed that Pratt and Roper are prime suspects, considered dangerous, and that use of deadly force authorization has been given Provincial Authorities by an international task force investigating the matter.

I had already gotten the drift of this, but the shoot-to-kill verbiage shook me. What the hell was going on? International task force? Billy eyed me suspiciously as I finished the article, slapped it face down on the bar and polished off number six or seven. Before he passed a second sheet to me he looked to see if my eyes were focused. He talked to me in a low tone that signified serious business.

"John. Are you OK?"

I looked at him as steadily as I could and belched in a low resonating tone. It must have been a sober sounding belch because he pulled out an official looking sheet of paper and held it up.

"You NEVER saw this. Never heard about it and we never talked about your buddy. Right?"

He made me nervous. I scanned the bar for support. Jill was talking to some new customers at the far end of the bar. I swiveled back and looked down at the paper. It was a yellow teletype copy, the kind they got up at the County Sheriff's Department.

He started to hand it to me, but just then Jill walked over with another round. The moment was lost.

He paused and stuffed it back in his pocket. "Ah…I shouldn't say this, but I'll do you this favor. If he gets in touch with you, I'd hang up on him and keep my mouth shut. He's in real trouble. Go to jail trouble. Or worse."

"Wait! Let me see that."

Billy clamped a bear paw hand on my wrist like a vise.

"Back off! I think you're getting pretty close to overstepping. Go home. Get sober."

He got up and walked out of the air-conditioned cool into the hot evening humidity, an instant climate change known to anyone who has ever downed a cold one in a rural Wisconsin tavern.

Jill wandered back. "What was that about?"

A dangerous thing happened. I got an idea. "Jill, remember what you promised last winter?"

She looked down. Long story short. One of my current legal violations actually belonged to her. It happened in December. Her boyfriend dumped her for a coed at the U. She called me for solace. She wanted to go drinking so we drove ten miles out of town to Denser and got good and soused at the four corners roadhouse. She drove back, at least as far as the s curves on Highway P where she took the high side and slid into the cornfield. Upon inspection I found good news. The car was not stuck. I also found bad news. She had blasted both the driver's side tires off the rims when the car slid into the frozen corn furrows.

Sooner or later the county cops would do the bar time sweep and we would have had some explaining to do. She was drunker than I. And to tell the truth I didn't give a shit. I got in the driver's side and scooted her over on the bench seat. She started to fume and complain but I just turned the motor and heater on and jacked up the radio. When the cops came to cuff me and stuff me, I saw cold tears run down her cheeks as she wept. "I owe you. Anything!" That was December.

She snapped out of her reverie, her eyes wide with surprise and a touch of disgust.

Quickly I intoned, "No, no, no…hold on. It's not what you're thinking. Well it is. But not with me."

"What are you talking about?"

"Remember before the cops came that night how you were moaning about why you kept finding losers and why couldn't you hook up with a guy like Billy? That you'd give yourself to him in a heartbeat?"

Her face flushed. "I was DRUNK!" She looked down, but we both knew it was true. "Anyhow, I'm a step up from white trash, a bar keep. He's going places. Hell, his dad's a big shot in the FBI or something."

"OK. Here's the deal. What if I told you something that would guarantee you would get next to Billy?"

"Are you kidding me! What is it? Blackmail?"

"Here's where the 'anything' part comes in. You do have to do one thing. It's simple. If I tell you one thing that will lead to Billy and you hooking up tonight, you need to promise me that you'll pull a letter out of his shirt pocket when you can, read it and tell me what it says. It's about Caleb."

"You better be telling me the truth, but you get me with Billy and I'll read the damn note."

"OK, here it is. You two idiots want the same thing. He just told me he'd give anything for one night with you. He stormed out of here because he's frustrated and what you might call vulnerable…and lonely. You call him. Tell him you saw him leave and you're worried. Ask him if you can just come over and check on him."

"You're sure?"

"You ever read Cyrano de Bergerac?"

Actually, she had. She was smart. Smart enough to calculate the odds. Nothing to lose, everything to gain. She reached over the bar, grabbed the phone, dialed, listened and talked. Smiling briefly, she hung up. I heard her yell something to her cook as she grabbed her keys and raced out the door. The cook pushed through the swinging kitchen doors waving the purse she had forgotten but she was gone.

Chapter 6
The Life of a Spy

Winchester, Wisconsin
October 21, 1970, After Midnight

Billy heard the faint knock. He opened the door and she moved in close, putting her hand on his forearm and said, "How are you?"

He didn't speak, but put his right hand on her slim hip, and pulled just a little. Jill did not resist as she stepped in. She shut the door, dead-bolted it and slipped closer, gently resting a hand on his chest and playing with his top shirt button. Using both hands now, he pulled her in tight. She looked up and kissed him lightly as she undid his shirt button. Kissing without stopping, they took turns unbuttoning one another until he stripped off her shirt and she had done the same to him.

After an awkward fumbling with thick fingers, Billy managed to disarm her of her bra. "My God, you're pretty," he mumbled as he bent down to delicately lick her erect nipples. He kissed his way down to the waist of her shorts and tugged at the buckle with his teeth. When he stood up to hold her head in his hands and kiss her full on, she finished the unzipping and stepped out of her shorts and panties. He backed her over to a nearby desk, lifted her up on it and gently buried his face between her muscular thighs. Reaching up with one hand to caress her breasts, he used his other hand to cup her firm buttock and pull her close to his searching

31

tongue. Shortly she started breathing more heavily, gasping, "Oh," as she came faster and harder than she ever had in her life. At that, he stood up and pressed gently but firmly into her tightened wetness. When she wrapped her legs around him, he straightened and picked her up. Still engaged, he carried her into the bedroom and laid her on the bed. He straddled her, entered again and began the eternal dance which has carried men and women to a transcendental place since the beginning of time. His thrusting was violent but the look in his eyes was tender as she began to gasp anew. He clenched her, held his breath and pulled into her one last time with every ounce of strength in his body. With a gasp, he spasmed forward, lost his balance and collapsed the wooden bed frame with a crash that could be heard next door as they both moaned in heartstopping orgasm.

Then he was so still she was afraid that he'd had a heart attack. They lay like that for minutes, not speaking, barely breathing.

Finally, he looked up, swept back her hair, and said, "I believe in movies now."

"What in the hell are you talking about Billy?"

"You know, those movies, where there is some adorable girl with a figure to die for but she's kind of struggling in her life, and no one realizes just how great she is until a dork like me comes along and appreciates her. That's bullshit right? Beautiful smart women get put up on a pedestal. They are chased by the best and the brightest, and quickly snatched up to live happily ever after. Their lives never touch the lives of a regular guy like me."

He blinked, and continued.

"That's what I thought anyhow, until I met you. How on earth could someone as great as you, be here in this little town, waiting for someone to find you and tell you—hell, tell the world—how wonderful you are? But it happened, and I'm in that movie."

"Billy, you are full of bullshit. I was kind of cute in high school but come on… that was a while ago."

"Really? OK, here you go then. I'm no Romeo but I used to be a lifeguard so I know a little about the female body. Most girls, the best they look is with their clothes on. The rare ones, it's the other way. You're the rose. The more petals you peel away, the more beautiful you become."

"Billy, I think you are becoming a poet," she said.

But he was already asleep.

* * *

My phone rang.

"John, it's Jill. Listen quick. I've got it."

"Are you OK? Where's Billy?"

"He's sleeping. I can hear him snoring. Shut up and listen! I found the teletype in his pocket. Here's what it says."

She read.

CONFIDENTIAL   CONFIDENTIAL
CONFIDENTIAL International Crime Contact Control
Number Ont. 10-1210-70

To: Winchester Sheriff

From: Inspector Linley, Nakotah Rapids Office, Ontario Provincial Police

RE: 10-96***Murder Suspect

***The Ontario Provincial Police request your assistance in an inquiry about a former Winchester County resident, Caleb Pratt. Subject Pratt is the suspect in a double murder and potentially responsible for a third.

***We have checked with the Ely, Minnesota Sheriff's Department. Under warrant, they searched his apartment and found that he kept close correspondence with a former co-worker, John Short. He may try to contact Short or arrange for some type of meeting.

***We consider Pratt to be dangerous. The assault was inordinately violent. I will be forwarding documentation from our district magistrate, Hon. Judge Irvin Lacque, requesting your county's assistance in gaining wiretap and mail intercept approval from your state and federal court system.

***If you can help us, I personally guarantee you some of the best walleye and northern pike fishing our district can offer, guided by professionals.

"Shit!" I said, not the first time that day.

"John! There's more. In the funk he was in when he came home, he walked right by a big manila envelope on the floor. It's official looking with government seals all over it. "

"Read it."

"It's from Special Agent in Charge Kelly. That's his Dad! It says to arrest you at home. No one is to see it and he's to discuss it with no one, not even your sheriff. Then he is supposed to bring you to Madison where you will be taken into custody at the Federal Justice Building. He's flying in tomorrow and he wants it done ASAP."

Once more. "SHIT! I gotta go."

"Where?"

"I'm in the mood to do a little puttering on the old 42 GMC all of a sudden…..Oh, by the way. We're even."

"John, please be careful…Oh, and John?"

"WHAT?"

"I like being a spy."

Chapter 7
To Build a Fire

Eagle Chain of Lakes, Ontario, Canada
October 23, 1970

To make a fire you simply strike a match, touch it to the paper, and watch it lap its way into the kindling like a cat moving in on a ¼ pound butter wrapper. At home, in the fireplace, the wood furnace, or the burn barrel, you just do it without thinking about it. Lightning starts fires which men cannot prevent and it destroys thousands of acres of forest every year. When I was a little kid, my buddy set his dad's garage, and me, on fire while chasing me with burning plastic on a stick. Caleb's live-in girlfriend incinerated his motorcycle and old red pick-up truck by throwing used oil-based stain rags in a cardboard box in a corner of his garage. Anybody can start a fire. Except me.

The west wind blew another dose of snow down my neck. It was no longer a gray winter day, but an early winter evening. Snow, pushed by the west wind, seemed to come in waves as the sky darkened. The far shoreline across from my island was a stark Japanese woodcut in charcoal and white. I could not feel the holes in my bloody lip thanks to the numbing effects of the snow squall.

I fumbled in my old brown lineman's coat and found the second pack of matches. They were squirreled away in different zippered pockets, some even soaked in hot wax to make them waterproof. Most of them had been in the pocket too long, and the stuff had crumbled off. I absently thought of how I was going to clean out the pockets when I got home.

Home. I probably wouldn't see home again the way the fire lighting ceremony was proceeding. Nagging at the back of my mind was that Jack London story. The man never went home from the cold Yukon. He burned, then froze.

I needed focus. You see it in basketball. I coached a kid once who went on to play for the Wisconsin Badgers. He was a predator on the court. Even as a young kid there was a supreme concentration on his game face that blotted out cheerleaders' colors, shouts from the crowd, the glare of the lights, pep band trumpets, and taunts of intimidation from opposing players. I needed that focus. I needed to score…or die.

As darkness crept over the wilderness lake, I looked down on my meager kindling pile sitting where I had cleared the snow. The pile of dry grass, dead spruce needles, twigs, and paper birch bark awaited my next try. I peeled some cardboard from the battered box I had pulled from the truck hole and hoped it was not too damp. I tried restacking the combustibles, forming a three-inch high teepee of things that I assumed would burn.

I had optimistically stacked larger sticks and branches around the kindling which I had centered under a deadfall hemlock. The tree had broken off about eight feet up on the trunk and stayed attached, forming a lazy A shape. I imagined that as the fire burned cheerily along I would fill in the side to create a large reflector which would throw heat for yards. A sudden gust powdered the sticks with more snow and made a mockery of my plan.

I restacked one more time. My fingertips were numb. I struck another match. It flared brightly, emphasizing the pitch blackness of the evening. I leaned forward on my knees to shield the impromptu excelsior. I held the match until I began to feel my fingers burn. I held it a little longer.

It caught.

The flame snapped and sizzled and began to throw a little heat on my frozen fingers. I felt the skin stretch on my face and realized I was smiling. I settled down. Hasty attempts to make the fire bigger were sure to smother it so I eased in a small piece of cardboard, poked a twig under a bigger stick where a small flame licked the kindling, and began to very gently lean larger pieces of wood on the delicate teepee. My calf cramped, and I had to quickly roll sideways to avoid kicking the fire. As I kneaded out the knot, I felt a reassuring sting in my toes as the fire threw more heat. No frostbite. The flames snapped upward and fought the enveloping darkness. I was getting wetter and warmer at the same time. Smoke tickled my nose. I was alive. More that that, I was sober, unfrozen and proud of myself. I had beaten off terrible fatigue and the urge to just curl up and let Mother Nature deep freeze my troubles away forever.

It's funny how combinations of little things conspire to get us through life one day at a time. The snow was even letting up. My spirits lifted. I gathered every piece of driftwood to be found in the dark and then broke as many limbs off the scraggly spruce trees as I could reach. Not looking forward to the process, I removed my boots and socks knowing that I had to dry them. The snow stopped.

Late that night as I shifted heated rocks from the fire pit to my back side I discovered a Snickers bar in the lineman's coat. Last year it had been too mild to wear the warm old jacket which meant that the wormy candy bar had probably been there for at least two years. I dismissed that unfortunate assumption with two flashes of good news:

1. More protein

2. Too dark to see them.

Fearing it might be my last food for a while, I cautiously worked open a small tear in the corner, exposing just enough chocolate to allow me to take the tiniest nibbles with my front teeth—like an anorexic beaver.

The wind let up. I heard branches crack off in the darkness, and possibly the sound of something moving. I looked at my Timex and resigned myself to ten more hours of darkness. Everything I had was on top of me or below me in an attempt to provide insulation. In between fitful dozing I tended my home fire. The night crawled onward.

I dozed in fits and starts. The cheap little souvenir thermometer attached to my coat zipper read 12 degrees. Caleb had one for skiing, and he gave me one for deer hunting. Finally I noticed a faint graying in the east. Cold had settled in all of my body parts. There was a lot of throbbing but thankfully no frostbite. The boots, dry and hard, would take some flex work to get back in shape. Luckily I had a four-mile hike to Buckhorn Lodge's Cabin #2.

I dumped out the collection of things I had rescued from the 42. I found all kinds of equipment in the red deer hunting knapsack. It still contained last fall's supplies. There was a Buck knife, twine, plastic bags, Rolaids, toilet paper, matches, a thermos, an old Instamatic camera with half a roll of film and a John MacDonald novel. The rest of the stuff lying around came from the cardboard box which had been donated to the fire. A half can of coffee, two boxes of elbow macaroni, and some pancake flour had survived the night and the snow. I munched on a handful of frozen macaroni while I jammed the foodstuffs in on top of the hunting supplies in the pack.

The dry macaroni hurt my teeth, but at least I had something to put in the gaping pit that was my stomach. A handful of snow helped get it down and softened the hurt of my lip. I shouldered the pack and picked up the gun case which turned out to hold the .22, not the .30-.30. There was one box of shells in the pack at the stock end. I hoped I had not bent the barrel. The empty gun case made a good wide pad for the straps of the knapsack. I slung the rifle over my right shoulder and set off.

Chapter 8
Old Memories in a New World

Ontario, Canada
October 24, 1970

The rhythm of the walk gradually worked the kinks out of my back and dulled the lip throb even further. It would be all right now. I would see Caleb in a couple of hours and find out what this was all about. He had always been aggressive but I could never see him as a murderer. I remembered him at a joint school management-county services meeting, blasting a social worker for ignoring the burns on a nine-year old girl.

"I don't get it. A more pressing case? What could be more pressing than a little girl getting scalding water thrown on her! What the hell are you thinking!"

"Watch it Caleb," said Cary Houseman, our well-meaning but ineffective principal.

The nervous social worker nodded in the direction of her boss, who was busy appreciating the pine paneling in Cary's office as if it could shut out the troubles of the world. Stirring himself, Claude Palmer, the white-haired, florid faced, administrator of County Social Services shifted uncomfortably in his chair and cleared his throat.

"It's my understanding that this was a rare occurrence and that the child is safe now. The nine-year-old in question is but one of many troubled children we have on our intake list and…"

"Cut the shit!" Caleb shouted. He was angrier than I had ever seen him.

Palmer jerked his chair backwards and started to speak but Caleb interrupted.

"Goddamnit! Just last month Kelly had to go out and arrest the girl's mother because she was lying down dead drunk in the middle of County P trying to take out her own appendix with a butcher knife!"

Principal Houseman, a mild-mannered man who lived alone and was easily unnerved by violence, was startled out of his normal passivity.

"Caleb, you need to leave. Now. Please." Houseman said.

Houseman never was a tough guy. He sounded like he was begging. Caleb started to leave and then turned around and walked back to the table. He leaned forward and braced himself on the table with outstretched arms. The sinew rippling in forearms made them resemble thinly sheathed phone cable.

"Claude, you asshole if you would spend half as much time on your job as you do at the bar, that little girl might have a chance."

Now Palmer stood up. I knew what was coming.

"Young man, I hope you can sell your shiny red motorcycle, …ah, what is it, a Norton Commando, for enough money to hire an attorney because you will need one. And Principal Houseman, I do not think your school board will be at all pleased with my report on how well you manage your scruffy staff. Hooligans are what they are! Educational Hell's Angels. You should be ashamed of yourself!"

Houseman blanched and looked like he was going to faint. He brushed back his wispy red comb-over. He started to stammer an apology but Caleb cut him off by poking his thick index finger hard into Palmer's chest just below his tie's Windsor half knot. Palmer expelled a girlish yelp and tripped backward in his seat.

"As long as you're reporting on people Palmer, why don't you mention that 16-year-old Indian girl I saw you leave the Dew Drop in Barribeau with two nights ago. That group of bikers you walked by on the way to your Lincoln Town Car…I was one of them! One of the guys I ride with is her cousin. You should have been trunk music right then and there. I usually mind my own business. What a guy does on his own time is his life. But you're not getting the job done, kids are getting hurt, and I'VE HAD IT! So bring on your lawsuit, you lowlife, and bring popcorn and snacks for the deposition."

Palmer blanched. The uncomfortable silence in the room was tangible.

Houseman said, "Caleb, sit down. We need to solve problems, not cause them."

The lone female in attendance, a new employee of the social services department, studied the cheap carpet. She had already learned when to keep her head down.

Palmer stammered, "I was doing background research on another case. It was just another interview."

It was a nice try, but Palmer's lowered head told the school people all they needed to know. His dissembling pushed me over the edge too.

"So you're trying to tell us that your tavern visits are more important than keeping a nine-year-old girl out of the hospital? You jellyfish!"

"Let me start over please. We are terribly sorry that any youngster would experience such an unfortunate situation. We'll be finalizing our report for the court by next…"

Caleb flushed red and made a noise that sounded a lot like his Norton 850 kicking over. I jumped up and got between Claude and him. I leaned in toward his ear.

"Leave Caleb. Now. We made our point. Don't get mad. Get even."

Caleb stormed out and slammed the door after him so hard that Principal Houseman's Master's Degree fell off the wall, a shattering testament to the uselessness of the intellectual solution to corrupt bureaucracy. Palmer didn't look so good. Briefcases were closed, and chairs were pushed back against the wall. The Social Services people stood and moved to the door. That was almost it.

However, that was not it for Caleb. As we walked out of the office on the tile flooring of the old elementary school gym/lunchroom I heard the squeak of size 12 Chuck Taylors coming back around a corner. Principal Houseman saw Caleb first and responded with an uncharacteristic burst of profanity. "Oh shit."

Caleb marched up to Palmer, put both hands on his chest, and shoved him backward a step. Then he clenched his teeth and did it again and again until Palmer was backed up against the tile block wall. Palmer's face was an unearthly white and stretched tight like the skin of a pig. Suddenly his eyes rolled up and somewhere in his gray matter, the lights clicked off. His briefcase dropped to the floor and he followed, sliding down the block wall with a pathetically delirious grin, accelerating until his feet slid out, jarring his butt down hard enough to topple the rest of him over. The demolition of the man was climaxed by the audible click of his skull bouncing on the linoleum.

There was nothing but shocked silence. The social worker made a retching noise and squatted down on all fours as if she were waiting for the start of the 100 yard dash. No one moved toward Palmer until Caleb said, "I think that son of a bitch isn't breathing."

He leaned close to Palmer and put his ear next to the man's mouth. He looked up disgustedly and said, "Don't let me have all the fun here, if someone else wants to go first."

There was a shocked silence.

He propped Palmer's head back, cleared the air passage and prepared for mouth to mouth rescue breathing. Caleb knew the drill from years of lifeguarding. At the first puff, Palmer's chest raised visibly, his eyes popped open and he gagged. He tried to sit up but immediately collapsed again.

Caleb looked over his shoulder at me and said, "Johnny, since you have been so fucking helpful up to this point, do you think you could do one more thing and call an ambulance? I'm going home and take a shower."

He stormed out. A minute later we heard the Norton's two big coffee can sized cylinders kick over. Then we heard the rubber burn as he headed down Water Street, going through three gears too fast.

Palmer never completely recovered. He suffered complications from a minor heart attack according to our friend at the local hospital, Doc Mack. Social Services announced that Palmer had been put on long term disability, and a small retirement party was held. Three weeks after his retirement, I notice an article in the court calendar section of the local paper announcing divorce proceedings for the Palmers.

I shook myself free of the reverie when my cold feet made me realize that I had stopped hiking while replaying that elementary school showdown in my mind. Shivers of nostalgia mixed with the cold. I recommenced my walk, pondering the inner nature of a man who would place his lips on the lips of a man he despised in order to save his life. The clear day warmed with sun. I drew closer to my destination with one question burning in my mind. Could Caleb kill in cold blood? I tabled the question as I approached a stretch of dubious looking ice. Even in the coldest temperatures, water from Buzzard Lake manages to flow over the rocky tangle at the head of the falls. The drop is about thirty feet to lake level. As I approached the falls, I edged toward land, judging that it would be safer to bushwhack through scratchy tangled spruce and cedar than to risk the ice above the falls. I cautiously worked my way down the portage trail alongside the falls, steadying myself with the fixed rope left there by outfitters. I scanned the large pool and bay area below, known as Trout Hole #2. At the left side of the falls beyond the frozen foam sat the shack provided by Buckhorn Lodge. Tall white pines, rare for that latitude, marked its location from a distance. It's a prize spot, commanding a hefty rental fee in the summer because of its proximity to Eagle Lake and easy portages to dozens of other wilderness lakes west of it.

I was a new man in a new world.

Chapter 9
When I'm Dead and Gone

Cabin #2, Ontario, Canada
October 24, 1970

No smoke climbed into the clearing sky. The log cabin stood quietly guarding the falls. It looked like something out of a Christmas card. As I approached I saw no footprints in the fresh snow. I put my fingers to my mouth and whistled, startling the winter birds. No shouts of joy, welcome, or even the "Shut up! I'm trying to sleep" that Caleb used to hit me with in the old days after a hard night out on Mahogany Ridge.

Only the Styrofoam crunching sound of my footsteps disturbed the quiet as I edged up past the old aluminum Lunds left there year round for the fishermen. I saw no tracks, no smells of cooking, no yellow pee holes in the snow where you walk—Caleb's specialty. Once he peed on my tool box that I left on his step overnight after helping him fix something. I never forgave him. His only defense was that he had improved since our buddy Grits blew a gasket over Caleb's personal habits. That reformation was precipitated by a marathon training run impropriety of epic proportion. Caleb asked fellow runner Grits if he could borrow his spare headband for a little bit. A mile later, he ran ahead and ducked into a corn field where he used it for toilet paper.

The sky was bright and clear now. Sun shone down on the aging wooden boards of the cabin door. Rays glinted off freshly scratched metal, and I noticed the lock was broken. Someone had been there recently. I pushed my way through the unpainted door. Swirls of snow followed me into the dark interior cut by one swath of sunshine spilling through a window on the south wall. The stillness was disturbed only by the silent drift of dust motes in the sun ray. It was very cold inside. I stumbled over to the cookstove that I had used so many years before. Inside there were no glowing coals, just cold ashes. On top were dirty pots, kettles, pans, plates, silverware, all of it cemented together with frozen glop. Someone had definitely been there, and the housekeeping had Caleb's signature all over it.

I focused on the rest of the cabin as my eyes adjusted to the dim room. There was stuff all over, mostly food. Much of it was in boxes, some labeled to identify the contents. There were boxes of cereals, crackers, and a veritable grocery store lineup of flour mixes for cakes, waffles, and cornbread.

The food could wait. I needed heat. Compared to the previous night's struggle the fire came easily thanks to an ample supply of kindling in the wood box. In no time, the heat was reflecting from the bunk area in the far corner of the one-room shack. I cleared all the pots and pans and put on kettles of snow. I opened a box of macaroni and cheese and threw the noodles right in on the melting snow. After it boiled, I ate it all and kept stoking the fire. All of this activity sped up the slow moving waves of dust coursing in the sunlight in the otherwise dark room. I stared absently for a few minutes. Out of habit I avoided the mirror on the back of the door.

Where was Caleb? I had driven over 800 miles in a truck with no heater to the middle of nowhere. There were other dubious accomplishments as well—driving after revocation, stolen license plates, crossing the border carrying firearms and polluting the West Arm of Eagle Lake with the old 42. I half-heartedly cleaned the dishes rather than contemplate the consequences of my failed gamble to find Caleb. I nosed around in the supplies that were scattered everywhere. No one had been there for a while. I had missed him by a few days judging from the mouse nibbling that had been going on in the cabin. He was gone and I'd chased up here for nothing. With no truck I couldn't get him out and across the border even if he were here. Carolyn would have laughed at all of it. She always did when I'd go out to rescue Caleb. She'd answer the phone, look at me without covering it and say, "It's the irresponsible son of a bitch," and then she would laugh. Carolyn. On cold nights, she'd snuggle up to me and we'd make our own heat. No more. I wondered when the last time was that I had laughed.

It would usually happen about twice a year. Caleb's car would get stuck or the motorcycle wouldn't run, or he'd separate his shoulder in a bike race, and I'd get the call about one o'clock in the morning to come pick him up at some bar and haul him home.

Maybe he was coming back. He wouldn't just duck out without leaving a note. Who was I kidding? Ducking out was his M.O. Once, back home, two girls unexpectedly showed up at his trailer while we were trying to watch a playoff game on TV. He didn't have on his mind what they had on theirs, but they invited themselves in anyway. Their persistence in insinuating themselves into our affairs, as well as apartments, had earned them the moniker of the Cuckoo Pigeon sisters, with a nod to the old "Odd Couple" show.

At any rate, Caleb pouted in his chair for a few minutes, purposefully not leaving room for the sister perched on the chair arm to slide in with him. Then he looked at me pointedly, and said, "You wanna beer?" I heard the refrigerator door open and shut. I shifted uncomfortably as that was followed by the surreptitious closing of the kitchen door. Shortly after I glanced out the front window and saw feet under the rocker panel on the street door side of the Bonneville. The driver's door opened magically and something crawled in behind the steering wheel. The Cuckoo Pigeon sisters looked up when the big V-8 roared out of the straight pipes that Caleb favored. When the car pulled away, they looked at me and laughed coyly, "Oh, that Caleb. Where is he going?"

An hour later they still didn't know. I shooed them out assuring them that I would call if he had been in an accident. Actually, he was in an accident. In LaCrosse. He had escaped the Cuckoo Pigeon sisters so he could go to a local tavern to watch the game where he had gotten bored during the second half and bet a guy $100 that he could beat him to Sioux Falls, South Dakota. They gave the bartender the money. Caleb ran out the door, jumped in the Bonneville and 90 minutes later re-entered the atmosphere by plowing into a farmer's field on the high side of a curve in the bluffs above LaCrosse. I got the call about midnight.

He'd done it again. When would he learn?

When would I learn?

Apparently not before both of us ruined our lives. It was now late afternoon in the great white north. I stoked more wood into the sizzling black cookstove and felt the radiant heat singe my face. I took off my boots and sat down on the lower bunk, my spirits sunk as hopelessly as the Titanic. I crawled under the grungy blankets. As a groggy afterthought, I loaded and tucked the .22 in with me, barrel end to the door. It would be just a nap I told myself. After all, it was afternoon. As I drifted off, I thought not for the first time that year, that it would be good to just fade away into a warm darkness and never come out of it.

Dreams for me have always been in color and fast. Before I knew it the olive drab truck cab was again around me. Beyond the red GMC lettering on the steering wheel I could see silver bubbles and hear their escaping gurgle. I was underwater settling to the bottom of the West Arm of Eagle Lake. I was aware of my breath coming in shallow gasps. The door was jammed shut because of the pressure, and the window would not roll down. It was getting darker, and water was filling the cab. Panic time. I turned to the passenger side just as a shaggy monster burst through the glass and dragged me out of the truck cab on to the cold lake bottom with a hard bump.

I screamed and then screamed again as the underwater scenario faded. I realized that I really was being dragged across the cabin floor by a huge swarthy phantom in a flannel shirt. He heaved one more time with lumberjack hands and dumped me unceremoniously next to the cookstove. It was nearly dark inside the cabin. Only a small glow came from the stove, leaving the rest of the room in the shadows. He straightened up and held a flashlight under his chin like little kids do on Halloween and growled, "Johnny! You want a beer?"

I did not want a beer. I wanted out of my nightmare and into wakefulness. My body ordered coffee; thick, dark, and hot. I struggled to accept the living contradiction before me—Caleb's voice embedded in a bearded, aged visage. The hirsute image was impressive. As he turned to grab another beer for himself, I discerned a limp. Apparently the prolonged isolation had cured Caleb's longstanding inability to grow a decent beard. When we worked together he always blamed his pathetic attempts to grow a November buck hunter's beard on some Shawnee lineage in his family. Now, after God knows how long in the woods, he sported a growth of hair from his ears to his nose and down to the shirt collar. What it lacked in aesthetics, it more than made up for in sheer shaggy volume.

"What happened? What went wrong?" I wanted answers to questions that had burned in my head as I drove north.

"Later. Let's eat." He looked at my stubbly face and said, "The way things look you have your own story to tell."

"Where did you get the food?" I asked as Caleb carried in more firewood from a stock pile that he had established at the edge of the cabin. I stoked the stove again and put on the pot.

"You can have your choice. The pickings are good around here. The cottages toward the main road have great cupboards. The guide's lodge has a cellar below the frost line you wouldn't believe." He hosted a beer in salute. "In fact, I stayed there during that little blow of a snow storm." He left with a bucket to get water from the opening near the falls.

I looked over the unusual variety of supplies that Caleb had stashed in no particular order on the shelves, floor, and open pole beam ceiling. The shelves contained cans—tuna in oil, sardines, and some fruits in heavy syrup. Under the shelves, on the floor there were two sacks of flour. One had black flecks that I hoped made it buckwheat. The round cross joints were hung with what appeared to be dried meats, including some kosher beef salami from Kahn Brothers in Chicago. Caleb was no thief, until now. He had survived the winter at this cabin on his craftiness and what he called his borrowing power—the power it took to carry the things he stored back to Cabin #2.

Caleb pulled up his pants leg and displayed a hideous wound and told me the story. Over the course of the next two days I would hear most of it, but at odd times during the winter something would click inside his head and another small bundle of facts or fiction would spill out. Some parts I later found to be false. They had to be his own creation, but as I've researched, I found he was never far off in his visualizations. The story was not pretty. He asked me to think it over before I related it to anyone. In the end, I promised that no one would know the story while either of us were alive.

That's when I started writing.

DAN WOLL and JOHN W. LYON

Chapter 10
The Events of
September—Remembering

Cabin #2, Ontario, Canada
October 24, 1970

We were comfortable inside the small cabin despite the blustery October wind as Caleb began his story. His trouble had started back in September. He and his teaching friend, Gerry Roper, had weaseled a few days of leave without pay from their teaching jobs to enjoy one last trip on the water for the season. I listened to Caleb and made notes as he spoke. Soon I put down my pad and closed my eyes as his words melted in to a soundtrack for a movie that I saw in my mind's eye. It went like this.

It was unusually hot for early September in Canada when Caleb and Gerry Roper hopped out ten feet from the rocky shore of the big island on Cache Lake, deep in Quetico Provincial Park. They carefully waded the blue Jensen canoe on to the only level piece of shore on the island. Gerry, short and lean, wore cut off shorts and a sweatshirt revealing a slight sunburn. He pulled off the bandana that he had tied around his wild red hair and wiped his brow. Caleb slumped against a tree. He did not look like a canoeist. He was over six feet tall with slab-like arms that looked like they were used to holding a jackhammer instead of a paddle. The redhead pulled an eighty pound Duluth Pack out of the canoe, carried it over and dropped it at the feet of the bigger man.

"Come on," Gerry nagged, "get it in gear. If we keep sitting around here the flies are going to chew us to bits. Let's get the tent up and get out on the water and fish a little."

Caleb swatted a bug and responded, "Oh lighten up for Crissakes. We wouldn't even be here if it wasn't for me knowing that portage by heart."

Gerry countered, "Yeah, and if you'd ever crawl out of the tent before ten o'clock we wouldn't always be thrashing around at the end of the day when normal guys are sitting around the campfire having dinner."

Caleb grinned. He could never come out on top. Gerry would always get in the last word. In the short time the two young men had taught together they had become fast friends. They had been up to Quetico before on a short vacation and knew the area well. Cache Lake was their favorite spot. The ranger told them that very few parties had visited the lake and its outlet river that season.

Caleb picked up his paddle and pointed. "Let's paddle down the river to the old bridge. I could go for perch tonight." Although the perch seemed to be getting a little smaller each year, the old logging bridge was always good for a dozen or so of the tasty fish.

Gerry had already finished setting up the tent. He was fast in everything he did, a fast talker, fast runner, fast paddler. He had been an outstanding baseball pitcher in high school. His best pitch? The fastball. He never seemed to slow down. Caleb, on the other hand, was a plodder. Reliable, strong, a finisher, but not flashy. During the school year, Gerry would get his kicks out of playing basketball with the kids after school, chasing them down, stealing the ball, stuffing their shots and talking insufferable trash constantly. Caleb preferred swimming for hours at night on a nearby lake or the solitude of the weight room where he could think and daydream while he did his chin-ups and bench presses. They made a good team.

They hung their food in a nearby tree, grabbed up their tackle boxes and pushed off, Caleb in front and Gerry in the back. Even their positions reflected their personalities. Gerry was a skilled paddler. When he steered, the canoe went straight and fast. He never had to rudder or make adjustments. Caleb sat up front, kept his head down, and powered his big, bent shaft paddle through the water with machine-like precision. As they headed toward the Cache River outlet, they left a small wake. Noiselessly, the canoe ate up the three miles to the bridge.

Caleb spotted it first. "What the hell! There's a boat. Somebody's here." The young men could not believe it. There had been no signs along the river bank of any visitors and the Cache Lake campsites looked as if they had been unvisited for weeks. In fact, Caleb and Gerry had never before encountered anyone as far into the park as the Cache River Bridge.

They pulled up beside the long abandoned, caved-in, logging bridge. It sagged into the water in the middle. The weathered planks near the water line were slippery with moss. Careless anglers could easily slip into the icy river water there, garnering a splinter in the butt in the process.

The men got out next to the bridge and stomped through the shoreline weeds and mud. There sat an old square sterned Grumman, the kind that takes a small motor. In the boat were two red five gallon gas containers, full.

Caleb exploded. "Sonuvabitch! Do you know what this is? Some bastards drove in here with this boat. They probably got some fat-assed businessmen signed up for their 'special trip', haul them in here, with a few cases of beer and leave them for a few days. No muss, no fuss, no paddling, no portaging, and illegal as hell. That's where the big perch are going. These fish up here have a tough enough time surviving. It wouldn't take too many renegade trips to fish the bay right out. Look over here!" Gerry pointed to a fire pit.

He kicked at the remains of a campfire ring. Scattered around the edge of it were several half burned egg cartons and beer cans.

"Looks like they had a hell of a fish fry and I'll bet they wasted as much as they ate. Those bastards!"

Caleb leaned over and pulled out a fuel container marked Johnson Sea Horse, carried it up the hill to a nearby boulder field, and emptied it. He did the same with the other and threw them as far as he could back into the brush. "What do you think we should do about this? Just report it, or what?"

Gerry sauntered over. "I don't really give a rat's ass, but offhand I would say you're over stepping it a bit."

Caleb picked up one of the outfitter's oars, considered the matter and then smashed it against a granite outcropping. "With all due respect chief, I gotta disagree."

Next, he grabbed oar number two and pounded it furiously against a large pine tree. One of his swings sprayed Gerry with wooden shrapnel. "Hey, watch out, you idiot!"

His partner's protest went unheeded as Caleb built up a head of steam. He eyed up a small boulder the size of a footstool. Using a weightlifter's classic clean and jerk move, he bent his knees, rocked back and yanked the small boulder up to the level of his chin. Gerry scrambled out of the way as Caleb staggered over to the boat, and all in one motion dipped and pushed the rock overhead where he balanced it briefly before crushing it down on the bow of the outfitter's boat. It crumpled like an empty beer can.

"Not cool, Caleb. I hope I don't ever have to answer for this temporary insanity."

Caleb shrugged. "Man, this place is ruined for me." His anger had passed.

"Are we done?"

As they paddled back to camp, Caleb hung his head, as much in disappointment over his loss of self-control as anything else. His battles with his personal demons always seemed to end up hurting his friends somehow.

The next morning dawned cool and clear. For a change, Caleb was up first. He seemed in a better mood after the prior day's depression over finding the motor canoe. They ate early while the fire's heat still felt good in the cool of the morning. A steaming pot of coffee loses appeal as the sun climbs higher in the sky. Usually breakfast was granola, but they always packed in one special meal on their trips. It would not have been recommended because of the bear problem, but they had carried in a pound of bacon and a dozen eggs to celebrate their arrival at the hidden gem of Quetico Park—Cache Lake. After that, it would be all dried food and whatever fish they caught.

The Cache Island campsite was a beauty. The west end of the island was open and elevated, allowing a breeze to blow through the site and keep the area relatively bug free. The view up river was the thing postcards are made of—lake with a rocky shoreline in the distance and trees. The nearest shoreline looked as if the overhanging cedars had been trimmed up to five feet by a platoon of gardeners. The guys knew that this was a sign of starving deer browsing as high as they could during the brutal winter. Their desperate attempts at survival left the tree line with an eerie manicured look.

The tent was pitched next to a small granite outcropping. Several ledges on the formation acted as shelves and a small dihedral formed a natural fireplace and chimney. Caleb started the fire rapidly, cheating a little by using some of the Coleman fuel from their portable cookstove. The dry pine logs burned down quickly and soon he was able to balance the frying pan on two of the bigger logs on the fire. Methodically he began separating the bacon, laying each strip out perfectly in the pan. As the bacon crackled, Gerry emerged from the tent, Ivory soap in hand. He stripped down and waded into the lake, yelping as he ran into the crotch deep water. In a couple of minutes, he was back grinning.

Caleb seldom bathed on canoe trips even though he was an excellent swimmer and much more at home in the water than Gerry. He did not like the cold water. He never had. When he was on the swim team in college, he would often arrive at practice early and stand on the edge of the pool and procrastinate for a half hour before diving in to begin his warm-up laps. He knew why Gerry did it every morning. On the days when he did force himself into the icy Canadian waters, he felt cleaner, fresher and more alive. The freshness always wore off because his dark side did not tolerate an excess of lightheartedness.

"You think you got enough bacon in there?" said Gerry as he looked at the black frying pan. The entire pound was bubbling away in an inch of grease. "Real high quality stuff, Caleb. I can feel my arteries plugging up already."

"Nah, you've got it backwards. This isn't the part that plugs things up. This just kind of lubricates everything so the eggs can slide way into the places where they don't normally visit and really do the job. Give me that paper towel."

Caleb began to fork the pieces of bacon and lay them on the paper towel to drain off. When he was done he poured off most of the grease and began cracking eggs into the pan. Gerry pulled out a big loaf of French bread they had dragged along and began slicing it for toasting on a stick. They finished at about the same time. What took thirty minutes to prepare disappeared in three. Gerry did not drink coffee but Caleb did. He threw the egg shells into a pot of water along with a half cup of coffee, dug around in the pack for a couple of hard candies and pulled out the James Bond book he had brought along. He would be incommunicado until the coffee was consumed.

They fished after breakfast. That morning Caleb caught a lake trout. The sky and the few high clouds created an inviolate white and blue impression. The wind blew the canoe slowly across the huge lake. The men trolled big crankbaits as they drifted. They had just moved to a corner of the lake near the inlet of a small creek when Caleb got lucky. He clipped another swivel and several ounces of weights on the lure and dropped it over the side, backreeling slowly just to check for depth. He had just started to retrieve the heavy tackle when a big fish jolted it ten cranks off the bottom. Fish were not supposed to bite lures hung with extra sinkers to test for depth. But this one did. It was to be the last bit of luck he would have for a long time.

Twelve pound test was on Caleb's line and little skill was required to drag the silver and black two-foot long trout up to the surface. Gerry netted it and held it up.

Caleb carefully pinched the lower jaw of the fish between his thumb and index finger. "Take a picture."

"Let's wait until we get back. I don't want to dig around in the pack for the camera now." Gerry said.

"This guy's not going back with us. He's going home where he belongs. He's too perfect to be up here with us."

Gerry took the picture and Caleb carefully lowered the trout back into the lake. It darted down and disappeared. It was the only trout they caught that day. They fished for another hour and then headed up the river. On the way, they silently paddled into a small bay and surprised a moose standing in the chest deep water. Caleb backpaddled to a distance of about fifty feet. The adult bull finally looked up when the shutter on Gerry's camera clicked.

They had lunch in the canoe sharing Gerry's two quart mix of lemonade. Caleb dug around in the daypack and came out with a pound of Swiss cheese, Ritz crackers, and two plastic bags filled with gorp. The softened cheese tasted good. Just when they were getting too comfortable, they would become conscious of the sweat rolling down their back, or the flies buzzing around the hot granite slabs on the shoreline. They paddled lackadaisically as they munched.

All in all, they were about as comfortable as it is possible to be in the north woods. The noon day sun shone overhead. The fresh air and exercise on the lake had made them hungry. They ate until they were sleepy. Caleb finished chores by dipping down and filling the water bottles again. He flipped one back to Gerry who was yawning.

The previous day had been brutal. They had paddled six hours without stopping in order to get to the final portage into Cache Lake. The portage was over two miles long and crossed two large swamps. Most guidebooks warned that even veterans could expect to spend a full day finding the way the first time. Few people attempted it. Caleb had been there before, but it still took them two and a half hot miserable hours. They each carried a huge Duluth Pack. They traded off carrying the canoe every fifteen minutes. The muddy swamp bottoms sucked their boots, causing their thighs and calf muscles to burn with strain at every step. There were deer flies as well as the ever present horde of mosquitoes. An unprotected portager would not last long slogging through the bog and bushy terrain with both hands immobilized while balancing the canoe. The upside down canoe filled with marauding insects. Head nets were a necessity. Heavy work gloves, long sleeved shirts, and long pants also had to be worn even in the hot humid weather to prevent their bodies from being chewed to pieces.

The second swamp was so deep that they had to flip the canoe over and float it across the mud, sometimes grabbing onto it to avoid sinking up to their necks in the fecund ooze. Fatigue pounded them, causing mistakes. Twice they lost the portage trail and had to put down the canoe and bushwhack around for ten or fifteen minutes to find it again. Pushing through the heavy brush on the final ridge between the swamp and Cache Lake they were stung by bees. Caleb threw down his load and started running as soon as he saw the telltale thinning of treetops which gave away the hidden shoreline. Despite his dislike of cold water, he ran fully clothed into the chilled waters of the Cache until he lost his balance and fell forward in icy refreshing surrender.

Now, a day later, things could not be finer except for the fishing prospects. Caleb rigged a red and white daredevil and trolled it across the deep holes of the lake while Gerry silently paddled. Later the men switched to crankbaits, but their luck remained unchanged. Gerry found a leech when they drifted near the shore. He rigged it on a slip bobber rig and tried different depths for a half hour. Nothing doing. By two o'clock in the afternoon, Gerry was seeing Caleb's conservation act with the trout in a different light. "Seeing as how you threw back the only fish we caught, I think we've got a little problem for supper tonight unless you expect a main course of Grape Nuts and rice."

Anything was possible with Caleb. Gerry's mind drifted back to the prior spring. They had taken a short trip to the Flambeau River in Wisconsin. Caleb was in charge of food. When they set up camp, Gerry and the other partners discovered that the food pack contained a six-month-old fruit cake that a student had given him for Christmas, a jar of peanuts and a quart of Jack Daniels. Fortunately, they caught a walleye but Caleb's credibility as an outdoor chef had been suspect ever since.

"Gerry! What are you doing? Yo!"

Gerry shuddered and roused himself from his memories of meals gone bad with Caleb.

"Nothing. Listen. Junk or no junk, the bridge is still good for a quick meal. Let's go down there for a little bit. One hour of fishing should do it."

Caleb reached in the daypack again, and took the last of the hard candies. "No problem."

Chapter 11
The Events of September—Return to Cache River Bridge

Cabin #2, Ontario, Canada
October 24, 1970

Caleb looked up and scratched his heavily bearded face as he surveyed the food strewn about the cabin. "Pour me some coffee. I'm going to need a little help to get through this next part. I still can't believe it. Part of it needs to be settled if we are ever going to go home. There's some other people in this story, including...you're not going to believe this...a guy we knew back in Madison. They're dead now. They had it coming. Problem is they've got important friends who don't want anyone to know what happened to them. Now remember. This happened back in September and I've been through a lot since then. It seems like I'm imagining parts of it, but Johnny, the key parts are right on."

Caleb continued his story.

"I'm going to tell you about a guy I knew a little back at the University of Wisconsin, and some redneck guide named Lucky LaJeunesse. Don't ask me how in the hell the two of them got together. They're polar opposites. I know something about LaJeunesse because I went through his stuff after he died. Piece of work, big guy, about 6'4," 240, kind of hard fat, with mean little pig's eyes. Complete

59

asshole. The other guy was a kid Gerry and I knew a little at college. He was one of these guys you run into in the gym or weight room. I never knew his real name. They called him Elbie, and he was OK for awhile. He was on the crew team and I heard he got cut or something. Then my buds in the weight room told me he got kind of crazy. Our last year in school I only saw him once or twice. He was hanging with a bunch of radicals and railing against the establishment. Whatever. I never liked him much. Gerry was kind of into that protest thing so he knew Elbie better. Last we ever saw Elbie on campus, he was getting in the face of some frat boy down on Langdon Street, lecturing about imperialist pig rich guy lackeys. Kind of funny since he was East Coast prep school himself before he turned into Che Guevara. Anyhow, I know more. I know about their friends, what they were doing, Lucky's town, other stuff. I don't know how I know all this. I got hurt. Maybe I heard them talking. I don't know. But this is the deal…"

I could tell that Caleb was fantasizing about some of the details throughout the narrative. He knew what they had done to him and he knew for sure what they did to Gerry. In his mind's eye, over the past months of solitude, he had come to know Lucky LaJeunesse and friends intimately. Caleb would always be my friend. If we were ever to get back to civilization, I hoped that he would be the same old easygoing guy, but as he talked, I could tell that there was a part of him that was broken. He had a hollow look in his eyes and mannerisms I had never seen before. He kept hitching up his pant cuff and rubbing a grotesquely scarred and atrophied calf muscle. He stammered a little, and paused a lot. That bothered me as much as anything else. He had always been proud of his speaking ability. Our principal always used to have him give the Back to School Welcome to parents. He used to brag that he was a member of the National Thespian Society until the night the owner of the Dew Drop Inn overheard, misunderstood and kicked him out.

Now he stuttered, looked down at his wound, pawed at invisible demons behind him, and stopped himself in mid-sentence. In the time that Caleb had haunted Cabin #2, he had created an entire family history to buff the reality. Whether the family history was true was not important. The crucial facts made sense and the most crucial fact was that we were in deep living color shit. I was aware of Caleb leaning toward me talking more intensely. I sat up and wrote down what he said with a ball point pen that hadn't been used since the last cabin resident marked down northern pike holes. Caleb took another look at his disfigured leg and continued. He looked off to a far place in his mind that was miles away and two months back and drifted in to an omniscient narrative of the following story.

In a town 30 miles north of the Provincial Park, at about the same time Gerry and Caleb were eating bacon and eggs on Cache Island, a young man named Elbie wasn't feeling very good at breakfast. Elbie shouldn't have stayed out until one o'clock drinking Labatt's in downtown Nakotah Rapids the night before, but why the hell not. To come so far unseen and unknown, and then get involved with another criminal! He spent the night drinking with a sociopath named Lucky, getting their story straight and trying to move ahead on the details of his escape route and his chance at a new life. Maybe it would all work out. Thank God Lucky didn't know how much money he had or how he got it. He only knew there was some for him if he could sneak a young punk south across the border. So for a hundred bucks and the promise of another hundred if they made it, the deal was sealed and Elbie went home and crashed in Lucky's junky old boathouse.

Lucky came storming in at seven a.m., hacking, spitting and hollering for Elbie to get up and get going. Elbie would have liked to sleep off the hangover in the cool dark boathouse, but Lucky was on the prowl, feeling ornery and looking for company for coffee.

Leaning on the counter of the Blue Arrow Café, finishing his third cup of coffee, Elbie finally felt like talking. "What the hell are you getting me up so early for when we don't have to leave until four?"

"Why don't you just change your damn tone before I rub your nose on the griddle. That might shut you up in front of all these fine people." Lucky waved his hand at the regulars sipping their morning coffee. Most averted their eyes when the grizzled old man with the absurd muttonchop sideburns looked at them. His head was the size and the shape of a 25 horsepower motor and the eye on the right side of his large veined nose wandered spookily.

Elbie rubbed his throbbing temples. "Sorry, I didn't mean it. I got a bad one this morning. Look. Let's start over. You might be right about starting earlier and eating at camp. What about your wife?"

The regulars had gone back to their business and there were no more stares.

Lucky LaJeunesse replied, "I told the wife about us going early and she said she wasn't feeling too good. She don't look good neither. Think it'd be best to let her get some rest for a change." He stood up again behind the red stool. "So we'll do it this way college boy. Drink up. Let's hit the road."

They headed back to the dock in Lucky's beat up Ford F 150. A peeling white sign that said, 'Lucky's', hung just out of square above the gray shack's door. Yesterday Lucky had outfitted a few day rentals and a one week group, but they arranged with Carl at the next pier spot to come over later to check them back in.

By the time they loaded their gear and gas, it was almost noon. They had a tent, sleeping bags, a couple of Homelite chainsaws with most of the red chipped off, a machete, and a cooler of food. Lucky tucked in a couple of bottles of blackberry brandy with his rain gear. Then he packed in the artillery. Lucky never went anywhere without his private arsenal. Hunting season was open for Lucky anytime and anyplace. If he saw a moose, they would just have to take the time to quarter it and pack what they could in a spare cooler no matter how much of a hurry the damn college kid was in. Or Lucky might leave the whole carcass to rot. It didn't matter to Lucky. The pulse of the gun kicking in his hand was the same feeling some men had during sex. If the target was alive, it was all the better. He liked to shoot.

He tucked in a Browning 12 gauge pump shotgun, and his pride and joy, a new .44 magnum revolver. He had helped himself to the oversized revolver when he saw it on the seat of a new Continental with Illinois plates. Dumbass berry pickers hadn't even locked the doors. Wonders never cease.

Elbie was pissed, but smart enough not to show it. The old redneck's temper could cause the whole deal to sour. He had to trust the guys in the suits who had gotten him into this mess in the first place. They were the ones who steered him to Lucky. They were the ones who promised that if he did as he was told, the old trapper would sneak him back across the border to Ely and set him up with a new identity and a new life to replace the one he had just ruined.

He wished he was as confident as everyone else.

"Don't worry," Elbie's contact had assured him when he called in from the pay phone in Peterborough. "No one will spot you crossing back if you do it in the Quetico wilderness. We will take care of you. "Searchlight" himself is monitoring the operation. He bet a lot on this. You're going to be OK."

Right. That was just before he had been discovered by the cops. How they let him sneak out of the boarding house they were hiding in and escape was destined to go down in the history of all time law enforcement screw ups, but it had left Elbie with a sense that everybody was looking for him. For starters, it made him suspicious of the supposed, no-sweat crossing back into the States through the Quetico Park. He knew there were more and more hippie outdoor types who didn't seem to have anything better to do than hang out in Provincial Parks. They were not about to be in cahoots with the cops, but nonetheless, this was not the time to meet anybody.

Apparently Lucky had a deal with the guys in the Nakotah Rapids Ranger station, but when Elbie asked him about the details of the American border crossing at Prairie Portage, Lucky only mumbled something about those jackasses not being smart enough to pour piss out of a boot if you wrote instructions on the heel.

"All you need to know college boy," growled the old man, "is I got friends in high places with the Provincial Police and they call the shots between here and Cache Lake. Let's roll."

Chapter 12
The Events of
September—"He's Running!"

Cabin #2, Ontario, Canada
October 24, 1970

The October wind picked up outside the cabin. Caleb interrupted his story again and listened to the icy sleet make a ticking noise on the window of the shack. He got up and went over to the cast iron wood stove. He put on an old kitchen mitt, opened the door and stoked it with a few smaller logs. He grasped the blue-flecked enamel coffee pot, warmed up his cup, then turned and looked at me, almost apologetically, and said,

"I know you're wondering how I'm privileged to the exchanges between Lucky and Elbie before I ran into them. I can't explain it, but once I did meet them, bad things happened to me. Some things happened while I was in a daze. Maybe I heard parts of this story retold. Maybe I'm imagining it, but it makes sense. Bear with me, because eventually, I did meet Lucky and Elbie in living color, and unfortunately that was as real as it gets. So somehow I know or feel that this is pretty much how they got from Nakotah Rapids to Cache Lake." He took a deep breath and picked up the story where he left off. I was beginning to realize that he was telling it in the third person to minimize the pain of the retelling.

* * *

Lucky and Elbie mounted beat up olive-drab three-wheelers, punched the electric starts, and headed off down the trail. They made good time on the trip south. Elbie hoped that the old man would not go off the deep end before they met the float plane on Cache Lake. If everything worked out, his contacts would pay Lucky, give him a new identity and bank account and help him sneak past the American border crossing. He suspected that if he died in the effort to sneak back in the country that would be OK with his "friends." One way or the other, the old Elbie had to disappear.

The government had a healthy interest in his prospects for a long life. But they needed complete deniability, hence the cloak and dagger re-entry into the country. From Nakotah Rapids, Elbie and the grizzled old guide drove their ATV's on trails as far as they could to Stanton Bay on the impassable Pickerel chain of lakes and bogs. Lucky packed supplies into a motoring canoe with practiced hands. The old five horse Johnson purred at the first pull and they were off across the fertile green bog lake, past one small island and into Rawn Narrows, which led further south to another hidden set of ATV's. They emptied the canoe and then pulled it in under a spruce deadfall and threw a camo tarp over it. Back on three wheelers, they followed a narrow poacher's trail up to the higher ground near a long abandoned logging road deep in the woods which would lead to the decrepit Cache River bridge and the final water crossing to the pickup spot on Cache Lake. The plan was to camp for the night next to the old bridge and wait for the plane at Cache Island the next day.

* * *

Caleb and Gerry paddled away from their camp back toward the Cache River and the fishing hole by the bridge. The wind had died down and the sun was in and out of puffy clouds. Powerful strokes moved them swiftly across the half mile of open water between their island and the mouth of the Cache River. Once on the river, they steadied their pace. The current was not strong but the shallow spots demanded close attention. Careful navigating around submerged boulders was required. Twenty minutes passed in silence before they reached the bridge.

The center of the old logging bridge had given way many years before. When it caved in, it created two ramps sloping to the center of the river from each bank. Caleb and Gerry edged the canoe over toward the north bank and pulled up next to the sunken wooden structure. After tying up, they gingerly stepped out on the sloping wooden surface. The timbers were in pretty good shape, but greased with algae, so they were slippery. The year before in May, Caleb had lost his footing while holding up a stringer of perch for a picture. He slid down the steeply slanting boards into the icy pool of moving water. He still bore the scar where he had driven a splinter the size of a pencil into his thigh.

They began casting small Mepps spinners downstream. Gerry's first cast produced the biggest perch. It seemed to work that way at the bridge. The big ones were always first. After twenty minutes, Gerry had five and Caleb had four perch over ten inches.

"Let's knock it off Gerr. It'll be getting dark soon. This is about all the fish I want to clean today. It should be enough if we cook up the instant rice."

Caleb had his back turned, but Gerry could hear him chuckle.

"Fine, let's clean them here. We'll keep the mess away from the campsite."

They carefully walked up the bridge with the string of fish. Gerry looked over distastefully at the vandalized boat.

"You degenerate. The place looks like Sanford and Son now thanks to you."

Gerry looked up. "You hear something? Listen!"

Caleb cocked his head and stared down the trail leading away from the bridge. "Somebody's coming! It sounds like a dirt bike or something."

Caleb looked over at the crushed bow of the boat and the splintered paddles. He felt his stomach turn over while a chill pulsed up his spine. The noise was getting much louder. He looked over to Gerry. There was nothing to say. Nothing to do but get out. Gerry opened his mouth and started to move just as Elbie's three wheeler came into view down the trail. Lucky was right behind him.

Elbie saw the two men standing at the edge of the river, dressed in grubby cutoffs and holding a stringer of perch. His startled expression mirrored theirs. Then he and Gerry locked eyes in a supernova of surprised recognition. Before either of the two young men could speak, Lucky pulled up two feet away from Gerry and shut off the machine. Hauling himself off with surprising dexterity and speed, he stuck out his jaw and bellowed, "And who might you be?"

Caleb and Elbie were about to say something but Gerry opened his mouth first. "Frick and Frack."

Lucky recoiled like a snake and unleashed a vicious blow, knocking the lighter man down with a clubbed fist. The punch came fast but did not surprise Elbie. He knew this was headed toward terminal ugly the moment he recognized Gerry.

"Are you nuts? Lighten up old man!" Gerry had regained his feet and his voice. The fish lay in the dirt.

Lucky turned back to the three wheeler. He drew out the .44 with his baseball glove sized paw, pointed it at Gerry and roared, "You're in a pile of trouble, faggot."

Lucky walked over to the damaged canoe keeping the big handgun pointed in the general direction of the two fishermen. He surveyed the crushed bow and broken paddles, then turned to Gerry. The revolver was gripped so tightly in his right hand that the hammer had lifted off the rest. Caleb and Elbie stood paralyzed by the potential violence, oblivious to each other.

Gerry made the first and fatal move.

He reached out to push the long gun's barrel to the side. His clutching motion caused Lucky's trigger finger to constrict tightly. The barrel of the gun issued its death warrant. The hole going into Gerry's flannel shirt was the size of a quarter. The exit hole would have been the size of a baby's fist, but the only ones to see it would be the perch.

While the concussive echo of the .44 was still in the air, Caleb woke from his daze and bolted straight ahead into the brush and disappeared. Elbie's shouted warning, " He's running!" followed him into the woods.

Chapter 13
The Events of
September—Night Swim

Cabin #2, Ontario, Canada
October 24, 1970

I held up my hand in a stop sign and said, "Caleb, are you OK? You wanna take a break?"

He sipped on his coffee and said, "John, I've had this inside bottled up for nearly two months. It's almost Halloween here in this godforsaken shack, but in my head, it's still September and I'm thinking of all the different ways this could have gone and Gerry would still be alive. I need to get this out."

Then Caleb said a word I don't think I ever heard come from his mouth. "Please."

I shrugged, sat back, and the story unfolded.

* * *

Lucky looked up slowly. He had a gob of tobacco and spittle running down the side of his chin. His floppy planter's hat had fallen off. His face was red, but his rage had passed. As Gerry's twitching body lay in the shallow muddy river's edge, he stepped back to the ATV and holstered the .44. Then he reached into the trailer that he had pulled behind and fished out the Browning 12 gauge. After unzipping it, he loaded it with double ought and went back to the Jensen canoe. Carefully, almost daintily, he pushed Gerry's prized boat into deeper water and then fired all five shells into it. The expensive canoe fragmented in an explosion of aluminum and fiberglass.

"I don't think our berrypicker buddy is going anyplace. Shorts and a T-shirt… an hour in the brush…sawgrass and bugs will have him chewed down to nothing."

Lucky rested the gun. He pulled out the blackberry brandy from the raingear and took a quick sip to clear his head. After tipping the bottle, he continued, "Hell, we're just gonna sit here. In a little bit, he's gonna come out and beg me to shoot him. Want a sip, sonny?"

"Why not?" said Elbie wearily.

Elbie sat on the tire, and looked at the floating debris from the ravaged canoe. Behind him lay Gerry's body, half submerged. The slight current floated one arm up and down in a preposterous farewell wave, as the body cooled in the shallow water.

Meanwhile, Caleb was in mud up to his waist. In the thirty minutes after the shooting he had covered less than a mile. He scrambled east toward the big lake roughly paralleling the river. Clad only in cutoff shorts and an old Paavo Nurmi marathon T-shirt, he was already bruised and scratched from crashing around in the brush and thorns. A small but determined buzzing cloud of insects surrounded him. Their stings and bites were unrelenting. As he stood to catch his breath, he frantically swatted, itched and scratched to no avail. His breath came in sobs. His aching leg muscles swelled from exertion and lactose overload. Physically exhausted and emotionally destroyed, he stared at the blobs on his shirt that he thought were mud. He realized as he squatted in the muck that he was looking at small parts of his best friend.

He pushed deeper into the swampy area. Over the noise of insects he could hear the angry sounds of a two stroke engine revving up. The pulse throbbed in his ears, and the incessant hum of the bugs made it difficult to tell the direction that the machine was heading. The noise faded. It was now nearing sunset. The twilight would last about an hour. He did not know if it would help in finding his way or just make him a clearer target. The river had to be near. He forced his way south through the mud and bushes. The second growth forest was thick with deadfalls, he scraped his legs and back crawling over and under the downed spruces with their prickly needles. Recklessly storming over one last deadfall, he came to the Cache River and slid down the bank into the current. The cold river numbed the pain and itch. He headed up stream toward the lake and then paused. Slowly, he turned, edged over toward the bank and began working his way back toward the bridge and the fading pink light that had been sunset. He had run for what seemed an eternity. Moving efficiently in the river, he was alarmed to discover how quickly he arrived at the last bend in the river before the bridge. His heart raced again. He knew that given the chance, the madmen would kill him too.

The bridge was silhouetted against the western horizon. Caleb discerned no movement along the shore. He looked at his watch and waited. Twenty minutes later, something moved. Caleb crouched low behind a fallen birch tree. He was beginning to shiver. There was a sharp report of a branch breaking followed by a splash. Caleb's frayed nerves gave way. As he turned to bolt, a moose moved out into the channel. Caleb began to shudder. Softly at first and then much louder, he wept. There was no one to hear him.

Later, as the cool evening settled in, he waded ashore at the bridge. It took him a minute to locate the body. He reached in Gerry's pocket and pulled out his wallet. Gerry was not very sentimental but Caleb knew that it held a picture of his girlfriend, Dee. Over their last campfire, he had shared that he intended to ask Dee to marry him. The wallet's contents were ruined but Caleb resolved that if he ever got out, he would tell Dee what Gerry never had a chance to say. Nothing else in his life made sense, but strengthened by his resolve to preserve a piece of his friend by carrying his unspoken intentions back to Dee, he turned upstream and began to wade the river toward Cache Lake.

* * *

Lucky was rubbing his hand over the holster of the .44. His eyes had a dry shine that made the whites look large and out of place in his dark bushy face. The way he moved his head slowly and deliberately, nodding to himself while speaking, made Elbie suspect that he was finally losing it.

"Seein' as how musky bait over there wrecked our boat and I blew up theirs, we need to get another to get us out on the lake for the pickup plane tomorrow. You take this three wheeler and trailer, go back to the last portage and haul that canoe over here."

"Why don't you come with? I don't want to get lost."

"What the hell's the matter with you?" Lucky spat out the words. "The cops told me you was some kind of secret agent. Secret agent my ass. You're a pussy. Follow the trail and get going. I got to stay here because if asshole #2 comes back,

I need to take care of him. You follow? Now git goin'. It's late. You get to the portage, camp there and be back here at sunup."

A rustle of leaves announced a shift in the night air as a cool wind passed through the sugar maples. Lucky went over to the three wheeler and tucked some odds and ends into the pockets of his favorite pair of bib overalls. His ragged bedroll had a belt strap attached as a sling that rested on his left shoulder. He would spend the night in the woods waiting for his chance to finish things. He kneaded his forehead with two sweaty fingers the size of bratwursts and said, "Now I'm gonna scout around. You get yourself up before daybreak. No shitting around. Meanwhile, I gotta find out what happened to that other son of a bitch. If somehow that berrypicker survives, there might be big trouble."

Something scary was happening in the old man's head. Lucky rubbed his forehead with his thumb, the contrast of the half twilight behind his barrel body expanding his movements. He tightened his gun belt and tied the holster string to his thigh. The Browning shotgun came out next. He held it like a priest holds a chalice. He snapped it back, savoring the rich solid clicks of the blued steel mechanism, then reloaded it and slid the safety on. Then he motioned and Elbie got on, kick started the ATV and rolled out of camp.

It was almost midnight by the time Elbie found the last portage. He unrolled his sleeping bag. Fall was normally a welcome time of year. It made him think of football nights back in high school when he was an All-American boy with a crew cut instead of a long-haired fugitive. He could not ever remember being so tired in his entire life. Driving the ATV had given him too much time to think. He was scared. Inside the Timberline tent it was cool and very quiet.

A shaft of soft white light from the full moon came through the end screen and illuminated the stored gear at his feet. It would be a clear night with no frost; Elbie was anxious. Something inside his chest felt like it was going to burst. He yanked his sleeping bag up around his head and pulled his knees to his chest. He thought back to his first days at Madison. He thought about his crew team jersey with the Big W on the chest. The vision morphed into a red landscape of a burning building and exploding plate glass and brick.

"Oh god, oh god, oh god don't let it be."

He moaned for a long time. Somehow, someway Lucky was going to find out what he had done. The old man was just crazy enough to blackmail his rescuers even if it meant double crossing whatever rogue branch of the FBI had secretly set this nightmare up. Lucky had seen too many scams of his own to miss this one. Elbie could not come up with a plausible lie to answer the questions the old man might ask tomorrow if he really set to thinking about why a black float plane from Quantico, Virginia was flying in with a portfolio for a dumbass long hair college kid. Did Lucky read the newspapers—especially those from August? If Lucky figured out who he was and what he had done back in Madison, Wisconsin, Elbie might be auctioned off to the highest bidders for the reward on his head, or hunted to the ground and shot.

Elbie thought about it some more as he hunched over in the darkness. An owl screeched. A rodent scurried under the packs. High in the pines the wind sighed. Then it was still.

* * *

Two hours after leaving the bridge, Caleb came to Cache Lake. The last section of the river was very wide. He had been able to wade up much of the river but it had been necessary to swim the last quarter mile where the water had no discernible bank but instead wound its way through a vast swampy wetland. Solid footing existed nowhere along the edges of the channel. Slowly Caleb breast stroked out into the great lake. As the bay broadened, a silhouetted tree line began to take the place of the reeds and brush. His feet touched bottom and it was rocky. He scrambled up on a large flat boulder near the shore.

The full moon glided through the high clouds and cast fantastic shadows and outlines. He could see his island across the bay. Hunkered down in the fetal position, he shivered so violently that his vision blurred. His head was splitting and the hot sting of insect bites began to intensify as the numbing effects of the water wore off. Healthy, he could have made the swim to the island in fifteen minutes. In his weakened condition, he knew there was no guarantee that he would survive the attempt. His situation was poor, but he was much too aware that there were no ideal options. He had to get back to shelter and food or he would die. The longer he waited, the slimmer his chances became.

Fortunately the wind had died down and the lake was calm, reflecting the full moon and the clouds like a mirror. It was easy at first. Caleb was halfway across before the fear overtook him. He tried to fight off the unrelenting anxiousness. His stroke was still powerful. He was awake and alert. The fear was not rational but that knowledge made it no less palpable. He switched from the breaststroke to a powerful crawl and began to kick harder. That was a mistake. Within five minutes, his right leg was cramping severely.

Terror replaced fear as he coughed on some water while he tried futilely to knead the cramp out of his calf. He had had leg cramps many times before while working out. He knew that he could swim through them by letting his legs go limp and pulling with his arms alone.

The lake was black and immense. He thought about how deep it was. The topographical map indicated 112 feet. What was on the bottom and what would it be like to sink down to it? He had never been so frightened.

He had also never been so alive and so aware of his own existence. An electric buzz of perception and self-awareness ran through him as another cloud drifted across the face of the moon. He looked up and knew that more than anything, he was not ready to die.

Rolling over, he began to swim carefully letting his legs drag. Going back to high school and the UW-Madison swim team, he was used to workouts of two thousand meters or more. Habit took over and fear receded. Sometime later that evening, his fingertips touched a rock. He stood up in the chilly air and waded ashore. He stumbled up to his camp, crawled inside the tent and tried to make some sense of the day's events as he nestled in his sleeping bag. Far off, a loon called a solitary cry of empathy, but he was already asleep.

Chapter 14
The Events of
September—Rock Star

Cabin #2, Ontario, Canada
October 25, 1970

I looked at the old wind up Big Ben alarm clock we had found. Both arms were pointing straight up. I said, "Caleb, It's midnight." He replied, "No. It's not midnight. It's a sunny morning in September on Cache Island and you're going to listen to what happened next. John, look at me. I killed people."

The wind had stopped and I was aware of a surreal silence interrupted only by the ticking of the clock and the beating of my heart. He had my attention.

* * *

At daybreak, Caleb walked to a spot on the west side of the island where a section of shore rose up in fifty foot granite cliffs. After hiking to the top, he looked over the edge and saw a small, but flat ledge ten feet below him. The rock face was fractured and jagged with hand sized cracks crisscrossing the face. The ten foot downclimb would have been trivial for him a few years ago when he was climbing big walls in Yosemite Park. He was as strong as he had been then, but the fluid climbing moves which were once so natural were now foreign and awkward.

He sat down and dangled a leg over the edge. The hardest part of downclimbing was the beginning. Some rock climbers think of climbing as crawling up and down a page of type. The cracks are words and sentences. Hand holds and secret wedgings are found within the letters. Some of the letters on this page were erased—where he had hoped for an H or an F, there was a lower case i. He twisted and lowered his other leg over the precipice while supporting himself at the waist. The granite scratched his stomach as he slid down until his chin was level with the edge. With the powerful confidence that comes from doing a hundred chin-ups a day, Caleb gradually straightened his arms until he hung at full length. His feet touched a large hold. Placing them carefully, he took the weight off his right hand and inserted it in a jagged deep crack running diagonally at his waist level. Shifting his weight to that hand, he simultaneously lowered a foot to a golf ball-sized protrusion. He wedged his other hand in the waist level crack and lowered himself again. Hanging only by his wedged hand jams, he gently dangled both legs in full extension one more time. His tiptoes touched the ledge. Caleb let go of the crack and landed catlike on the two foot wide ledge.

He turned around and saw that he was about thirty feet above the water. When he lay down he could not see the lake at all, only the opposite shoreline. He would be very difficult to spot from below. Even more fortunate was the placement of an alcove at the back of the ledge. When he jammed himself into that small cave, he could not see the top of the cliff above him. If he had to hide, this would be his place. The island was too small to hold any other spots. Only an experienced rock climber would consider climbing down the overhanging face. The fat man who had shot Gerry appeared to be many things but a rock climber was not one of them. Caleb was not so sure about the younger man, but anyone downclimbing would be very vulnerable to a sudden grab and shove. Whether they were mountaineers or not, they appeared capable of relentless and ruthless tracking. He had to prepare for the worst.

The climb back up was easier. He put his sleeping bag, four quarts of water and three days worth of food in a pack and lowered it onto the ledge along with some plastic baggies. He did not know how long he would be on the ledge and his mind retreated to seven days hanging on the face of El Capitan where bodily waste had to be contained in baggies, and flung off a belay ledge for obvious reasons. That housekeeping accomplished, he returned to the camp one more time to prepare a less passive form of defense.

The small crag behind the campsite overlooked a tiny bay. It too, dropped off steeply to the lake. The water below the overlook was deep. Gerry had discovered it on their first trip and had always taken a few high dives each visit. He never would again.

Caleb hauled over several rocks from softball to bowling ball size. As he worked, he thought of a similar beautiful lake and an old girlfriend. His memory flared bright as a flame…back to a time years ago at an alpine lake. Time waited as he remembered mornings making love to a tall red-haired beauty in the spruce trees at the foot of Mt. Conness.

In his mind's eye, he saw the tan line on her thigh which marked the beginning of an alabaster paradise and passionate beauty that he had still had not gotten over. He used to tease her mercilessly, holding her back to give all her tensions time to build to an unbearable peak. When finally she began to curse and pull at him with frantic strength, arching impossibly wider for him, he moved her into a final gasping release. As he emptied himself, a tremendous tide of tenderness and affection and aching need would sweep through him. He knew that he would never be able to let her go. Nothing was going to separate them ever…until the next day. Making breakfast, he carelessly let the backpacker's fuel container spill on the campfire igniting a Molotov cocktail and their tent. He had been lucky to throw the bomb out on the talus rock before it burst into a fireball. Common sense trumped passion. When she finished telling him what an idiot he was, the beginning of another failed romance had been marked along with the start of his belief that he was a fool to think that women valued him as anything more than a hard body.

He thought about that. Then he went back to the tent and got a gas bottle and brought it over to the rocks. Caleb scrambled down to the water dragging his orange sleeping bag. At the shoreline he lined up several bowling ball-sized rocks in a line and spread the colorful bag over them. He had created a six-foot long tube that might be confused with a covered body from a distance.

* * *

While Caleb was preparing a primitive defense, Elbie had rejoined Lucky after his night in the woods and was following the old trapper through the brush to Cache Lake. It was like trying to keep up with a bear. Lucky hated canoeing for the sake of canoeing and had rammed the three wheeler and canoe trailer through an overgrown logging road until it petered out a half mile short of the lake. Now they were carrying it all. Lucky crashed through the prickers and the brambles as if they were not there at all. Elbie struggled to keep up. He was supposed to be carrying the rear end of the canoe, but in actuality, he was being dragged along. The warming sun added to the discomfort.

"Hey, will you slow down?" Elbie said.

"Sonuvabitch boy! We ain't got all day. Keep up."

It was another five minutes before the pair fought their way into the lake. They set the canoe down in about a foot of water and Lucky got in first lifting the bow of the boat almost two feet out of the water. Elbie grabbed on to the bow gunnels and stepped in, leveling the canoe slightly. Lucky propped the Browning in front of him. He wished he'd brought some more slugs along. He did as much hunting in the spring and summer as he did in season. "Violatin" they called it in Nakotah Rapids and Lucky was the best, or at least the most prolific. He liked his Browning.

"That asshole's got to pay. Just like his berrypicking buddy." Lucky was in a startlingly bad frame of mind and it frightened Elbie.

They were on their way. They paddled slowly toward the island as Caleb and Gerry had the day before. Their canoe moved just as steadily, if not as swiftly. Caleb saw them coming. Their canoe was several hundred yards from the east end of the island. If they landed on the small beach just below the outcropping where he had planted the diversion, he might have a chance. If they did not see the orange sleeping bag, or if they circled the island and landed on one of the bigger beaches, he was in trouble. Spread out before him were a box of matches, his filet knife, two liter containers of Coleman fuel and several large rocks. If Lucky and Elbie did not land near him, he would have to gather up the fuel and matches, and then hide. He had no delusions about his chances in that event. His pursuers were no strangers to the woods and they would track him. He felt that it was unlikely that even if they figured out his ledge hiding place that they could get down to him but anything was possible. He wondered if he should jump off and kill himself if they found him. He wondered if he could.

The canoe closed the distance quickly. Lucky was a bull and Caleb remembered that Elbie had been on the University of Wisconsin crew team. Lucky's ugly voice boomed out and echoed across the lake to Caleb. "He should be back in there someplace screamin' his guts out and going crazy from the bugs. Lost and scared and crazy is what he should be. Sonny, you ain't been to jail. You wouldn't like it. You an' me killed a berrypicker and one got away. That's all there is. He's probably half-dead by now, but maybe he ain't. We won't know for sure until we find their camp and make sure he ain't there. We'll bury all their stuff so nobody will ever know they was in here. You see what I'm sayin'?"

Elbie felt something bunch up in his chest, his face flush, muscles flex and days of rage spew out his inner feelings. "YOU GODDAMN SON OF A BITCH PECKERWOOD BARNYARD SCRAP REDNECK. Shut the fuck up! I'm out here cause I killed a guy in cold blood. Blew his ass up. I blew up a damn building! People are looking for me. Bad people. I don't know who to trust. They say they are going to help. I got reason to believe they will kill me. They might kill you too, you goddamn idiot. I don't give a fuck. You shut your mouth or I'll fuckin…"

Lucky was raising the Browning at Elbie when his face went white at the sight of something on the shore behind Elbie and the bow of the canoe. The old trapper lowered the weapon.

"Look over there! That looks like a guy."

There was an orange clad figure prone on the shore not a hundred yards away. A hawk wheeled overhead. The morning sun reflected off the water which gently lapped against the side of the canoe.

Lucky pointed and said, "Take it in over there sonny."

Caleb readied himself as they approached the outcrop. He kept down and out of sight, but he had to have a good position when they passed under him. God help him if they spotted him when he rose up to make his move. He could hear the paddling and voices coming closer. He dared a peek and saw that they were moving in and pointing ahead to the beach. Caleb recognized the giant bulk of the man wearing the straw hat and blue bib overalls. He had a shotgun. The canoe drifted closer.

Up above, crouched behind a large egg-shaped boulder, Caleb lit a match and held it away from the backpacker's gas bottle. When he moved it next to the bottle, a three-foot plume of flame whooshed out the end. He heaved it like Bart Starr used to wing it at Lambeau Field. It nailed Lucky in the chest and bounced off and into the canoe. Lucky's shirt and planter's hat were instantly engulfed in flames. The canoe looked like the base of a fresh barbeque pit. The big man yelped and jumped up capsizing the canoe. The Browning flipped into the water and disappeared. When Lucky bobbed up, he saw Caleb. The old man was not a very good swimmer and thrashed wildly for the canoe. Elbie had already grabbed onto it when Caleb heaved the first boulder. It hit the canoe and caused both men to lose their grip on the aluminum craft. Lucky started to go under. He was in deep water and in trouble. Caleb's second rock missed everything, but splashed near enough to the old man to disorient him and cause him to gasp in more water. Elbie reached for a flotation cushion just as Caleb's last boulder landed square on the younger man.

79

There was a horrible clunk from Elbie's skull as the rock hit him above his right eye. Blood spattered on the water, the overturned canoe, and Lucky's face. The old man roared. Holding on to the edge of it he reached into it and fished in the water filled canoe with his free hand. The hand came out of the water with a huge revolver in it. Instantly, Lucky pulled the trigger, taking a wild shot. Caleb heard the explosion and simultaneously felt the pain. He sat down in shock and looked at his right leg where a large piece of flesh was hanging loosely from his calf muscle, exposing bloody sinew. The huge slug had glanced off the rocky escarpment and nicked him on the ricochet. The flattened hollowpoint bullet had peeled the muscle and skin from the upper calf. The bleeding was profuse. Ripping off the nylon webbing he used for a belt, Caleb knotted it and wrapped it around his leg, just below the knee. Using the filet knife, he cut a six inch length and used it to tighten it into a tourniquet.

He knew that if the old man did not drown, he would be coming. He pulled himself up, his injured leg dangling uselessly. With agonizing deliberateness, he worked himself up the wall and limped back to his tent. He had no idea where Lucky was. Quickly he tore open his tackle box and took out a roll of duct tape he kept for utility repairs. The tourniquet had to stay tight and he had to have both hands free. He had about three yards left on the roll and he used all of it. Starting at the knee, he wrapped it around and around the tourniquet, pressing the flesh back in place as best he could. When he was finished, he knew that he had all but cut off circulation to his leg. He could worry about that later. It wouldn't be the first time. Years before in Yosemite, he had lacerated his arm badly halfway up the big wall. No bandages were available, so he and his buddy Al wrapped the forearm in duct tape and finished the climb the next day. It wasn't much fun peeling off infected scabs the size of bloody corn flakes, but he lived. Hopefully, the duct tape would come through again. A splashing down at the shoreline startled him. He struggled off back toward the cliff and his hideout as quickly as he could.

Lucky's chest burned. He had almost drowned after Elbie had been hit by the rock. The effort to stay afloat, grab the canoe and fire at his attacker all at the same time was monumental. Gasping for breath, he saw his partner floating face down in the bloody water. The little son of a bitch had the radio transmitter in a waterproof bag. If that went down, he couldn't set up a meet with the very dangerous men who were counting on him. Clinging to the canoe with one arm, he had reached out and lifted Elbie's head out of the water by the hair. Either from effort or the sight of the boy's face, he lost his grip on the canoe. Lucky had never experienced fear until that moment. He thought he was going to drown. In the most terrible exertion of his violent life, he thrashed and struggled furiously, gagging on water and fighting to keep a hand on both the canoe and his injured partner. Somehow, he ended up splashing on to the beach. Now Lucky was kneeling next to Elbie. The transmitter was gone but maybe the plane would come anyway. The boy was still conscious but dying. Lucky knew that. He had been around the dead and dying often enough to know the look.

He did not know that he was dying too.

His great body had finally overtaxed his heart. In every possible way, he felt worse than he ever had in his entire life. There was a sharp shooting pain in his arm that aggravated the fury he felt as he looked at Elbie writhing blindly in agony. Lucky had tears in his eyes. That never happened to him for any reason. Something was wrong.

The old man stood up slowly. A searing pain shot through his chest almost driving him to his knees. He grabbed a nearby birch tree and held on until the pain passed. When it did, he looked down at his empty holster. He could not remember how it happened, but was surprised to see that sometime after firing a shot at the berrypicker, the revolver had disappeared. He took out an ugly Bowie knife from the sheath on his side and started up the rocky path toward the tent. At the tent, he found a roll of bloody duct tape. The berrypicker had apparently been hit badly and tried to do some doctoring before running. An obvious bloody trail led into the woods toward the top of the cliff on the west end of the small rocky island.

Five times Lucky had to stop and lean on trees to catch his breath before he reached the cliff edge overlooking Caleb's hideout. The bloody trail continued right up to the brink. A bolt of white pain jolted Lucky again. He blacked out for a second and came to on all fours a foot away from the edge. The flat rock in front of him was smeared with sticky dark red. He cautiously leaned over and saw a blood splattered ledge directly below him.

"YOU SONUVABITCH! I KNOW YOU'RE DOWN THERE AND I'M GOING TO KILL YOU!"

Caleb pushed himself against the back of the shallow cave. He could hear the old man moving above him. Both men were breathing in gasps. A shower of sand and pebbles fell down on Caleb followed by the clattering of Lucky's huge knife dropping onto the ledge directly in front of Caleb. As it rattled to a rest, its deadly polished blade reflected in the sun

Above, Lucky clutched his shirt as he sagged to one knee. A wave of vertigo engulfed him as his tortured heart exploded. His last view was of crystalline Cache

Lake and graceful cedar trees leaning over the opposite shore. He tumbled forward and dropped over the edge. Caleb screamed as the body bounced at his feet. One of the boulders that created the shelf he stood upon broke off from Lucky's impact and plummeted to the rocky shore below, carrying Lucky along. Caleb looked down and saw Lucky lying amid the rocky debris, the knife now jammed crazily into his side.

The climb up was not as difficult as the previous descent. Caleb's injured leg was almost useless, but between his good leg, strong arms, and leftover adrenaline, he had all the power he needed to negotiate the holds. He limped back around to the shore and found Elbie. The young man was breathing and lying in a pool of his own blood and vomit, but miraculously, still conscious.

Elbie tried to move his head and groaned. Caleb looked at him. "It's you isn't it? Elbie, my ass. It's L.B. Leo, right? Leo fucking Burt. I knew you were useless in the gym, and they cut your ass from the crew team and now look what you've gone and done."

The most wanted man in America, Leo Burt, spasmed and whispered, "I was a plant…secret arm of the FBI. They recruited me, helped me build a rep as a war protestor. I infiltrated peace meetings. The bomb…said it would turn people against…peace movement…said the building would be empty. They had to get me out of the country to save their own asses!" He sucked in a small gulp of air and coughed up blood. Weakly, but in a voice driven by an angry heart and furious mind, he promised, "I wrote it down. Every word, name, promise and secret phone numbers in Washington. I have a letter. I hid it all in a locker at the Badger Bus depot in Madison. Take the key…my pocket. Tell …"

Then he died.

Caleb, who had never seen a person die in his entire life, had now witnessed the violent deaths of three people within twenty four hours. He was reeling from the shock of the past day, but he had his wits about him enough to understand that he was in the center of a vast conspiracy, holding a secret that could get him killed. It began to rain.

Caleb rolled Elbie on his side, fished out the key, and carefully placed it in his own pocket. He waded over to the trapper's canoe which had drifted to shore. There was a bunch of nylon webbing in the boat. Caleb knew from climbing that it was strong and would last almost forever. Carefully, he wrapped it around Elbie's body from head to toes, knotted it and then tied the loose end to a large empty Duluth Pack the trapper had laying in the half sinking canoe. Then he wrestled the dead campus radical into the canoe. He began carrying rocks. One at a time, he filled the pack until there was no more room. Then he cinched the leather straps tight. He found a paddle and slowly worked the boat out to a fishing hole he knew of off shore. He looked back at the shoreline and saw that the rain had already washed away the blood where Elbie had lain. He grabbed both gunnels and began rocking the canoe sideways until he got an edge under. More water poured in, the canoe tipped and the pack plummeted to the bottom with the body trailing. He knew from fishing, that they had a hundred feet to go before coming to rest on the icy black bottom.

Caleb left the canoe and slowly swam back to Cache Island for the last time.

DAN WOLL and JOHN W. LYON

Chapter 15
The Events of
September—The Key

Cabin #2, Ontario, Canada
October 25, 1970

I interrupted. "Are you telling me that Leo Burt blew up Sterling Hall in Madison, Wisconsin as some kind of secret counter intelligence move against the peace movement?"

Caleb said, "I think he had accomplices. I don't know about them. The bombing happened in late August. I don't pay much attention to news anyhow, and Gerry and I were getting ready to go canoeing. What I do know is that Leo confessed to me on his death bed and I've never seen a guy show more remorse. Why would he lie? He says some rogue arm of the FBI cooked this up, convinced him that no one would get hurt and there was something in it for him."

Caleb was getting wound up and I did not want to light him up but I had to protest, "You really think people in our own government set the bombing up?"

He threw the dregs of his coffee on the floor and grabbed one of the brandy bottles he had stolen from a nearby cabin. He took a long pull, wiped his lips with his sleeve and said, "Listen."

It was 1:00 a.m.

* * *

Back in what was left of camp, Caleb crouched at the front of his tent. He used Gerry's portable stove to make some hot water. He numbly studied the scene, dipping a tea bag into his cup, and tried to massage the feeling back to the lower part of his leg. He sat for several hours, drinking tea and nibbling on candy, when he saw a seaplane.

The seaplane circled the island once before landing. From where Caleb lay, he could see two canoes lashed to the pontoons and official markings on the plane. Although it had only been a few hours since Lucky's body had smashed on the rocks below, it seemed much longer. Between the shock brought on by his wound and the horror of seeing a falling body hit so hard that rocks broke, Caleb was totally disoriented. He was not too delirious to understand that if he was unable to contact the men in the plane, he was going to die.

The seaplane landed on the south side of the island, giving Caleb a stretchy feeling of panic in his stomach. He tried to calm himself. Who knew why the plane was here? It was not out of the ordinary for park rangers to touch down on beautiful lakes like Cache for lunch or simply to enjoy the scenery for a half hour or so. After a while he heard voices. He could barely contain the rising panic he felt. The bow of a canoe poked out from behind a big boulder at the end of the island. Soon he could see both paddlers. One had an uncased, scoped deer rifle propped up beside him. The paddler in the stern was also armed. In a minute, another canoe appeared bearing two more men looking like trouble.

"Hey! Over there! Look at the mess. What the hell!"

Voices came from the other canoe.

"Shit, that's a guy. It's that trapper. Hah! It looks like our friend has changed his name to Unlucky."

Then there was laughter.

After that Caleb could not hear what they said. One more time, he hobbled back to his ledge and lowered himself down. Lucky had not had any trouble finding him, but Lucky didn't kill him. He slunk back into the recesses of the shallow cave.

The canoers beached their canoes directly below him. They got out carefully and quickly. Two went over to Lucky while the other two jacked cartridges into their rifles and scanned the surrounding area. One of the men kicked Lucky's lifeless leg, and Caleb could hear a harsh laugh.

"Guess those boys in Washington, D.C. won't have to worry about this old peckerwood talking. Now we need to find this Elbie character and solve their other problem before this all gets out of hand."

They dragged and wrestled Lucky's carcass over to the shade. It took all four of them to do it. Breaking into two teams, they began to climb up the broken easier rock on the side of the cliff. It wasn't long before Caleb heard noise above him.

"Shit, will you look at this blood! Goes right over the edge of the cliff. Now what in the hell? His damn gut must have hurt and he walked right off the edge. Let's go."

"Wait. This is weird. Look over the edge here. See how it's all puddled down on the little ledge right below us.

"You're right. Is there any way we can get down there and look at it?"

"If you trust me to remember how to belay, you can tie on and climb down and I'll keep you tight anchored to this tree here."

Caleb heard the sounds of uncoiling rope, a delay, and then grit and pebbles falling down on the ledge. He looked around. No exit. Almost unconsciously, he reached into his pocket, pulled out the small locker key and swallowed it. More grit and dirt fell and then his heart jumped at the appearance of two feet dropping down in front of him. The knees bent and a face appeared. The sight of Caleb sitting there in a puddle of blood almost startled the man into backing right off the ledge, but he recovered quickly.

"Boy, I don't know what you are doing here or where you are from, but you are in a whole hell of a lot of trouble. I don't like heights and if you mess with me now while I'm standing on this ledge, you're dead meat." He unholstered a very large hand gun and pointed it at Caleb.

The flight back to Nakotah Rapids was not pleasant. They bound his ankles and wrists agonizingly tight. It was superfluous. Even if Caleb's mangled leg had permitted some sort of locomotion, he was already going into shock, fading in and out of a nauseating reality. Despite his stupor, the men in the plane kept up an incessant and aggressive line of questioning, punctuating their queries with kicks and slaps.

"How'd you end up on the same island with Lucky?" There was a kick to the ribs. The voice was harsher and louder. Caleb knew it was not going to get any easier.

"I don't know." Caleb saw the big hand arc through the air before he felt and heard the resounding slap.

"Son, we know you're a part of what happened to Lucky. You got one damned chance for things to go halfway easy. Now what happened and what did they say!"

"Boat flipped...packs went over...don't know...honest..." He was kicked again. This time it was the leg that had already seen damage.

Caleb rolled over on his side in the small plane and vomited, and lost consciousness.

* * *

When Caleb woke up, he was wearing a threadbare hospital gown, but he was not in a hospital. He was in a cell, his leg throbbing something awful. It smelled heavily of antiseptic and was in a wrap as thick as a cast. Looking around he verified that he was in a jail. He was the only prisoner. There was a sink and a toilet at the end of the narrow room, leading Caleb to believe that he was actually in an old bathroom which had been converted into a holding tank. Otherwise, the room was bare.

There was a plastic gallon milk container filled with water and a cold but surprisingly large hamburger lying next to the old army cot. He drank half the water and forced himself to eat some the hamburger bun. He felt better. He went back to sleep.

Sometime later, Caleb heard footsteps coming down a flight of stairs. The door at the end of the room opened, letting in a rectangle of natural light. Two men entered. One of the men was large and doughy looking, wearing blue jeans and a red checkered flannel shirt. The other man was short with a neatly groomed mustache. He wore a badge on his dark blazer. As he came closer, Caleb could read his name, "Linley."

Linley opened the cell and came in followed by Flannel Shirt. Quite correctly they assumed that Caleb was in no condition to try anything, although he recognized that he was a little stronger. Linley sat down on the foot of Caleb's cot. Caleb felt a searing pain as the man settled down. Flannel Shirt remained standing and opened up a small notebook.

"Young man, we have a dead guide on our hands named Lucky LaJeunesse. More disturbing than that is the fact that we know he had a very important passenger. Does the name Leo Burt mean anything to you?"

The shock of hearing Burt's name jolted Caleb but thanks to his weakened condition, his mind was ahead of his reflexes. He didn't even blink.

"I only saw the crazy hillbilly."

"This is a matter of national security. I must warn you. As unbelievable as it seems, we are authorized from the very top to take whatever measures are necessary to extract the truth from you. Before he began his poorly planned escape, the missing Mr. Burt communicated to us that he had something we needed. He told us it was locked up and that we could have the key and location if we picked him up in Quetico. When we showed up at the meeting place, he was gone, his guide was dead and we found you. You see where this is going?"

Caleb doubted that they would kill him until they were sure that he did not know anything. That was the good news. The bad news was that they were going to torture him in the meantime. What the hell...he could always tell what he knew when he could not take it anymore.

"Well sir, let's begin with introductions. I am Inspector Linley. Who are you?"

Caleb's voice was dry and raspy but it held conviction. "My name is Caleb Pratt. I was canoeing in Quetico with my friend. We were attacked by that man. He killed my friend and followed me to the island. I was lucky. He wasn't."

Linley and Flannel Shirt exchanged smirks.

"Actually, he was. What about Burt?"

"There is no Burt. Just the crazy old man! I suppose you're not interested in getting me a lawyer or a phone call?"

Linley laughed. Then his face shape shifted into an emotionless mask.

"Well Caleb, I do believe you are responsible for the death of a respectable Nakotah Rapids sportsman and an innocent young tourist, even though you only admit to one murder."

His voice was quiet, but intense. He continued in a sarcastic tone.

"Now what you are going to have to explain is why you killed them and what happened to their personal belongings. Especially those of the young man."

Caleb felt an urge to share what he knew, but it was becoming more and more apparent that the inspector and whoever he represented, had two problems— finding Burt's cache, and eliminating anyone who knew of its existence.

"I did not murder anyone. The crazy bastard killed my friend and tried to do the same to me. I have no interest in anybody's personal belongings but Gerry's and mine. I do not know what was in that canoe, if anything. Maybe it fell out. And besides, I keep telling you. There was no Burt, whoever the hell that is."

Caleb could not trust anyone. He decided to repeat the facts.

"I was attacked. My friend's dead, my leg is killing me and you're worried about some missing key! What kind of cop are you!"

"I wish I could believe you Caleb, but the fact of the matter is that this case has implications I cannot reveal to you. I think you know more than you are telling. Until I hear more, you will receive no more medical attention. In fact if you continue your obdurate behavior, we may be forced to subject you to some physical duress during our next questioning. I will give you three days to think it over while we complete forensics on your friend and your victim...till then."

He was all talk, no listen. Abruptly, he got up and left. Flannel Shirt closed up his notebook and followed. He gave Caleb a dirty look and slammed the cell door shut so hard that the reverberations hurt Caleb's ears.

The cell that Caleb was in was actually a dead end hallway which had been converted into a confinement area. It was eight steps from front to back. The walls were aging red brick with crumbling mortar. None of the bricks were loose. The floor was cement covered with chipped and peeling red paint revealing a sub layer of paint. Two bare incandescent light bulbs hung suspended at each end of the room. They were controlled by a switch out of his reach. He could see the switch and the rest of the hallway through the steel bar door that kept him imprisoned in the filthy cul de sac.

Hours passed. He thought about the key. He had no natural light, but Flannel Shirt visited him regularly with what Caleb estimated to be supper then breakfast. Things were going to get moving sooner or later and any modesty in looking for the key would cost him his life.

The plastic container of water or spoiled milk was a staple and solid food ranged from left over picked at chicken bones to a peanut butter sandwich. It wasn't great, but he was living. He forced himself to eat. The next day he felt better.

When the inevitable occurred, he steeled himself for the unmentionable search for the key that had to succeed. He remembered a time when he was only three or four and his parents thought that he had swallowed the little hook off of a toy tow truck. They seined through his movements for days. Finally, his dad decided that if he had swallowed it and it hadn't killed him by then, it probably wasn't going to and they gave up. If his mom and dad could do it, so could he. Especially when his life was at stake.

He got lucky for the first time since he set foot on Cache Island. Thanks to his diet of stale food and tainted milk, the search was quick. The silvery surface of the shiny locker key attracted his attention and he fished it out with a minimum of discomfort, all things considered. He looked around for a hiding place and settled on the toilet tank. He lifted the lid and reached down in the cold rusty water and placed it in the right hand corner.

Caleb prided himself on his stamina and recovery speed. His stubbornness was paying off. He tried walking back and forth, knowing that he was irrecoverably damaging something in his leg, but at the same time he was exploring compensating muscles which were allowing him to override the pain and the damage. As the blood pulsed and he adjusted to the pain and his strange gait, his mind focused on one thought. Revenge.

Linley came back one time. There weren't many questions and even less answers.

Flannel Shirt had held him while Linley beat him savagely about the face. Linley didn't hit particularly hard, but he wore a signet ring that had cut through the stubble of his beard and made vicious lacerations on Caleb's cheeks and chin. Toward the end of the beating, Linley made Caleb cry out from pain. The only thing that kept Caleb from talking was that he wanted to kill these men. If he talked and they executed him, he would never realize his vengeful obsession.

As they left, he looked up and muttered, "You said you were going to give me a few days before subjecting me to…what'd you call it?…duress."

Linley cooed, "That's exactly right. This is not duress. We are merely putting you on notice as to what duress might entail."

After Linley left, Flannel Shirt came back and tossed a can of Band Aids in through the cell door and laughed. Caleb staunched the worst of the bleeding with the band aids. From what he knew of first aid, he should have had a dozen stitches. He slept with his face pressed against an old dirty pillow to apply pressure to the Band Aids.

He woke up before the next meal arrived and looked around his cell again. Despite some makeshift carpentry, the steel door was formidable, and the rest of the small rectangular cell was windowless. There would be no miracle escape.

Chapter 16
The Events of
September—"All Aboard!"

Cabin #2, Ontario, Canada
October 25, 1970

"Whoa!" I interrupted again. "You did NOT fish through your own shit for a key."

Caleb grinned for the first time since he started talking, reached into his shirt pocket and pulled out a small locker key. He flipped it to me. I ducked.

"Hey! Don't lose that." he said.

I threw the dregs of my coffee on the floor and grabbed the brandy bottle from him. "Go on," I said, as I took a big pull and winced.

Caleb recommenced his story. It was 1:30 a.m. and the wind began to howl.

* * *

The cell was cheap, ugly, and escape proof. Caleb got up and hobbled back and forth a few more times. The pain in his leg was worse, but his mobility seemed to be increasing.

He studied the cell door. It did not go to the ceiling. The old hallway walls rose fully three feet higher than the top of the hinged cross hatch iron grillwork that

93

formed the door. The jail door reminded him of ones where they locked up the bad guys in the old cowboy movies he loved. The cell was about five feet across. It was about the same width as the dorm hallway he and his mountaineering friends had shown off on in college. Except for his bum leg, he was stronger now than he had been back then. He put his good foot on to the first cross bar of the door and hauled himself up. So far, so good. The next cross bar was higher up, but using the strength in his arms, he was able to hop up on to it. This put him in a position chest high with the top of the doorframe. There was one more cross bar on the cell door, a foot from the top. This was going to hurt some, but not as much as staying. He braced his good foot on a vertical bar and pulled up again until he could get his bad leg on the top bar. Excruciating pain. Quickly he lifted his good foot up and alongside the other. In that position, he was crouched with his hands less than twelve inches above his feet, jammed up on the top bar.

He could only hope that he had calculated the frequency of his keeper's visits correctly. There seemed no way that he could maintain his present position for more than ten minutes or so. He knew however that his body was capable of more than his mind currently told him. If worse came to worst, he could probably last a half hour.

He painfully and carefully downclimbed and practiced reclimbing the barred door several times in the following hour. Each time, the pain got worse but his skill improved.

One hour later the guard had still not come, and Caleb was tense. He decided to climb up one more time to his perch and begin counting. He told himself that when he reached 500 he would get down. He was on three hundred twenty three when he heard a latch at the top of the stairs outside the cell rattle. Adrenaline surged, blocking out the pain. Faster than he would have believed possible he reached out with his good left leg and braced it on the wall nearest his feet. Like a man who did this every day, he then stretched over to the opposite wall with his right hand while holding himself into the bars with his left. When his right hand was flat and securely braced against the wall, he took a deep breath, pushed as hard as he could and let go of the bars. He reached over quickly with his free hand, increased the pressure even more and then lifted his bad foot off the bars and lightly placed it alongside his good leg planted horizontally against the wall. He was braced wall to wall arched over the door opening and parallel to the ceiling. To someone coming down the stairs, he was completely out of sight.

"Son of a bitch! Where did he..." Flannel Shirt was not the type to think things over before acting. He burst into the cell as soon as he could get the key into the lock and turn it. Caleb never even had time to be nervous. It just happened. He let go and dropped squarely on Flannel Shirt's head and shoulders crumpling him immediately to the floor.

Caleb had never done any serious wrestling. His high school didn't even have a team when he was growing up. But he won his share of the few fights he was in because he had mastered one move that wrestlers refer to as a head steal. Caleb knew it only as a choke hold. Years of weight training and rock climbing had given him the power to make it a very effective tactic.

Pumped up by pain and fear, Caleb had no problem overcoming Flannel Shirt. He was aware of Flannel Shirt's ears and neck turning crimson then purple as Caleb relentlessly increased the pressure. When the muscle tension left the jailer's shoulders and neck, he let go. Flannel Shirt made a little burble and then lay on the floor, still. Caleb checked the man's pockets for anything useful. No knife but there was a set of keys and some change. Checking the wallet, he found a twenty and a couple of singles. The other stuff would do him no good.

Caleb limped out the door, almost tipping over the gallon milk jug that was to be the most substantial part of his breakfast. Three steps out, he stopped abruptly and rushed back in. Crossing over to the toilet, he lifted the tank lid and retrieved the little locker key.

He cautiously hobbled up the stairs, attending carefully for signs of activity. He held the jailer's heavy key ring in his right hand, a poor weapon but his only option.

When he reached the top of the landing, he stopped, gathered his nerve and listened before opening the door. He took a deep breath and stepped into a small office of some sort. It had a desk, counter and a couple of file cabinets, and an old wood floor. The venetian blinds allowed the gray street light to filter in, revealing particles of dust suspended in the air. A clock said 5:46. Soon the sun would rise.

The room was empty. Caleb opened what turned out to be a closet and found a black leather flight jacket adorned with the Canadian flag and black and gold emblems informing everyone that the wearer was a member of the Nakotah Rapids P. D. He looked down and saw a large gray and red gym bag. There was a jogging sheriff in town. He ripped out a pair of black gym shorts, a heavy cotton sweatshirt and a beat up pair of Converse running shoes. The running outfit wasn't designed for the Canadian fall but it was a lot better than a hospital gown with nothing underneath.

He pulled a counter drawer open and found a dented, tin cash box. A twinge of homesickness flashed through him. It reminded him of the cash boxes carelessly left in the small school office after games. They were usually not locked and neither was this one. Inside were a stack of fives and singles plus more change. He kept the bills.

Caleb limped over to the window and moved aside the blinds. Looking outside, he saw a lone street light reflecting off a tin-sided building proudly proclaiming itself as the Nakotah Rapids Farmers Cooperative Mill. Beyond that and the road were the railroad tracks. The morning C.P. Rail freight train was moving a car marked Soo Line from the main line to the siding. He quickly picked up a map of Ontario that was filed in the rusting display rack on the counter, then moved quietly out the door to the deserted street.

Hidden by a stack of railroad ties, he watched as the train crew's brakeman gave the end car's coupler rod a tug to disengage it from the rest of the moving train. The maneuver was sometimes known as the slingshot.

The switchman, up the line twenty yards, stood waiting at the switch standard. The lone boxcar was slowing down behind the train because of the drag of squealing hand brakes. As the last car that was still part of the train cleared the frogs, the switch was thrown and the Soo boxcar rolled by itself on to the siding. The brakeman swung up the grab irons to the top of the car and cranked the brake wheel but it was almost unnecessary. It coasted to a slow stop at the loading dock. The operation was a game of skill and coordination between the engineer, switchman and brakeman. The conductor walked up the tracks quite a distance, leaving his caboose empty.

Looking back at the rest of the train parked on the main line, Caleb saw a car carrier three cars ahead of the caboose. It was a relic, but it was loaded with new Canadian made full-sized Chevy pick-ups. It looked like the place to go.

Limping down the tracks he picked up a rail spike that had worked loose from the siding track and pocketed it. He was constantly looking for weaponry. Grabbing on to the ladder on the side of the car carrier, he pulled himself up, hand over hand, to the top rack, hoping the train would not recouple as he was hanging on.

He moved to the second truck in line. As he expected it was locked but it only took a couple of quick smashes with the rusty spike to knock enough out of the window to unlock the door. He climbed in and rolled what was left of the window down and out of view just as the train slammed together one last time and began crawling ahead.

Caleb found Nakotah Rapids on the map and from the direction of the impending sunrise, surmised that he was headed west on the C.P. Rail tracks. That guess was confirmed an hour later when the train rolled through English River. By then he had peeled back on the wrap on his leg. He found it ugly, but to his minimal medical knowledge, satisfactory.

Studying the map he wondered what was familiar about the area ahead of him. As he traced a finger along the C.P. rail line between Ignace and Kenora, he remembered a past summer trip when he had fished and drank beer with John for two weeks on Eagle Lake. That had been in June. It was prime tourist season, but even then they had seen very few people on the far West Arm of Eagle Lake. It was now getting deeper into fall, and many of the outpost cabins on the lake would be deserted. Caleb needed a place to hide, to recover, and most of all to think. The whole winter didn't seem too short to recuperate.

It was afternoon when the train rumbled into Vermillion Bay. Caleb was prepared to jump off regardless of the consequences to his leg, when the train slowed. Fortunately a car change was necessary. Caleb climbed down as soon as the long train's wheels slid to a stop just short of the town limits. The temperature was mild for late September but the running shorts were not enough protection.

He did not know how much his battered leg could take but he had to get into town. A plan was forming in his mind. Resting every hundred yards or so, he managed to get to Main Street.

He went to Vermillion Bay Grocery Cooperative. The sign above the door bragged, "We aim to serve you Better." He prowled the aisles with a cart ignoring the bemused looks of the clerk. When he checked out, twenty five dollars made him the proud owner of the biggest Duluth Pack he had ever seen in his life. It was a huge canvas carrying pack—obviously used because it had Ish-nay YMCA stenciled on the back. It would have made sense to buy a cheaper pack but Caleb was not into ideal options. With fifty dollars remaining, he bought all the canned goods he could fit into the pack, along with several boxes of matches, a pair of red sweat pants, a stocking cap and a big screw driver. Acceding to an odd compulsion, he turned back, bought a pen, a postcard and a stamp.

He was getting nervous. Caleb knew the yellowing bruises visible on his face and leg would make him stand out anywhere, let alone in a town of 200 people. But Canadians get used to strange Americans buying strange supplies up north. The checkout clerk paid no attention to the haggard looking stranger.

Outside, he arranged the food in his pack and slipped on the sweat pants. A mail box was just outside the municipal office. He scribbled on the card, affixed a stamp and dropped it in the mailbox. The sun was setting as he limped down Bay Street to a boat landing behind a sketchy looking outfit called Larry and Cathy's

Spruce Tree Lodge. Larry and Cathy appeared to have closed up for the season because there were no lights on in the lodge. All the canoes were stacked and chained together except for one old Grumman which was visible through the cracks in a smaller decrepit boat house near the lake's edge. The door was padlocked, but the old cedar boards were dry rotted. One good pry with the big screwdriver popped off the hasp. He dragged the old canoe over to the lake.

Caleb's luck seemed to be changing. He struck the mother lode of survival supplies on his first break-in. He methodically began to shuttle what he needed out to the lake. He might as well have been in a ghost town. Empowered by a feeling of fatigued recklessness, he stopped worrying about being observed. Later that night he would wonder at his boldness, but it's easy to be bold when there is nothing to lose. His luck held.

Healing time in a secure location was his driving motivation. Although his destination was only 20 or 30 miles away, it would put plenty of distance between those who were hunting him and his hideout. He would probably be the only human for 10,000 square miles for the entire winter. The two main lodges in the area had closed for the season. Owners, for years, had taken the money that their prime Canadian locations earned and high tailed it back to winter homes in places like Illinois. There would be no disturbing visitors at the primitive outpost cabins. The one Caleb was thinking of was tucked in a bay accessible only by canoe and portage. There would be no reason for a stray snowmobile to head that way because there was nothing but wilderness for a hundred miles in three directions.

On his first trip to the shed, he took an old-fashioned but well stocked Plano tackle box and a nice Berkley Cherrywood rod with a Garcia Cardinal reel. In addition to the usual tangle of hooks, lines, spoons, and jigs, the tackle box also contained an old fashioned army knife, dull but heavy. On the second trip he took two paddles, a cushion and a canvas tarp. He also found a full length rubberized poncho and a filthy army blanket.

He paddled off south and west into the setting sun. By moonlight he was able to reach a small bay at the end of Vermillion Bay. He beached the canoe, then wrapped himself up in the army blanket and canvas tarp. He rolled over and used the heavy army knife to punch a hole in the top of a large can of Dinty Moore beef stew. He wolfed it down cold. He laid back and went to sleep as the Northern Lights flared overhead in cascading sheets of blue and yellow.

When he woke up, it was raining gently. He was a damp muddy mess. He could have killed for a cup of coffee, but the search for dry kindling would have eaten up precious time. Someone might check the boat house, and he wanted to be far away in case a sharp mind pieced together the trail he had left.

It was fully ten more miles of paddling to the place John and he had found by the Buzzard Lake Falls years ago. The light rain and overcast day made him gloomy, but it also discouraged any other boaters. The windless day was perfect for canoeing. Despite the natural awkwardness of solo canoeing, he made good time.

He kept to the shore and only once did he see other boaters. The noise of the motor carried a long way off through the fog. He tucked in tight against an overhung cedar tree while the boat sped by a hundred yards off shore. They must have been late season muskie fishermen judging by the fact that he could see poles. They were as thick as broom handles and stood out even in the fog.

At about noon, the light rain turned into a cold downpour. Caleb had on the poncho which slowed his paddling but it covered him up. If he shifted positions frequently, he didn't cramp badly. He was chilled and developing a painful sore throat, but the wind stayed down, and no one else was on the lake. An hour later, the rain changed to wet snow.

Two days later the lake was frozen over, but by then Caleb was holed up for the winter in what the outfitters at the Buckhorn Lodge referred to as "old cabin #2."

* * *

Caleb looked up at me. Half of the brandy bottle was left. He took a pull and handed it to me. I did the same and handed it back. In that fashion, we silently finished the bottle, covered up the best we could and went to sleep. As I drifted off, I reflected that our shed was almost identical in size to Thoreau's Walden Pond retreat. Henry David said, "In wildness is the preservation of the world." I wondered if our wild desolate place at the end of the Eagle Chain of Lakes could preserve our lives.

DAN WOLL and JOHN W. LYON

Chapter 17
The Bear Facts

Cabin #2, Ontario, Canada
November 24, 1970

Caleb and I spent the next few weeks reconstructing and melding our stories into a coherent outline of the terrible series of coincidences that had led to the deadly intersection and ruined lives at Cache Lake. Meanwhile, October bled into November, more snow came, and the cabin food supplies began to dwindle.

One afternoon, Caleb was poking through our belongings for the hundredth time. He turned away from the pack, straightened up, then reached down into the pack again and flipped a box of .22 shells into my lap.

"John. You're a hunter. Hunt. Get me a rabbit."

I fiddled with the shells. There were one hundred of the little brass rim fire cartridges packed neatly in the clear plastic box. Actually there were fewer because I had not repacked the box after the last hunting trip the year before. What that meant was just under a hundred rabbit dinners. That is if we were the world's best hunters. Even Olympic biathlon contestants miss some of their shots. The gun stayed behind the door along with the fishing tackle most of the time. There was no way we could hope for great luck with the .22, because I was out of practice and Caleb was not a distance shot without his glasses. They were back in Nakotah Rapids.

Conservation of ammunition could be important if we had unwanted guests. There was even some talk of a moose hunt, so we decided to save the shells for something we really wanted or needed to shoot at.

Snares were the answer. Caleb came up with the materials as we talked one night in the cozy log cabin.

"Something strong and flexible is what we need for rope to make the loop," he said as we sat in candlelight after a dinner of steamed walleye and watercress.

"How about some fish line? There's some 20lb. test in the red tackle box I borrowed from the cabin on Walleye Lake." He took the candle resting on its Mason jar lid holder over to the boxes behind the door. He came back with the whole box a minute later and we pawed through the contents.

"The trigger will be the trick, I said as I dug through the stuff that was layered in the bottom. "Shit! Too many loose hooks in there." I carefully pulled my hand from the box. Trailing from it were several hooks attached to a couple of spoons. Although they were not the official Daredevil, they looked good, but not on my fingers. We pondered different styles as I wiggled the hooks from my fingers in the candlelight. Caleb stoked the woodstove up again and put on more water for tea.

"We'll tie a loop in the end, then run a loop through the end loop." I worked the stiff plastic with my hands, curling the line and tucking it through the first loop as we sat at the plank table.

"So, now what?" Caleb was holding the spool.

"We tie your end to a thin tree branch that we pull down and let the rabbit catch itself."

"What is the trigger?" Caleb was skeptical.

"Oh, you know, we'll just lay it on the ground and the bunny…"

"We better think this over." Caleb poured more tea.

By late evening we thought we had a suitable answer. We practiced and pretended how it would work until we thought we had it right. Like all great inventions, the first time wasn't perfect. Two days later we held another meeting to redesign the snare.

Outside, we cleared the snow away on one of the rabbit paths we found. The snare was suspended from a small birch tree. Later that day we checked. Empty. We'd had a customer but it had left without paying with its life. The bait was cornmeal on a bed of dried grass. The rabbit liked it because it was gone, but the snare had not tripped. The stick that was driven into the frozen earth had not been brittle enough to snap, nor loose enough in the ground to pull free when the rabbit tickled the line.

We rebuilt the trap. In the bright sun and snow, the inside of the fishing lures sparkled silver. We drove them at an angle into the ground, then flipped the modified treble hooks over to hold the line. The last refinement we made was to include five equally spaced hooks around the loop. That way we figured we had our rabbit doubly caught.

By then, we were getting tired of sitting and jigging for fish and checking tip ups. We had been lucky enough to find some grubs in a rotted log at the far end of the island. We saved them in the traditional Copenhagen container found in the cabin. My grandpa always said it gave them the right flavor. It worked. Caleb had customized a Berkley Cherrywood pole to a two-foot-long ice fishing rod. He lamented the ruination of a good rod until he pulled up the first lake trout.

As the days wore on, the rabbit snare was also a success. We baited up with a variety of cereal. It was my day to check the snares while Caleb pounded new holes in the ice for tip ups. He had developed them from a Daiwa spinning rod. It looked great in theory, and he was ready to go after northern pike. The bait of the day was perch. They are illegal to use as bait, but one more violation tacked on to murder didn't seem important. As clouds rolled in it seemed like a good time to lay in a supply of food before the next storm.

At the first snare we had been lucky again. I shouted to Caleb across the lake as he took a break in the chiseling. An area with brambles and low browse could keep several rabbits happy, even those long gangly snowshoe hares. I tucked the bunny in the back pocket of my blue skier's jacket.

The second snare was the other way but not far from the cabin along the edge of the falls. I reached the area quickly on the cross country skis that Caleb had found in one of the cabins. Hunting there had a bonus attraction because of the plentiful blueberry bushes on the high ground past the falls. My plan was to pluck enough of the frozen berries for some kind of cooking.

The snare was gone.

In its place were large paw prints that I did not recognize at first. They were fresh. I was in the process of putting a name to them when I smelled something awful. I had skied through some dark fresh bear scat. With that, a pile of black brush near a birch tree came to life and transmogrified into a large black bear. His low growl shut down my pancake daydreaming and turned on the fight or flight mechanism. Although bears hibernate, it was only November, and this particular one was still on a singular mission to chow down before the big sleep.

He turned on me from a distance of 20 feet. His face was bloody. In that frozen moment, I realized we had trapped a bear. He did not think it was funny. As he squirmed and rubbed at the silver thread of the leader with hook shanks circling his snout, his low growl turned into a bellow of anger. He moved toward me as if he knew I was responsible for the pain. He looked like he wanted to pay me back. Payback is a bitch. I saw the ebony shine of his claws and sensed the hatred of an animal in pain. I could not turn around on my skis. He would be on me in a second.

There was an opening in the brambles and blueberries ahead, so I charged ahead through the snow, passing the bear before he could reorient for a charge. I skied downhill in a tuck back to the lake's surface. Normally bears are afraid of men. I thought that once I was in the open area of the lake he would leave me alone. The experts say bears do not like open areas like frozen lakes. He lumbered after me.

I had gained a good lead by the time I hit the lake. I made a beeline to the cabin. My path took me across the bay near the falls. The black horror behind me was picking up speed in the open. Bears can move amazingly fast, even the sleepy ones. Caleb had seen me by now and at first did not understand what was going on. He told me later he did not know why, but he cut in front of us at top speed, 100 yards ahead. Our strange parade rolled across the ice.

Moving across the snow covered ice was easy. I had never considered myself an expert skier, but I was hard charging in gigantic diagonal glides. Caleb reached the cabin door first and fumbled with the latch. I was speeding toward the shore line where we had made a hole to scoop out drinking water, when I heard the crack and splash. I turned my head to see the bear disappear in the lake. But he would be back.

Caleb had the .22 down when I reached the door. He was working the lever as I unclipped from my skis and scrambled up the path. The bear was trying to crawl out of the hole. He kept breaking through the ice, but as it broke, he was working his way toward shore. Then he stood and climbed out. He shook himself out just like my Mom's old black lab. I watched, sucking air, fascinated and terrified at the same time.

Caleb shouted and moved around me with the small caliber rifle. The bear was closer and had pulled most of the hook laden steel leader from his mouth. It hung to the side, held only by the end hook. I could see his giant yellow teeth at the side of his mouth. Fresh blood drooled down his wet lips and chin. He roared and moved forward.

"Shoot! Maybe it will scare him." I knew a .22 shell wasn't much.

"It won't! It won't fire!" Caleb was staring at the weapon with a combination of fear and anger. The bear, leader still trailing, was picking up speed and beelining toward the cabin.

"In! Inside! I ran past Caleb and into the cabin. He turned, jumped in and slammed the door, and dropped the cross bar to its catch.

The bear was right behind. He scratched the door harmlessly until he found a grab hold on a diagonal brace board and began prying. The door shattered like so much kindling.

"The safety. It won't fire unless you squeeze the lever action tight to the stock when you pull the trigger." Two more boards gave way. The bloody red snout and teeth showed through the crack.

The gun cracked loudly inside the small cabin. The bullet sang by my head like a bottle rocket.

Caleb told me later that he remembered what an old friend had told us when we helped him butcher a steer at a farm. Make an X between the opposite eyes and ears, point, and shoot. The bear dropped with a thud on the door step. No twitch or groan. Just dead bear.

We skinned out the bear, saving the fat for lamp fuel or whatever. The meat made an interesting change from fish and rabbit. Not good but interesting. We had never tanned a hide before. I had read where the Plains Indians chewed on skins to soften them, but I could not feature that. One of the camping books borrowed from one of the cabins suggested using a mix of urine and fish oil. For a temporary measure, we just scraped the hide's insides, rubbed in salt, and nailed it to the weather board siding. It would stay there freeze-drying for a few months. By then we might have the answer.

However, by then, we were starting to develop another problem.

Chapter 18
Two Is the Loneliest Number

Cabin #2, Ontario, Canada
December 1970

I could tell you about day-to-day existence in the north woods. The way we survived off the fat of the land. How two friends made it through the rigors of the Canadian winter. Let me tell you about the loneliness. It is a creeping wonderment underlining your belief that you will never again be close to someone. Oh sure, you talk to the guys at the gas station, the kid at the check out or whatever, but what about that certain someone? When the sun sets at three in the afternoon and stays down until 8 a.m. you have plenty of time to think about that.

Caleb and I did talk. In fact his story kept showing up at those odd moments when we would stop on the trail to rest, or in the evening while I'd whittle. He might be trying to redo one of the old fishing rods when he would remember something, look up and tell me another nightmare. He fiddled with that locker key a lot.

But talk wears thin. Case in point. How many fishing trips do you ever hear about that last more than a week? They can't last longer. All the jokes are told, stories caught up on and confessions made that are going to be made. Even with our careers, and quite possibly, our lives on the line, after a while we were talked out.

We had a moldy John MacDonald paperback to share on a per chapter basis with the dishes at stake if one gave away information concerning the next chapter. The second week, we mostly had work time, eating time, sleeping time and quiet time. The third week, we had work time, eating time, griping time, and snoring time.

As I talked with Caleb those first days, then weeks, I decided that he was working his way back to normal. Gerry's death slid into the background, while we began to figure out what the hell was going on with the Quetico ambush, Burt, and the mysterious document hid away in the Badger Bus Depot in Madison.

Our own government had encouraged a depressed ex-rower to help a couple of other young people blow up a building for the good of the cause and to make anti war protestors look bad. It went south, a guy died, and now their red, white and blue solution was to kill some more people to avoid the truth from coming out. Destroy the village to save it.

We discussed going back to the States. It could not happen until spring. If we hitch hiked long distances now, we would stand out because there were few tourists. In the warmer weather of spring and carrying a few props, we would blend in as men on a fishing trip or even bear hunters who had car problems. To cross the border at Fort Frances, we could jump a south bound freight train or borrow a boat and cross Rainy Lake.

He and I talked about the tragedy. I encouraged him. It was Psych 101 at work. The winter would be his therapy—and mine. I wanted to puke when I realized I was imitating those loser ministers and counselors you run into who say, "by helping others to find themselves, I hope to find myself…".

We had found ourselves all right, and we were in a very dark place.

Grousing and bickering started to seep into our serene cabin life. It started with coffee cups. When I dropped in at Cabin #2, there were 2 cups on the shelf. Two cups, two guys. Great. Wrong. The oversized, orange one with a happy face on it was in one piece. The other was a white chipped cripple with no handle and the words "BITCH BITCH BITCH" printed on the side. Whoever was first to the shelf had the honor of the smiley face. Second place received the cripple. At first it was funny. Then one night, as we worked on our projects, I accused Caleb of hiding the smiley face so I could not use it. Things became intense.

Caleb thoughtfully answered, "Where would I hide it? Dumbass."

"Under your bunk, behind the wood box, anywhere you wanted."

My blood pressure began to rise as the joke wore thin.

Caleb looked out the shack window at icy white stars and whispered, "Why would I hide the smiley cup?"

"So you could use it all the time?"

I was working on a long wooden sled runner. I began tapping it in the palm of my hand.

His face reddened. He looked down carefully at his hands, then pulled up his pants leg, examined his wound, picked a scab, and finally exhaled deeply.

"John. This is bullshit. Let's have a beer."

He went over to the icebox in the far corner on the north wall. We had the old green army blanket draped over our dwindling supply of Labbats. I realized that a crisis had just passed. I felt the need for more defusing.

'We'd better make a beer run one of these days."

I looked over at our stockpile as he withdrew the blanket. Necessities were important.

"Hey! Here's the cup." He held up smiley face and carried it back along with the two bottles of beer.

Somehow I felt he had planted it there. Then I remembered checking the larder before supper. I'd been drinking coffee to warm up. "Sorry. I forgot." I did not look him in the eye. The next cabin raid included three coffee cups as well as beer.

Chapter 19
"We Are Not into Ideal Options"

Cabin #2, Ontario, Canada
March 6, 1971

Loneliness.

It set in. The weeks blended together and we had more and more quiet time. We went out of our way to be polite. The unspoken rules were in effect. Ask, don't tell, offer the fish fillets to the other one first, let the other guy make the choice. The weeks wore heavy. Christmas did not help. Caleb dragged in a three-foot-tall Charlie Brown Christmas tree and decorated it with fishing tackle. It cheered us up initially but it was not long before the euphoria turned to nostalgia and then depression.

There were two kinds of weather: blizzards and roaring blizzards. Even in a nice little shack, survival was still contingent on tunneling out to stashes of fire wood that he had made in October. It was a load of lonely time. Finally I decided that aside from the long term goal of escape back to the states, we needed a short term one.

Goal setting, the buzz word that makes middle level employees roll their eyes heavenward, scratch their heads, and rattle Rolaid bottles now seemed important. We needed a goal. Not increased fish production, snare setting, quality, or higher yield moose hunting. We needed to beat the loneliness game. There is only one cure. Caleb brought it up at a fine snowshoe hare banquet one night.

"We need to do something fun."

Goals don't have to be in behavioral objectives for Caleb.

"What are you talking about? I'm supposed to dance? Listen to you sing? Oh wait, I forgot how much fun it is to watch you peel calluses off your feet."

Sometimes we forgot about polite.

Caleb paused, looking up from the new hasenpfeffer recipe, a blend of corn bread and yellow cake mix biscuits covering tender rabbit, mixed with three cans of vegetables found below the frost line in a cellar of one of the bigger lodges.

"No. NO. Let's go to a town. See a show. Take in the sights. Prison can't be worse than this. I'm the guy who killed someone. You just get a hand slap. I've had it. I'll take the risk. You need to choose. We go, or I lose my mind and you are stuck with a crazy man."

"Let me correct you. Not one murder—THREE. And I'm already stuck with a crazy man. Officer Linley is out there with his dog, King, after you for murdering people, we've got...ah...no licenses, guns across the border, illegal bait and littering."

This was all depressing talk. I was feeling sorry for myself. What the hell. How bad could it be so I finished with, "What if we get there and it's "Dumbo," or "Snow White and the Seven Dwarfs?" Caleb put the goal in words I understood.

"Let's go meet some women."

We toasted with Trout Pool Number Two water having run out of beer the day before. Caleb turned serious for a minute.

"John, once, the first time I climbed El Cap, I had a hundred feet of rope out below me when I came to a move that I did not know if I could handle. It's on a pitch they call Hollow Flake. The name of it scares climbers all over the world. If I started it, there would be no reversing. It was a move that I would have trouble with in a gym—two feet off the floor. Live and in person, 2000 feet off the deck, a slip is a death fall.

I made that move. I risked my life on purpose for a rock climb. If I say let's go —I mean it. So maybe I should go alone. I've got to get out, and frankly, as it stands now, I don't have a lot to live for. If this goes bad, let me say this. I'm gonna make it end game. They'll have to kill me and maybe I'll welcome it and take some of them with me. Are you up for that?"

"Hey, Caleb, this is me. My WIFE just ran off with another guy and got herself killed. Now I wonder if she ever gave a shit about me. People in my hometown think I'm a drunk. They're right. And most of all, I have broken umpteen state and provincial laws to end up in the freezing shithole for months with a friend who tells Twilight Zone stories every night starring himself. Life's not exactly seashells and balloons for me either. What do I have to lose? Remember the night we stuck the car and stole the log skidder? Let's make something happen."

A trip like that takes planning. It was several days in the making. The cottage want list, or what we came to call, the CWL list was reviewed and pared down. The cross country skis and boots we had liberated from the nearby cottages, were cleaned up and waxed. We assembled light packs that could be expanded for the trip home. The CWL grew again after I reviewed the latest reading material rescued from another cottage, Saturday Evening Post, June, 1964. Also, we wanted Jello chocolate pudding, cheese of any kind, milk, fresh vegetables, cooking oil and popcorn. And beer.

The trip planning replaced the boredom, grousing, and sullenness with an anticipation of adventure, cold ones, and women.

It would be best to be in town on a weekend. It was hard to know for sure what the date was because the days were blurred by overnight hunting forays and a hangover or two. The date might be important. We tried to guess the day of the week. There would be more local people congregated plus skiers and snowmobilers into party on a weekend. We planned our departure to allow us to arrive on a Saturday morning—best as we could figure. We considered disguises. Lumber jacks and loggers all know each other in the small town of Vermillion Bay. With our accents, there was no way we could pass as locals. Vacationing cross country skiers might work, although we appeared rather seedy. Some things could not be improved. As Caleb often muttered over the winter, "We are not into ideal options."

The day before we left was clean-up day. We washed our clothes in the largest kettle we had. As far as personal hygiene, I suggested a Polar Bear Club outing, but Caleb was not having it. We settled for scrubbing up the best we could with water heated over the stove.

I took a lot of Caleb's hair off and shaped his beard using a great pair of scissors we found in a high end cabin. It was not as good as Ron the butcher's work but it was an improvement. Caleb then worked on me. I was not as desperate, but I did need some tune up work.

The trip started with high hopes. The weather was great–daytime highs in the teens with no foreseeable storm. At least that's the way we interpreted the little barometer/thermometer combo nailed to the wall of our hovel. We left the cabin with clean clothes, finely waxed skis and an adventurous spirit. The route would retrace our path on the lakes until we intersected the CNP tracks again. At that point we would have to bivouac somehow, get through the night, and then ski in first thing the next morning along the double main line which had an access road. It would be packed down so we would be able to make great time once we hit that.

I worked up a sweat in the morning sun. There was a light wind of three to seven miles per hour. It was a great morning to be alive, as they all can be. I had forgotten that. I think back to that morning often. After an entire morning of steady skiing and most of the afternoon we were disturbed by the first mechanized noise we had heard in months. It was disorienting and unsettling until an accompanying seismic tickle and rumbling reminded us of our destination—train tracks. We were there. It was time to look for a camp as the sun dropped to the horizon. Once up on the tracks, we noticed a small shed a quarter mile down the tracks. It was a maintenance shed and it did not take much to break in. We were hungry so we ate all of the jerky and canned beans we had brought for supper and breakfast. Filled up, we leaned back against each other, pulled our coats tight and despite the cold fell into a hard sleep after the day's exertion.

We woke up cold and stiff but eager to get going. Caleb was whining about no breakfast, so I surprised him with two candy bars I had squirreled away. When he asked me why I hadn't told him last night, I just gave him a look. Forbearance was never his strong suit. If he had known about them the night before, there would be no breakfast. Fortified, we hit the railroad right of way, moving quickly with our breath icing up in the crisp sunny air. In an hour or two we knew we were getting near town when we started to see fresh snowmobile tracks pressed into the trail. Every twenty yards or so, the handy work of last summer's maintenance crew was evident. They had replaced ties on the main line using Fremont track repair machinery. I could tell by the stacks of short ties that they left behind at the rail side. The machinery pinched the ties so hard and violently in two places it severed them. Caleb stopped and looked at the machine for a long time, almost as if in a trance. I coughed, and he looked up, "Umm, sorry, I was thinking of something."

He'd get like that.

We had packed some heavier jackets to wear later in town so that we could fit the role of vacationers. I also brought my wallet. We had discussed the merits of bringing any ID along. Easy choice for Caleb. He had none. I brought my wallet. I figured if we needed it for a minor situation, exchanging currency for example, it would arouse suspicion if we did not have anything. Currency was not a word we had used much in the last month or two. I did have some. When I left home, I cleaned the freezer, Carolyn's inside joke for cold cash. I always wondered why she had a fear of being without money in an emergency. That's why she told me she put the money in there. I believed her. Then.

Shortly before her last car ride, I teased her about why she really had it stashed.

"…in case you died," she joked.

I said, "Don't be foolish."

She died and I was foolish. But not foolish enough to leave the money. When I counted what I had grabbed, it came to 450 dollars in small bills. Little did we know that it was going to buy us a lot more than a few drinks and a night out.

Chapter 20
Something in Store

Vermillion Bay, Ontario, Canada
March 6, 1971

"How are you boys today? Looking for something special, ey?"

It was the manager of the Vermillion Bay Grocery cooperative, looking very official in his white apron, white shirt, and dark pants. He was standing by the checkout scratching the back of his white folded paper service hat. It covered the top of his head, and I guessed, a bald spot, while showing a thin fringe of salt and pepper hair. He had watched when we unclipped our skis and leaned them against the exterior of the old tin sided building along with the small sled we were pulling to haul a load back. He could have been the butcher. We found out in a few moments he was.

"We just need a few supplies. Nice store you have here."

I was ready for common conversation. Caleb gave me a wary look, then rolled his eyes, as we moved past the entry and down an aisle away from the manager.

"Just ask if you need help, ey?" He turned back to a rack of toys and do-dads that had been there too long. Christmas lights were still in the window. I felt a little stab of nostalgia for happier times. Christmas at Cabin #2 had been silent night, moody night.

"Christmas," I said to Caleb, when we were further down the row of canned goods. "What a night of warm special memories, ey?"

I mimicked the shopkeeper's Canadian style.

"Look, never mind OK. Let's get the stuff and get out."

He scrutinized the list as he moved down the row. "Stop talking so damn much. Let's not take any chances. EY!"

"Right."

I moved to the pudding section. Seeing even this mom and pop style grocery store sent my mind into a food frenzy. Snack Canyon beckoned! Rice Krispies, raw onions, potato chips, spaghetti sauce all called to me from old white perforated metal shelving. Only the thought of an upcoming restaurant meal kept me from chowing down right on the old maple floor, well polished by the shuffling of thousands of boots over the years. I wandered over to the cheese rack. Not much compared to Wisconsin but good enough. We met the butcher again at the meat rack. We went for some steaks, two whole chickens, bacon and varieties of lunch meat that would give us a change of pace for a few days anyway.

We rounded out our staples list with unforgivable junk items and bottles of Jack Daniels. Caleb rationalized that we needed them to prove that we were on vacation. The stumbling block was more .22 shells. We were afraid of arousing suspicion. Caleb was considering stuffing them in his pocket when the butcher came up behind us.

"On the trail, ey? Been on it myself but not much this winter. It's pleasant in this nice weather which actually we get quite a bit of, at least compared to Churchill, ey."

We moved over to the checkout together and I handed over some twenties as we chatted. Caleb kept things rolling. He could not help it once Churchill came up.

"You worked in Churchill? I've always wanted to canoe into Hudson Bay from one of the rivers that runs through Churchill. I've read that the ice is on the rivers for eight months of the year, but you can catch trout with a safety pin. I want to try it."

This time I gave Caleb the wary guarded look.

The grocer counted out the change in Canadian. He gave us the exchange rate as near as I could tell but rounded off the small change in his favor.

"I worked up there for the Hudson Bay Company 14 years running their post. I liked it, but it wore thin on the missus. I thought the polar bears were plenty of excitement but we've been down here three years now and it's good. My name is Kent. Maurice Kent. Folks call me Kentie."

Kentie seemed to be affected with logorrhea which I had previously only run across in a crossword puzzle. I figured it's important to play along with the natives. You don't want to stand out in a crowd.

"Hi Kentie. This is Clark. I'm Lewis. We're on a holiday for a little bit, mostly skiing and hiking.

"Clark and Lewis? Sounds familiar."

Caleb gave me a look that would kill, but it was too late.

Clark turned to the magazine rack, passed over a tabloid claiming an Ontario woman had given birth to an alien and selected the Times-News.

"Gotta keep up with the civic events you know." Caleb casually pointed to the side column of the paper which announced that the United States government was taking steps to increase pressure and surveillance of radical groups accused of agitating and provoking violence on college campuses. A side article announced the death of some liberal activist in a car accident. The evidence of drugs in his bloodstream undercut his accusations that the FBI was actually instigating incidents with double agents for political purposes and that evidence was being suppressed.

Caleb gave me a meaningful look that Kentie interrupted.

"So you young fellas up from the states having any luck meeting cute girls on the trail?"

Caleb laughed. "I think we were on a different trail. We didn't see too many."

"I believe you think I'm fooling, mate. There's a bunch in town now from some college. They usually start out later—about now, and get back in time for supper at Carol's down the street."

He finished packing our things and shoved the huge brown bags our way.

"This is the story of our lives," said Caleb, "always ahead of our time."

"I guess you can still catch them at the Snow Ball then, ey?"

He wiped his hands again in his apron using the style and practiced manner of a long time shopkeeper.

I looked past Caleb to the end of Kentie's index finger and followed it to a home made poster stapled to the note board.

10th ANNUAL SNOWBALL SATURDAY NIGHT AT CAROL'S
8:00-11:00
Meal served at 9:30

**Winners of Labatt's Powder Puff
skiing events to be announced
following the buffet.
Dance to the sounds of the Meltones
$5 cover at the door.**

"So that's the deal at Carol's, a winter party," I said. "I'm always ready for a social outing. Sounds like fun."

"Where are you boys staying?"

Kentie looked over curiously.

We were ready for that.

"We've got a mobile home parked out by the tracks a couple of miles east of here. Just thought we'd ski in for exercise and supplies."

There. I'd done that nicely. Just like we planned. Now it was supposed to be Caleb's turn to add some filler for the story. But what I heard instead was, "So tell us about the dance."

There was a look in his eyes I had not seen for awhile.

"Yeah, tell us about the dance."

Maybe that look was in my eyes, too.

Kentie was warming to his task. He wiped his hands unconsciously again and said, "It's just like it says there on the sign boys. Plenty of girls, and not just those stuck up college ones. It's the biggest party all season except for last fall when Sergeant Conwey's youngest daughter got married to Albert. Couple of the boys said it was a shotgun deal. Nobody believed it at the time but she's in full bloom now. That Albert, he's a quick one you know…"

"Sergeant Conwey? Who's that?"

The words came out before I could control them.

"Master Sergeant Wendel Conwey? He's assigned to the district. Actually he works out of Dryden, but he lives here and keeps law and order on the highway and in the district."

Caleb interrupted. "But what about the dance?"

"It will be a good one. Last year it took two other officers plus Sergeant Conwey to settle down the Galle brothers, Clint and Keaven. Every year, they come in from logging, get a little tight and need to let off a little steam. It used to get out of control until Sergeant Conwey showed up. He's a hard man. They might try something again, but I suspect things will be fine."

He continued. "Etta and I are going. We enjoy the food. They have a Bar-B-Que that cooks outside all night, and about nine they set up buffet tables for everyone. My Etta, she really dolls up for this one."

"You mean it's dress-up?"

I knew we couldn't handle that. He chuckled.

"No, of course not. You've got to wear ski clothes if you have them but if you don't your lumberjack clothes are fine. The only rule is…ah heck, there are no rules, only guidelines."

I made arrangements with Kentie to store our packs, skis and sled in the back unheated room in the store. He said the food would keep fine, and we could pick up our things there any time in the afternoon or even at night. All we would have to do is just knock on the back porch door because he and Etta lived upstairs and would be glad to open up the back. He smiled as he palmed an Abe Lincoln. He was a friend for life. The fire in my wallet was cooling but only slightly.

We walked down past the five store main drag past Dorf's Wear for Men, The Cooperative Hardware Store, Sid's Take a Sip Café, and Carol's Fine Food and Drinks. Just around the corner was a weathered white frame building topped by a small plywood sign which proclaimed it the Vermillion Library. Carol's opened at 5:00 p.m. and corresponding signage on Sid's Café announced that the cafe closed at 5:00 pm. We marveled at the symbiotic nature of small town businesses. We went back to the hardware store to see how we could get them to donate some .22 shells to our adventure. The trick was getting the donation without the contributors' knowledge. No problem. They were just out on the shelf waiting for me to empty six boxes into my pockets while Caleb went up front and bought some beef jerky and nail clippers. You'd be surprised how easy shoplifting is when you have decided you have nothing to lose. Then it was off to Sid's for a lunch we had dreamed of for months.

The brown fiber board walls were covered with Saturday Evening Post covers. I took a calendar count. Good restaurants have a minimum of three tacked up, preferably four or five. Sid's had four along with a Formica counter, mixed tables, and an unmistakably tantalizing greasy spoon aroma. Two men in plaid wool shirts looked up as we tap-danced across the wet black and white checkered tile floor in our cross country boots to one of the many empty tables. One of them muttered something about "wood fairies."

Caleb might as well have been a peckerwood magnet. He had a cellular dislike of rednecks, even though he looked more like one than they did. They could sense it. He stepped to one of the good old boys, cocked his head and emotionlessly looked at him the way Ali stared down Sonny Liston. They traded dark curious looks until I poked Caleb hard and told him to knock it off. An older lady, hair dyed silver-blue, wearing a black and white plastic name tag announcing "Vi" approached us. She held her black pen poised at a precise angle, ready to record our choices. We sat down.

"What'll you have boys? The specials board is over there on the wall, but I'll get you some menus too."

"Coffee for starters," I said, contemplating our first meal in months that we did not have to shoot, hook, or snare.

"It's been a while since we were faced with such a selection."

At first she thought we were kidding. The wrinkles on her face softened and turned to a smile when she saw that we were sincere. Vi returned with our coffee and handed us clear plastic folder menus. We ordered the lasagna off the specials board as she poured strong brown café coffee into sturdy white ceramic mugs. She placed our order with the chef by laying the green food check face up on a chest high pass through window behind the counter and stools. Then she came back to us in a flash to chat.

She was friendly. Caleb kept his head down, but it did not slow down Vi. We found out that Sid and Carol (of Carol's) were husband and wife. They shared a common kitchen. He ran the Take a Sip. Carol ran the tavern because Sid was too old to stay up until the last ones left. She rolled her eyes to let us know what she thought of the last ones. Caleb stared off into space for a moment. I think he wanted a membership in the last ones club.

The food came quickly and we started to work. Vi left us for a moment when she saw the knives and forks start to move like hockey sticks at a face off. Our chipped white restaurant dishes held brick sized portions of layered cheese, ground beef, and white noodles slathered in a spicy tomato sauce that oozed out from the stack.

Vi returned with garlic bread. She made small talk about the dance, then lowered her voice.

"Stay away from those guys." She used her eye roll again.

They're the Galle brothers," she said, using her pen tip to point out the two swarthy looking men hunched over a table by the window.

"They are nothing but trouble. In fact, they were in a big fight at the last dance."

Something should have clicked in our fool heads, but the food had disabled our warning radar. The plate of bread slices was placed between us. By the time I finished listening to Vi, the bread had disappeared. Caleb and I ordered seconds on the lasagna. The guys to stay away from looked over at us.

Sid stuck his head around the kitchen pass-through window and joked, "We won't have to wash these plates. Look at this. You boys licked them clean! Vi, give them some more French bread. We want to keep customers like these."

The shaggier Galle brother who was returning from the rest room gave me another dirty look as he grabbed his mackinaw. They left, apparently having decided to waste their afternoon and pollute the air elsewhere. We planned on reading the paper and exploring the rest of the town, killing time before the dance. Maybe we could even sneak in a snooze at the library. We'd done it in college.

"I'm glad they left." Vi said matter-of-factly, as she brought more of everything to our table. "They are always trouble and even more so when they've been drinking."

"I'll remember that Vi." I said thoughtfully.

DAN WOLL and JOHN W. LYON

Chapter 21
"Good Evening, Sergeant"

Vermillion Bay, Ontario, Canada
March 6, 1971

"The girls said they'd be by later because they wanted to change clothes and fix their hair, but they will be here," Etta said proudly.

"They're just up for the weekend this time. Usually Ranae and Linda stay with us but we are paneling and painting our living room and all the furniture is in the guest room. Kentie is such a handyman. Why even when we were in Churchill…"

"Is everyone ready for another Labatts?" I interrupted as politely as I could. I stood and noted bottle levels. A full round was in order. Hearing no objections, I left, avoiding a story that I felt we were destined to hear several times. I walked to the end of the bar to signal the square-jawed older bartender.

Etta was winding up for another of her Kentie stories when "Clark" came over to me on his way to get popcorn. We talked in the corner by the old-fashioned theatre style popcorn machine. I had operated one of these when I tended bar in college. On the lower shelf I found the coconut oil, plopped it in, and set the timer switch. The measurer was on top of the popcorn tin next to the butter salt. In two shakes, the kettle was stirring. The place was now filling with a happy, noisy lumberjack, ski crowd. Brassy red-haired Carol, smiled and waved to me from across the room. I thought we were fitting in. "Clark" was not so sure.

"We made a mistake coming here. First of all we're going to be stuck with probably two of the homeliest women in North America, and secondly, I've had my fill of Canadian jails." His hubris was wearing off.

"We can't hang around with the nosiest two people in town and expect our cover to hold up much longer."

The kettle was sizzling. The first kernel popped.

"Clark, YOU were the guy who was interested when old Kentie suggested it would be fun to meet these two single sweethearts sight unseen. He told you about the cop who might show up, but that didn't bother you. Do what you want but I am entering the terminal don't give a shit zone, and this here, it's my re-entry vehicle."

I waved a bottle of Labatts at Caleb, then did a finger pointing number, and reminded him how all of this had come about in the town clothing store which also belonged to Kentie. After lunch and a nap, we had gone there to buy new underwear. Etta had appeared from behind an aisle and wandered over to chat because of course, she filled in at Kentie's store. Before we knew it we had promised to meet her two nieces at Carol's that evening, just to get away from Carol.

Now we were there for the moment of truth. Our attention was drawn back to the popcorn machine. Things were really happening there now.

"Caleb, I mean, CLARK, now it's your turn to choose. I've bet all my chips on doing whatever the hell I feel like, for the first time in months. You said you were in. Damn it, this was your idea! Let's do it up big time."

I turned back to the machine, flipped the kettle over, poured it out and reset it. Clark chugged his beer and looked at me.

"I'm in. Remember the log skidder? We said what the hell that night and it all worked out fine."

We went back to the table with Kentie, Etta, a dish of fresh popcorn and four more beers to wait for the girls. When they came, we could not believe our good fortune. They were cute. Maybe not Playboy cute, but wholesome, healthy and fun. The bad news was that lots of other guys thought the same thing. The girls were continually asked to dance by every townie in the place. However, their small town roots betrayed them and they kept orbiting back to the comfort of Kentie and Etta. Our friendship with their kin eventually gave us the upper hand.

Our best foot forward approach seemed to be working. We went to the restroom to discuss this pleasant state of affairs while the band took a break. It's funny how things can be down so low one minute and going through the roof positive the next.

Caleb reviewed the girls' strong points.

"Not bad. I take back everything I said about Etta."

I tried to stake the first claim.

"I kind of like Linda. She's well read and a terrific conversationalist."

Caleb shook his head.

"I suppose you came to that conclusion without considering the fact that under that bulky ski sweater she has a balcony you could do Shakespeare off of?"

He washed his hands like a surgeon at the undersized sink mumbling some sort of blessing about running water. I, too, washed and enjoyed the efficiency of modern technology as applied to heating and moving water. We exited the men's room and hurried down the narrow hallway almost bumping into one of the Galle brothers. He barely gave me a glance but he studied Caleb for a minute before moving on to the restroom.

The exterior walls of Carol's were made of old cement stone work, just like the foundations of most well-built barns. The worn but beloved building had a history going back to the first days of the town. It had been a blacksmith and manufacturing shop at first. It sat empty for years until Carol bought it. Then came her romance with Sid and the rest was history. The bar was along the side. Behind was the shared kitchen. The main room was chopped up in several levels with the lowest and largest being a slightly raised dance area, enclosed by a railing. An old juke box rested over in the far corner by one of the old barn style windows.

We had staked out a table near one of the sets of steps leading up to the dance floor. The band, as stated on the banner, was the Meltones. They were better than expected for a group of four locals fronted by a bearded Cordovox player. He knew what he was doing. He sang a perfect lead, right on key, undisturbed by the acoustic hell created by the plank floors and ceiling. The crowd loved it. There was no sign of the rough stuff Kentie had warned of but the night was still young. More people kept coming in the door and money was changing hands quickly. Our plan was to be gone before anyone got rowdy. Etta had managed to seat herself between Kentie and Caleb. I was at the end of our round table booth, bookending the two girls between Caleb and me.

As I viewed the bobbing, undulating, mass of humanity on the dance floor, I thought of a snake pit. A few too many beers made it easy to squeeze my eyes and see snakes heads and fangs instead of stocking caps and hairdos. The silver red

Meltone spotlights created an impression of a syrupy blood red haze. After months in the Canadian winter, I was not ready for this crowd.

Kentie startled me.

"Here he is now!"

I sensed a moment of truth. Caleb looked away.

Kentie stood up and stretched out his hand to greet a black and silver haired officer dressed as a Sergeant of the Provincial Police. His black tunic and striped pants indicated that he was probably just off duty—or still on.

"Good Evening, Sergeant. You remember our nieces Ranae and Linda? And these are our new friends from Wisconsin, Clark and Lewis."

The Sergeant turned to me and shook my hand with a paw the size of an outfielder's glove, then turned and examined Caleb. Carefully.

Uh-oh.

"Young man, it's a pleasure to meet you. May I ask if you…"

CRASH. A plate glass window shattered in the front room.

"SARGE! HELP!"

We all ran and looked in time to see two lumberjacks whaling away on each other out on the slippery sidewalk. Sergeant Conwey stepped through the glass window, almost daintily, and then waded into the fracas. He threw the upright lumberjack across the hood of an F-150, which caught the attention of the other combatant who was trying to regain his footing. Things got real quiet. Conwey addressed the bearded warriors.

"We're going downtown boys. The rest of you, help board up that window and mind your own business."

Fair enough. We rejoined Kentie, Etta and the girls at the table, just as Carol announced that the food was ready. Two long tables covered with white cotton tablecloths were piled high with meats, potatoes, hot dishes, Jellos and a few lonely salads. By the time we filled our plates, the fight was forgotten. The meal was outstanding. I was amazed that there were not more cookbooks featuring Canadian cuisine. I was considering seconds on the barbequed beef until Linda informed me exactly what mammal I was enjoying. I pushed back from my plate, understanding why there aren't so many Canadian cookbooks.

After dinner, it was time for the ski awards. The emcee stood up, put two fingers in his mouth and brought the crowd to silence with a piercing whistle.

"Folks, due to an unfortunate display of rowdiness, Sergeant Conwey will be unable to present the awards, so I…"

He was interrupted by a cheer and shouts of "Conwey!, Conwey!" as the giant sergeant re-entered the room and headed toward the bandstand. He accepted the microphone.

"Folks, all is well in the good town of Vermillion Bay. Let's honor our ski champs."

Applause.

Everyone clapped and hooted as the winners went up and accepted their medals. Most were hotshot types and purebred racers, but a few of the locals earned shining moments on the bandstand. The local female winners were especially cheered as the Sergeant kissed them and gave them hugs and pats on the back that migrated suspiciously to the south. What the hell. Apparently Conwey felt he had earned the right after years of duty in rural Canada.

Linda told me later he had had offers to transfer and move into the fast lane of advancement a number of times. The Commissioner himself had been a partner with Conwey in the old days up at Churchill and had wanted Conwey's logic and common sense at the Provincial Headquarters. Conwey always turned him down.

The band started up as the last award was presented. The Sergeant was swept up in a crowd of greeters. He stopped at nearly every table, went the length of the bar and even took a peek in the kitchen. His smile disappeared as he stopped purposely at the Galle brothers' table. Kentie informed us that these were indeed the two ne'er do wells who had dropped in unannounced at Sergeant Conwey's daughter's wedding reception. Ultimately, they were given the plate glass window exit (apparently a Vermillion Bay favorite) and reduced to unconsciousness by the hulking Sergeant, but not before his daughter was in tears.

He hadn't forgotten and it was clear that he had the full attention of the Galle brothers. The tough guys averted their eyes and mumbled agreement with whatever directions the Sergeant was giving them. It would turn out that their attention span was not so good, but for the time being, the crowd nodded assurances and gossiped quietly about the bullies. Kentie leaned over and said, "Conwey's a great man. We don't talk about it but he saved my life one night in Churchill. He may bend the law once in a while to preserve the peace, but he is the most honest man I know. I've staked my life on it in the past and I'd do it again."

Linda squeezed my hand and motioned toward the Meltones who were launching into a Canadian cover of "Devil With A Blue Dress On." We moved up the steps to the dance floor when the slithering snake pit premonition struck again. Once was enough. I froze which backed up Linda, Caleb, Ranae and everyone else causing a general humping, bumping, spilling of drinks and a "What the hell?"

chorus. As we all unfroze, I realized that we had stopped opposite the Galle brothers who were descending at the same time.

"Aye Linda, I haven't seen you since the Conwey wedding, ey. Ready to do the dance with me tonight?"

"Get away, you slimeball bastard or I'll have the Sergeant come over here and beat you until you cry like the big baby you are."

She turned looking for Conwey, but the brothers scooted away, eyes glowing with smoldering hate.

Waltzing with snakes seemed safer than going back in the bar with the Galle's so we eased our way into the dance crowd as the Meltones sax player put down his horn and crooned "Strangers in the Night." At first Linda's body felt stiff and tense, but as we danced I felt her begin to melt against me. Finally she rested her head on my shoulder. I felt like I had come home. I was aware of her scent and how delicate her tiny hand felt in mine. The night was young and full of promise. I had not felt so alive since my courting days with Carolyn. I remembered back to a dance where passion overtook and we two-stepped out the door and ended up in a haymow on a blanket.

In between dances, a friendly young skier made the mistake of noticing what a good time we were having. Although he probably was close to the same age, Caleb's ordeal had left him looking twenty years older. The big blond haired kid had a tipsy walk and a cock-sure smile that said he was on top of the world. He sidled up to Caleb and said teasingly, "I hope I can have as good a time as you are when I get to be your age."

Caleb's eyes flared but I gave him a look. He took a pull on his beer, considered, then replied, "Keep your mouth shut and you might get to be my age."

The blond kid kept his smile, but his eyes signaled comprehension and he wandered off.

Caleb laughed.

"You know, this is about as much fun as you can have with your clothes on."

It was my turn to consider. The band was playing "Sleepwalk," an old favorite by Santo and Johnny. I looked sidelong at the girls and said in a conspiratorial voice, "Maybe we can remove that qualification."

Just as I was about to propose a change of venues, a heavy hand clapped on Caleb's shoulder.

The Sergeant.

"Boys, I almost forgot, what with all that plate glass window excitement. I hate to disturb you, but I want to see some identification. I'm really sorry guys, but this will just take a minute."

I reached for my wallet and handed him my valid Wisconsin Driver's License.

"Fine, fine John. I probably would not have even asked if it weren't for that Clark and Lewis crap."

He turned to Caleb.

"And you?"

My mind raced as the hulking policeman stepped toward Caleb. Just as Conwey reached out for the non-existent identification, Keaven Galle passed behind me, with a shiny brass knuckle guard on his right fist. Necessity is the mother of invention. Kentie had just bought another round of beers. They were set in foursomes all over the table, some full, some half full, some not full at all.

I grabbed a full one off the table, hooked my left index finger in the loop of Keaven's unbelted pants, pulled and slid the bottle upside down into his pants. Immediately foam formed at the belt loop top and at the floor where his boot ended. His consternation passed quickly. He grabbed me by my shirt and pushed me backwards.

Into the Sergeant.

This made the Sergeant glum and once again distracted him from Caleb. The Sergeant collared me and tossed me aside in order to get at Keaven Galle. I felt like a human ping pong ball. Galle was winding up to throw an empty pitcher at me, which he did with brutal force. I was always good at ducking. So were the girls. Kentie, standing next to his friend and chatting with Carol was not so lucky. He took a glancing blow on the ear from the 40 ounce missile.

I was feeling momentarily smug. That lapse of attention nearly cost me the face I'd carried since I was a baby. Clint Galle had come running over to take a swipe at me with his beer bottle, and I was just able to duck out of range. His follow through brought him face to face with Caleb, who drained a full pitcher of beer over his head and then railed him right in the nose with the empty pitcher. I heard nose cartilage collapse like breaking celery sticks. Blood spurted over all of us. Clint staggered backwards, holding the bloody wreck that was his nose, grabbed an ash tray with his other hand, and threw it wildly at me. It conked the blond skier in the temple, wiping the shit-eating grin off his face. Ski boy wobbled, then sat backwards on the barbeque sauce table, setting in motion a tsunami of sticky, dark red, sugared tomato juice, barbeque, and Jello. Several passers-by immediately stepped and slipped, knocking over Carol in the process. The blond skier regained his feet. Not wanting to be outdone, he grabbed a sauce bowl off the surviving table and sent it across the floor, stone-skipping style. The crazily spinning spicy dish splattered dancers, drunks and brawlers alike.

Sergeant Conwey bulldozed through the crowd after the remaining upright Galle brother when the gentleman bartender caught my eye. He waved us toward the bar. There was a duck under to connect the bar with the kitchen. He motioned us to move quickly. Somehow he had all our coats there waiting and we took them. There were stacks and stacks of beer in the way. Caleb grabbed a couple as we hustled around the corner of the bar. I threw a twenty on the bar and grabbed a bottle of whiskey and we were off. The Meltones were packing their instruments. The rhythm guitar player had rendered a marauding lumberjack senseless with a powerhouse Mickey Mantle swing of his white Fender Telecaster which now hung in two pieces connected only by six light gauge strings. They were done playing.

No problem.

Someone took a break from the brawl, cranked up the jukebox and punched in "Street Fighting Man." I looked back one last time. Kentie and Etta were pouring the last of the popcorn on a vaguely human-shaped barbequed mess on the floor which at closer inspection, was indeed, the Galle brothers. I was glad we had made enough buttered popcorn for everyone. Sergeant Conwey was fumbling for his second set of handcuffs. The night was still young.

Chapter 22
Lights Out

Vermillion Bay, Ontario, Canada
March 7, 1971

The Pinewood Motel was a long one story brick building. Our room was at the end. It was cold inside so Caleb turned on the gas space heater. I had a better idea. I grabbed Linda and pulled her back into the small bathroom, shut the door and turned on the shower as hot as it would go. The bathroom was so small that there was not enough room for both of us to get undressed at the same time. I allowed her to go first and being a gentleman, offered to help. Soon we were inside the steamy metal shower stall. Although the white metal stall was stained with dark rust blotches and the shower curtain had an interesting strain of mold, the ambiance was perfect.

Linda's towel was wrapped around her blond hair for protection, but the rest of her was there for me. While we lathered and rinsed each other several times I found out that we were about the same height, her eyes were sparkling blue, and she was a dark but natural blond. We were just starting to get more involved when there was a gentle knock.

Caleb cracked the door, and whispered, "How about a trade?"

I pulled Linda's hips against me and hissed, "Is he kidding! I've dreamed of this. You're wonderful"

"I think he means the shower, not me...although I could be enticed." She smiled mischievously and blew into my ear.

I could listen to her all night. I felt myself turn to Jello. That is, parts of me turned to Jello.

"OK. We'll dry off and make a switch."

"Lights out and into bed." Great words from my past but when my father had said them, I don't think this is what he had in mind.

The small pine paneled bedroom had two queen size beds. We set up shop in the farther one. Linda laid down as I straddled her and gently scratched her back between her shoulder blades. She was no stranger to physical work because her shoulders were tight with muscle, which aroused me even more. I kissed her from her shoulders all the way down to her feet and back up again. She groaned softly and rolled underneath me. Her nipples were tight and erect when I licked them. Her hands searched. We worked together, finding, feeling and fitting. I pushed myself up slightly and worked my chest back and forth gently rubbing her breasts each time.

She began to tense and clench and then she ordered, "Come here."

Something was going on in the other bed but our cries and gasps drowned them out. I was happy for the first time in years.

A knock at the door interrupted the post-coital bliss and napping. All of us sat up and froze, until we got our wits about us. By prearrangement, Linda went to the door. Caleb and I quickly moved behind the door, full bottles in our hands. Days later we would laugh and wonder how Ranae was able to keep a straight face. From her position in the bed, there was just enough light coming in the door for her to directly observe our naked rear ends as we crouched, with upraised beer bottle weapons in our hands.

We heard, "It's me, Kentie. Are the boys in there? I've got to talk with them. Conwey will be on his way here soon."

Linda had opened the door as far as the chain would allow. I looked around the door and saw Kentie dressed in a parka, heavy pants, and boots. It was snowing hard on a night that seemed ageless, but no longer young. Beyond him in the falling snow sat Etta in the car. She was in a robe, waving and smiling dumbly between the sweeps of the wiper blades. From the light of the street lamp, one of the dozen or so in the whole town, I could see that the trunk was part way up.

"What's going on Kentie?"

I slid a pair of boxers on and fumbled my pants up my legs. Caleb was doing the same. Linda worked the chain lock while Ranae turned on the bathroom light to let us see without being blinded.

"Conwey wants to talk to you, I think. He was not too pleased about what happened at Carol's and when he locked up the last hooligan, he remembered he still had not seen Lewis' ID. I told him you had a mobile home out by the ski trail because I knew you were off with the girls instead."

"And?" Caleb said as he grabbed his shirt and sweater.

"Well, he thought he should get right out there before the snow got too thick and have a visit with you."

Kentie looked around the room and took in the disarray of towels, bottles, suitcases, backpacks, bras, and boots. It looked like the Rolling Stones' road crew had shacked up in there.

"I thought I better find you so you could be prepared to talk with him because I've got a feeling maybe all of your identification is not in order?"

He looked nervously out at the car through the snow, then at our disastrous motel room, and then back at Etta.

I let out my breath.

"Kentie, you are so right. Sergeant Conwey is right to want to talk with us but this is not a good time. Someday, I will tell him the truth, but not now."

"I figured. Well, I brought your skis and the rest of your packs so you could hightail it for now and chat with him later at your convenience. He's a good man, and I'll hold you to it that you get back to him."

"You are a good man Kentie, and we thank you for your kind thoughts." I said, as I zipped up a wind breaker and bent to finish slipping on my ski boots. I moved to the other side of the door, kissed and hugged Linda, then still holding her hand for a moment, backed out the door.

Caleb unclenched from Ranae and followed me outside. Brushing fresh flakes from the trunk, Kentie and I unloaded the car and laid out the skis in the snow. We shouldered our packs and said our thanks. Etta waved and gave an unsure smile from the car.

The only movement in the parking lot came from the flakes of falling snow, accumulating quickly now. There were no sounds from the highway.

Caleb shook his hand, turned on his skis, then looked back over his shoulder.

"Kentie, we appreciate all your help. Someday soon, we'll get back to you about all of this. Boys, be careful, and remember, Conwey's your friend too."

It was my turn to tell a lie.

"Kentie, Etta, thank you both. We'll be back to buy you all a beer at Carol's soon."

It was still dark, but I was afraid he could see my eyes. I held my head up to the snow to wash away the tracks of my tears. What a wuss I was turning into. Or maybe I was growing up.

We skied out of town on a snowmobile trail that paralleled the road. I was rested and feeling good. The time alone up north with Caleb, hunting and cutting wood, had caused me to shed pounds, added muscle and had shaken me out of my physical funk. It felt good to feel good. Caleb was in the lead as we slid into the darkness. Our time was limited. Sooner or later, Conwey or someone would expand the search to the woods and outpost camps. Maybe the heat would be back off in the States.

But what about Linda? On the way back from Carol's she had told me more about herself. Marrying young to a mistake in the works had caused her to make career changes. She divorced and went off on her own, and survived. Nurse training and a part time job had been tough but she had made it. More work and an advanced degree had opened doors for her at several major hospitals. She told me that she felt she had her life on track again. Could I fit in the schedule?

We were at the edge of town and getting closer to the railroad tracks. The wet snow felt good on our faces as we glided beside huge, dark spruce trees lining the path. Our plan was to rejoin the access road that ran along the tracks until we reached our cutoff point to cross out on to the lakes and the long trek back to the Buckhorn Cabin #2. We would make the trip non-stop. We passed the last gas station at the intersection of Main Street and Highway 17. The lighted clock showed 4:45.

The stillness was interrupted by the humming of an early freight train. The thickness of the air conducted the low pitched rumble of the diesels and grind of the wheels like the giant bass speakers back in the rock and roll joints in Madison. The signals were not flashing yet, but the train seemed closer than it should have been. They usually slowed to 45 or 50 miles an hour through the towns but this one seemed to be pushing the upper end of 70.

The three shining Canadian style headlights from the eastbound freight blinded us as it roared down the rails. We turned from their glare and saw approaching car headlights from the north. The car was turning off Highway 17. The crossing lights were not working. The only thing the car's driver must have seen were stripes of white-lit snowflakes shining in train headlights as the diesel horn started to blast.

We stayed well to the side as the four black engines raced their megaton load of grain past us and onto the crossing grade, the lead engine's horn and pounding thunder of wheels under traction cracking the quiet of the snowstorm. The car's lights were finally shining on the Canadian Pacific Rail engines but it was too late. As slippery as the new snow had made the road, there would be no way to stop the car even if it had tire chains.

It was a highway cruiser judging by the blue and red light bar on the top. At impact, I could see the police logo across the doors. It had to be the Sergeant. Then everything was gone at high speed. Hooked on the front end of the braking train, the crushed squad car was dragged alongside as the behemoth train disappeared into the thicker woods a quarter mile ahead. The diesel horn kept on blowing with a mocking Doppler effect as the noise of the scraping impact died away. We stood in stunned silence until the caboose passed us. Then it was quiet. I dropped the pack from my back and put more kick in my skis.

Chapter 23
"We Have to Talk"

Vermillion Bay, Ontario, Canada
March 7, 1971

A few helpers were on the scene by the time we skied up the access road to where the train had finally been able to stop. The SD-45 diesels were panting in the snow a mile east of the intersection. Heavy duty flashlights from the cab provided illumination. They shone toward the crushed steel that had been a squad car. Some of the train crew had climbed down from the engine and were squirting CO_2 fire extinguishers at the sputters of flame. The twisted steel that had been the police car was showing licks of fire at its trunk and tires from the friction of being dragged. In the dark, you could imagine the rest of the car, but in the day's cold light there would be nothing to see. The locals would later shake their heads about Sergeant Conwey's miracle. He was alive.

"John," Caleb said, "can you see him?"

"Yes, he's pinned in by the radios. It looks like the crash pushed them into the seat." I replied.

We attempted to get him out of his car. It was no easy task because of the way the firewall had been twisted back into his legs.

Conwey started to come around as they worked on keeping the small fires from spreading. His voice was not that of a booming policeman anymore. "What the hell was that train…"

The police radio consoles were shifted toward the driver's seat and throwing small sparks.

I leaned in. "Conwey, It's me. John. Where does it hurt?"

I was bending in through what was left of the windshield opening. I climbed partway in, brushing more of the glass away. One of the trainmen shone an electric lantern on the front seat. The blood from Conwey's nose was mixed with his silver mustache. At his lips the blood ran off to each cheek.

I hollered, "Get the light down here. The pedals are tangled up in his legs and there's an oil slick all over!"

As I put my face closer to the floor to try to untangle things, I recognized the coppery smell as blood, not oil. There was a layer of it, covering the floor but I could not find the source at first. I was blinded by a light; then it was adjusted and I could see.

At Sergeant Conwey's right leg I could see the slice in his dress pants and a steady pulsing of blood coming from his thigh. Then I saw the radio's brackets. His leg had been slashed in some way by the sharpness of stainless steel supports. I looked down at the pedals to see how things were tied up and to take my mind off the cut.

"Best get me out boys. We haven't got much time before this car starts cooking."

His voice had less strength than before. I glanced up to Conwey's face and saw his eyes fixed on Caleb.

Broken bones or not, we had to get him out of there. Tongues of fire licked at the back seat. We felt them. The CP train men were running out of fire extinguishers. It was time to get Conwey out. Once again we were not into ideal options.

"Let's get going boys," ordered Conwey.

Conwey encouraged us in whispers while I worked upside down through the radio brackets to free his legs. The ¾ length working boots would have to go, so I slid the knife from my pocket. I slit the laces, and worked his legs free. Moving part way up in the seat I finished unclipping the front of the holster sling from Conwey's shoulder as Caleb undid the snap at the back. We made this into a quick tourniquet to slow the blood flow from the leg. The flames were spreading. There were hands everywhere as Sergeant Conwey's substantial torso was lifted and passed through the windshield head first toward the passenger side. As the rescuers pulled, I worked his legs around the cables, cords and wires that were everywhere.

Conwey groaned and rolled his head back and forth as we moved him. Once he was clear, I pushed back and scrambled out. The wet snow flakes felt good on my overheated face and cleared the plastic smoke smell that clung to my nostrils.

They laid Conwey on a sheet of plywood which had been placed on the hood, then carried him down the tracks farther away from the fire. Someone found a blanket. Caleb wrapped it around the wounded sergeant. I could see they were talking in low calm tones. Above the sputter and crackle of the flames we could hear the sirens of the Vermillion Bay Fire Department coming from town.

Then there was a heavy breathtaking crumpf of an explosion as the flames finally found a drip of gas from the gas tank. With enough oxygen and gasoline fumes drifting through the trunk and back seat, the whole works let go, sending car parts to junk heaven and lighting off the spare rounds of ammunition from the squad car's shotgun.

The snow was picking up again as I walked over to Caleb and bent down to the Sergeant's bloodied face. He was nearly out now, but he blinked his eyes open like an old china doll and looked at both of us.

"We have to talk."

Then he was gone again, a strong man taking refuge in an internal fortress where there was no pain, no feeling, no blood loss or throbbing head. His body would need the healing strength he held within.

I held his hand and arm as I knelt by him. There was still a strong pulse. I could feel the steel in his muscled arm and I knew that he would keep his word to talk to us.

Red lights flashed through the clouds of snow kicked up by the big tires on the rescue vehicles. The lights came down the access road in three sets, then circled the burning hulk of Sergeant Conwey's car. Quickly the fire was out as a freezing spray of foam sizzled on what was left of the roof. The Vermillion Bay Fire Department took fires in a personal way. These were not firemen for hire—the big city guys who put out fires in somebody else's neighborhood, give it their best shot for a couple of days, then go home, wash off the smoke and have a few beers to sleep it off. It was different in Vermillion Bay when the fire is licking at your front door, or your friend or neighbor's. We backed off as the intense rescuers helped the ambulance crew load the Sergeant. Then they were off and it was quiet except for a few who remained behind to watch the fire and talk quietly to the trainmen.

Now we were tired.

The catnaps we had managed the afternoon before in the small library were suddenly not close to enough. I could feel fatigue starting at my feet, filling me up, reaching to my thighs, and climbing. I was toast.

We turned and walked slowly along the steaming wheels of the train. We could hear a work train blowing its whistle and coming toward us on the other tracks. The three-car train stopped alongside us on the secondary line. The engineer shouted down from the old blackened GP-9 workhorse.

"Signal didn't work, ey?"

"No." Caleb turned back to his skis.

"Anybody hurt?" the railroad man asked from his idling powerhouse.

"Yeah, but he'll be all right."

I looked along the flatcar to the old work car and avoided eye contact. I tried to keep my thoughts from drifting back to the tangle of pedals and brackets and flesh on the bloody squad car floor.

We started west on our skis. The wind was picking up. It would be daylight soon, but it would be a gray and snow-filled one.

Chapter 24
Snowbound

Edson Maintenance Shack, Ontario, Canada
March 7, 1971

We missed the turn back to the cabin. When we came to the Edson switch shack, we knew we had gone too far. Snow was coming down so thick that all we could see were mounds of snow on either side of the rails and an occasional piece of railroad hardware sticking up through a kaleidoscope of blowing white snow.

Edson is on the map. Sort of. Fishing and hunting maps back then had it as a wide spot on the railroad, and in fact some highway maps showed it too. When you go there, you will find a dirt road, two machinery sheds, an old bunkhouse, a stack of bricks, and a shack marked "Dynamite."

We went for the bunkhouse. By now, my stomach felt it needed a sign marked "Dynamite." Too much fun, too much stress, and not enough Rolaids. I had always had a nervous stomach. After the fire in the back seat, I had had enough high intensity for a while. Knowing this about myself was one of the things that had helped me keep an even keel and a steady job. Moderation had always been a watch word and I hadn't watched it lately.

After kicking through the snowdrifts and tripping on broken icicles, we chipped away the packed snow to open the door. The shack was two rooms with an arch where they had cut away the wall to open things up. The second room must have been another shed that had been moved in. The walls were unpainted wood, but at least they were tight. No wind blew through. Two windows brought in a trace of dim white sunlight after it had been filtered through the blizzard.

It looked like heat could be provided by a square boiler-like chunk of cast iron sitting in the middle of the room. A sooty smoke pipe elbowed over to the wall and out. Hanging on a series of nails and pegs were a collection of utensils and an old porcelain coffee pot.

There was no one home, but someone had been there. Not too long ago. We were too damn tired to care. Thinking about how quickly the work train had arrived, it was probably the crew from the work train. The fire was gone but there were a few wafts of warmth from the ash pan at the base of the jury-rigged box stove. There were some barely glowing coals in the dust and the stacks of old firebricks were warm.

We rebuilt the fire using a few newspaper sheets from the classified ads section and splinters from old railroad ties.

"How did they get this weekend edition already?" Caleb remarked in amazement.

He went over to the south facing window to gain more light in the dingy shack.

Over his shoulder, I saw what he meant. It was the current edition of the Times-News. Current news. What luck. We had met the three-car train crew just before daybreak when they were approaching Conwey's wreck. They had to have somehow picked up an advance copy for it to appear in Edson for us.

"All the comforts of home!" I crowed.

"Yeah, but the paper was dropped off this morning. What about when they come back?"

I walked over and opened the door again. The snow was big, wet, and blowing sideways in gusts well over 20 miles per hour. Fifteen feet away we had felt our way around a tall signal tower on our approach to the shack. Now we could not see it from the door. In the thirty seconds I stood there, a pile of snow several inches deep accumulated inside the shed. I leaned on the door, sweeping the snow back, and latched it.

"No one's coming. Not today. Probably not tomorrow."

I looked over the papers stacked a safe distance from the fire box and found what I thought was the rest of the paper but Caleb was quicker.

"Sports pages!" he said with a look of triumph.

All brain activity ceased on Caleb's end as he enjoyed a rehash of overpaid NBA babies talking trash, dunking at will and generally pissing all over Dr.

Naismith's grave. Then he moved on to college sports and football. He muttered things like: "Shit, the Knicks are still winning. Somebody ought to guard that basket hanger Frazier for a change. I hate those bastards!"

Caleb was a Celtics fan. He grumbled.

"Oh great, look at this. UCLA is winning again. Well, that ain't lasting long. Woodens' too damn old and Alcindor is the last great center he's ever going to see, so you won't be seeing the Bruins in the Final Four again. You can count on that. Hey, and here you go. Baltimore versus Dallas in the Super Bowl. You know the Colts are gonna get their asses kicked. Dallas is the only football team in the country that can give the Packers a go year in and year out."

I went back to the fire. As soon as the headlines of the sports world wore off, so did Caleb. I moved through the routine of putting a pan of snow on to melt so there would be water to cook with, wash, and drink. Looking back, it almost seems like that is how I spent the whole winter, putting pans of water on to boil. That and breaking into cabins.

Necessity is not the mother of invention. It is the mother of breaking and entering.

Stumbling back out through the blizzard, we helped ourselves to the chunk wood that was piled on the ground next to a flatcar half filled with reject saw logs. Apparently the company brought log firewood by the car load, then had employees cut and split it on their own time if they wanted to keep warm.

The local crew seemed to like it warm because under the snow drifts, they had created a gigantic cache. We carried wood inside for almost fifteen minutes and created a wood pile.

"That has to be enough. I'm so tired I feel like hammered shit in a wagon track."

There was no way of knowing when the rail crew would come back to Edson, but as the storm continued to whip up more snow, and visibility went to zero, it was safe to assume it would not be that night. I could picture their diesel idling at the siding while they were warm and comfortable in the Vermillion Bay Motel while we were in their dump of a shack. Hell, they were probably making arrangements to have a leisurely dinner with Ranae and the new love of my life, Linda. Love stinks. I could not sit in the dark gray shack and think about it. I went out in the snowstorm to look around.

The machine shed had a couple of those putt-putt speeder cars made by the Freemont company of Minnesota, odds and ends of tools, and boxes of flares that could be strapped to the tracks to be set off when the weight of the engine's wheels rolled over them. These signal packets let the crew know that switches are set differently ahead and warn them that things have changed. Other boxes contained the standard twenty minute stick type flare for general use.

The other shed was the one that interested me. I took the lock off the door using a long pry bar from the other shed and walked into the dimly lit shack. Sure enough, there were stacks of wooden boxes that said, "Danger Dynamite."

When we were kids on the farm in the late 50's we would poke around in the odd places occasionally. One of the places I recall best was an old stone milk house that had been later designated the spray dope storage area. That was what one whole side was-stacks of insecticides, like lead-arsenate, 2-4D, and 2-4-5T. We did not play in there very much because it smelled bad. The real story was the other half of Dad's old building.

It was open to a kind of miniature attic. That's where we found the dynamite. There were about 40 or 50 sticks in the old wooden box tucked up in the rafters. Later we heard Dad tell that it had been up there since they had blown up stumps in the early 1940s. For us kids fooling around on a Saturday morning, it was a gold mine of fun and disobedience. Two neighbor kids, Frankie and Ricky were there. We spent the afternoon tossing the wet dripping sticks back and forth like jugglers. It was great. We broke a few open and looked at the soggy sawdust centers. But all good things come to an end, and this certainly did when our dads pulled in the driveway with parts for the baler.

We caught hell. Then they lectured us. Then they told us what to do. Kids were actually expected to listen and take responsibility back then. They made us carefully load it all in the repainted Radio Flyer coaster wagon and take it down to the old unused well by the pond while they fixed the baler. Two boys were instructed to balance the wagon while the third pulled it along. Our dads were WWII vets. Mollycoddling was not invented yet. Following directions was. We sunk the dynamite in coffee cans in the well. Only in high school did we find out how dangerous the stuff really was when it was sweating. The only regret we had, however, was that we never got to set any off.

I remembered my dad's directions as I examined the manufacture dates and all kinds of warnings on the box labels. In the corner, around behind the door, there was a metal cabinet that held two kinds of blasting caps. I grabbed up a handful of the flame ignition type with preplugged fuses and a few of the electric type, then walked over to the wooden boxes and stuffed six of the dynamite sticks in the back pouch of my blue ski jacket.

I don't know why I took the dynamite, but I did. Maybe it was because my dad never let us fire any off. Maybe it was because I sensed that our winter was going to explode one of these days, one way or the other. I jammed the lock hasp back on the shed as best I could in the swirls of snow that were coming down, then stumbled back to the bunkhouse where I hung the windbreaker beside the door.

We got to talking about why the current newspaper was at the shack and how the crew of the old GP-9 came to the wreck site so quickly. A few months later the story came to light after an inquisitive reporter tracked things down.

Fred, the engineer we met as we left town, had a brother Ross who worked for the Thunder Bay Daily as a route driver. Every weekend he was responsible for getting the papers delivered to the whistle stop towns along Highway 17 from Kenora to Thunder Bay. It also came out that Ross had a girlfriend who would welcome company if he could ever get away from his route. And his wife. So Ross cut a deal with Fred and the rest of the weekend crew. If they left early for their weekend inspection tour of the tracks and took the newspapers along with them, they could split a cool twenty five dollars American.

While the Canadian Pacific crew took over the paper route, dropping bundles at drugstores and grocery stores from Kenora and Oxdrift to Dryden and Upsala, smooth, old Ross ran a modified route around to the Thunder Bay Starlite Motel to meet his sweetheart and work a few things out. This happened about once a month. Ross couldn't afford any more, or maybe it was the old Catholic rhythm method. That worked for the train crew because they only had to get up early once a month.

They stopped the train at such odd hours that no one ever saw how they were delivered except a late drinker or occasional constable who received a complimentary copy of the paper for their silence and disinterest.

Because they started early and could not finish early, the crew usually stopped off for a few hours at one of the bunk houses to inspect things, relax, thaw a hidden beer, read the paper or one of the dozens of old Playboys that were shelved about.

The arrangement had its merits but it came to a screeching halt a few months after Ross' soon to be ex-wife called a reporter for the other paper in town and gave him a tip off about the delivery system. She had seen the old, dented newspaper truck her husband drove when she went to visit friends one weekend in Thunder Bay. A quick peek through the window was all it took.

As we sorted through our packs, we were unaware of the mousetrap game that miraculously brought the paper to the shed. I would find out later. Caleb never would.

I took one of the leathery-looking chickens and laid it to thaw near the stove. As Caleb went back to reading the paper, I searched around the two cupboards for some kind of roasting pan. I found the pan and cover part of what I wanted and made the rest from an old cast iron trivet that fit inside after I broke off the pointy ends. I then halved the chicken, put it in the pot, and threw in two potatoes from the supply of staples we had brought with us.

After carefully checking the fowl in the pan and covering it, we stacked bricks around it to complete our little Dutch oven and bake it for a few hours. I learned early in life that basting is important. Every time either of us got up to check the fire, we would drizzle a little water and broth back over the top using an old soup spoon that we found rusting in the sink. This meant restacking the bricks as we checked the dinner but it gave us an excuse to check the storm between naps in the late afternoon light.

Reading the Sunday paper was a treat. We were warm and relaxed. We had home cooking and memories of the girls. It might have been the best weekend of my life up to that point. It certainly was afterwards.

I read the paper differently, at least differently than Caleb or my wife or about anybody else I have ever met. This has allowed me to get along with those people. I go for the book section first. Most Sundays when I spot the top ten list, I clip it out and tuck it in my wallet to refer to when shopping. I keep score on which ones I have read and how much I liked or hated them. Book store people on occasion have asked me to leave when I have started to talk people out of buying a so-called best seller.

Reading the current book list made my eyes glisten with excitement. The Godfather was still a bestseller! Some new guy named Crichton had a bestseller. Probably never hear of him again. There were also unauthorized biographies of almost every active religious and political figure and Jacqueline Susann had the new Hollywood smut book off and sailing. Even the mass market paperback list looked interesting because a few months back, when most of those titles were in hard cover, I was too drunk and depressed to buy one. A warm shed in a blizzard in Canada makes a great place to read.

It was my turn for the front page and something caught my eye that had escaped Caleb as he raced for the sports page. A sidebar said there was a scandal brewing, and investigators were lining up the last documents to prove their cases.

It went like this:

SCANDAL!

Decorated Officer Under Investigation for Murder and Corruption

Spokespersons within the provincial government hinted Friday at the development of a scandal within the Ontario Provincial Police involving Master Sergeant Wendel Conwey, a highly decorated veteran officer. Lieutenant Jeffrey Aime indicated that Conwey is being investigated in regard to possible connections with the murder of Atikokan sportsman Lucky LaJeunesse and an unidentified canoeist. LaJeunesse and the canoeist were found deep in Quetico Provincial Park, apparently the victims of brutal assaults. In the past, there have been reports of illegal activities on the part of local individuals engaging in poaching and smuggling. It is known that LaJeunesse has prior convictions in these areas. An unnamed source theorized that Conwey, who has been warned about using unnecessary force in the past, may have let an interrogation get out of hand.

Conwey was unavailable for comment, however residents in the small town that he often patrolled, strongly disputed the allegations. Local businessman, Maurice Kent, was outspoken in defense of Sgt. Conwey. "Something stinks and it's not the smelt left over from the SnoBall. Sgt. Conwey is a tough one but he's not a murderer. He confidentially told me that the reason he's been around here so often is that there are real killers loose in the area that Headquarters won't take seriously. Put that in your pipe and smoke it!"

When questioned about Kent's accusations, Provincial Police spokesman Aime said that they were groundless and commented, "Mr. Kent will be put on note that his irresponsible behavior is impeding an investigation and he will be on a very short leash from now on. I suggest you get your information from people who actually know what is going on."

"Caleb. I think you better read this. It sounds like a story I've heard before."

The fact was that the accident was an accident. It was also an opportunity for higher ups to discredit a very sharp officer who was still critical of an August 30 failure to arrest American terrorists in Petersborough, and even more critical that his own current search for the terrorists had been tied up for weeks in red tape.

Kentie was right. Conwey was an honorable man, and he was figuring out that we were living proof of his suspicion that crimes in Canada had been committed to provide a clandestine unit of the American government with plausible deniability of a propaganda scheme gone terribly awry.

Chapter 25
"Think This Is the Edson Hotel, Ey?"

Edson Maintenance Shack, Ontario, Canada
March 8, 1971

The new day broke in a blast of white and wind. The howling had started in the railroad shack some time in the late darkness and sung all the rest of the night like the choir at an asylum. We stoked more wood on the fire throughout the night, but at dawn it was teeth-chattering cold.

This place was a dump. We called it Camp Dirt. Not only dirty and dingy, but poorly equipped, except for the great coffee pot. We had become spoiled at our hideout cabin because of our borrowed pots, pans, and various creature comforts collected from other cabins.

The outside temperature had dropped to well below freezing, and at best guess we were looking at a high of about minus 10 for the day. When it stopped snowing and the arctic high pressure began settling in, the temperatures would drop further. We would wait out the storm in the shed. There was no other choice.

We talked about ways to get squared away with the Buckhorn and return some of the stolen equipment to the other cottages in the area. If we ever managed to clear ourselves of the murders, it would be ironic—no, make that stupid—to end up in the hooch for vandalism, fighting in bars and petty theft. It was idle talk to kill time. The dead bodies were not going away, and we were fugitives in a not very secure hiding place, accomplishing nothing but more petty theft and vandalism.

We passed the time by making small discoveries in the small cold railroad shack. We started with a minor find of a portable radio that even had working batteries. We were poking around in an old cupboard mounted on the wall by the dry sink. I looked at it closely. It appeared to be about ten inches deep. When the cupboard door was slid open, I realized that the inside dimensions were not so deep. After clearing out thirteen old stained thick porcelain mugs, we solved the mystery.

The back wall of the prefab unit was plywood. As Caleb rummaged around looking for spices, he bumped it and it fell forward from its place exposing a hideaway. There was the radio. It even had batteries. It was the first radio we had come across in all of our winter's rummaging through northern cabins and sheds. Behind the radio was a pack of condoms.

"Look at this, not all of the coupling and uncoupling goes on outside I guess," smirked Caleb.

We spent most of the day keeping warm and being restless. Marginal entertainment was provided through our attempts to tune the radio by tipping, tilting and walking it around to various locations which allowed us to mix elevator tunes, polkas and old standards in with the static. We could not get any news. I browsed old magazines.

Soon, we also found out why so much wood had been split. The old wood boiler inhaled oak and maple. The birch chunks were quickly devoured appetizers in between the hardwood main course. By late afternoon, the wind quieted down and ceased whistling through the walls.

A new noise startled us. It was a medium pitched hum and low rumble. At first it was just a whisper in the wind, but it gained in loudness and intensity by the minute until, it sounded like a blower on a silo filler.

That's about what it turned out to be.

We put on our hats and coats and dashed outside to see a throbbing monster of a snow blower coming down the tracks. It sprayed the hard white crystals thirty yards beyond the tracks in a mist. There was a low diesel rumble under the sound of the spraying snow. Two grimy workhorse F units dressed in the old solid red C.P. paint scheme pushed the roaring machinery. They were probably beauties on the main line at one time, but now, 1416 and 1418 were being used for their strength on dirty, out-of-the way jobs. They moved down the main rail line, then backed all the way up to the switch and cleared the siding.

When hiding out, one does not welcome contact with the civilized world, but with our success in town and with the blizzard for a cover story, things might work out. If we could come up with a reason why we were outside in the first place, no one would question the fact that there was no place else to go. We decided we better invite the boys in for coffee since it was their shack. They were going to stop in anyway and there was no way to hide that we had been there. I just hoped they did not check the locks on the sheds.

"We saw the smoke," came the voice from the top of the ladder.

The engines were idling black chuffs of carbon in time to the rumble. A dark figure emerged from the snow blower's cab.

"What's to eat?'

The sound did not carry well in the thin biting air, but we could hear him chuckling. It was going to be OK.

Other figures were emerging from the blower and the F units. There were four men on the crew. The last of them stepped down into the snow and readjusted a pack. They looked like two sets of twins as they moved slowly forward through the hip deep snow. The large man who had first talked wore a black wool trainman's hat as did the last to come out of the idling engines. The other two had black and safety yellow striped stocking caps featuring the older Canadian Pacific logo. They all wore bib overalls and black work boots. They crunched their way into the wind-cleared corner of the shack. These did not look like the kind of guys who would hide radios and condoms. The cold was chilling us quickly through our light-duty ski clothing. We would do our explaining inside.

"Come in here and have some coffee."

Caleb carried in more firewood and closed the door behind. It was crowded inside, but it didn't seem gloomy now with voices and the orange fire glow from the stove door. The man who had come out of the cab first was the talkative one. He was the eldest among them. A disarming smile betrayed the threatening words, but at the same time his sharp eyes passed judgment.

"You boys must think this is the Edson Hotel, ey? You know we could have you arrested."

Caleb answered for once. Maybe he was starting to become human.

"You guys are going to think we're nuts but we bet some friends that we could ski all the way to Kenora. No rules, no guidelines. Just get there alive. As you can see from our packs and supplies we had no intention of breaking in or stealing but we didn't plan on this blizzard. That was stupid of us. We're sorry. We've got some money and we'll make good for the little that we have used. Most of what you see here is stuff we brought along."

The crew chief considered.

"To tell the truth boys, I wish I was with you. I'm old now and I miss being a dumbass and just heading out on an adventure. Besides, you make damn good coffee. Anybody here got a problem if we agree we never met these gentlemen?"

Three heads shook. We traded introductions and the crisis passed.

Coffee was poured for all from the old porcelain pot. We had used the time honored recipe perfected centuries ago by ranchers and lumberjacks. It included one of our precious eggs to capture the boiled grounds. I was surprised by their friendliness, but considering how well the locals had treated us in Vermillion Bay, maybe I shouldn't have been. In minutes a new batch of coffee was ready.

I poured and refilled as Caleb passed steaming mugs of the North's thickest and finest to those who thought they had rescued us. There might be more questions to finesse our way through, but these guys were just happy for some company and hot java. The guy with the pack reached down and pulled out a can of condensed milk in a wrinkled paper sack. He popped it open with a flick of his red Swiss Army knife.

"Here, would you want some of this in your coffee?"

They must have suspected my coffee making skills at first because everyone had some of the thick milk. I thought it made the coffee taste better too. I did not take too many positive things away from that winter but ever since I've poured condensed milk into my coffee.

We made small talk about the storm. The term snowbound took on new dimensions for us as the crew recalled past Canadian winters and favorite blizzards. The best I could do was to relate the previous winter's ice storm in Winchester that knocked out power to the little community for three days with devastating economic effects to local businesses and dairy farmers.

The train crew felt they had rescued us. They accepted the ski trip gone wrong explanation at face value. They stayed, sipping more coffee and smelling the chicken. Before they left we would have a feast. The guy with the pack produced another culinary magical trick by pulling out a couple of pounds of ground beef. The burger would turn into a late lunch casserole to go along with the chicken. The chief, who we now knew as Hunter, indicated that if they were going to eat with us they needed to get out and go up ahead a couple of miles to clear the next switch tracks. He said to expect them back for more coffee and food, as soon as they cleared up to the Badlands, referring to a section of track that chisels through a rugged high spot in the Canadian granite shield.

I was looking out the frosty little window watching the rotor spin in time to the throb of the diesel engines. Hunter caught my eye and grinned. His brown eyes sparkled with an enigmatic sense of humor and perceptiveness.

"You seem to like trains, ey? You wouldn't want to come along, would you?"

I was up and out of my chair in a snap. I looked over at Caleb.

"You guys will be OK?"

"I can handle the cooking and chores. You know what? I'm kind of tired of your face anyway."

I didn't think he was kidding. It had been a long winter. I needed a break too. I couldn't wait to ride the behemoth machine that had the ability to conquer winter.

Inside, Hunter said, "Let's get started." The engineer led the way to the door and the bright cold path beyond. The open door let in a blast of below-freezing air so we did not dawdle. The diesels' pulsing engines called to me across the empty air. Out there waiting was the steel monster, waiting to challenge Old Man Winter and I was going to be part of it.

We climbed the ladder and opened the door to the cab of the blower. The fireman handed me a folded newspaper saying, "Here. Run this into your buddy. He might want another dose of fresh news. I'll check the controls and be ready. Watch out for the hand rails. When it's this cold, they stick to your mittens."

Sure enough, just like a dumb kid's tongue on the flagpole, my wet mitten froze to the pipe railing of the locomotive. I tugged it free and finished my climb to the ground. I glanced at the front page of the paper as I approached the shack door.

Bold headlines across the top of the page screamed more bad news:

POLICE OFFICER HOSPITALIZED
AFTER STEALING SQUAD CAR AND
CRASHING INTO TRAIN!

Master Sergeant Wendel Conwey, already under investigation for...

What the hell. Caleb could read it. There might be something we could do later, but right then, I had a train to ride.

Chapter 26
"Pull Over"

Highway 17, Ontario, Canada
March 10, 1971

Two days after the train ride, we were standing out in the gray drizzle on a grimy highway bordered by spruce trees and snow banks, soaking. Not too bright, but we seem to have had developed a resume in that area over the winter. As Caleb put it, "Of all the stupid things we've done over the past few months...this is one of them."

But there we were reviewing our weather forecasting errors. As we guessed, the cold front had lifted but it was replaced by something much worse in an amazing quirk of the jet stream. Rain. Buckets of ice cold rain. It dropped, patted, dripped, drenched, and soaked everything. My skijacket had long since stopped shedding water. We were on Route 17, headed east down to Nakotah Rapids in a last ditch effort to get to Sergeant Conwey and the truth. I had a feeling that he owed us something, at least a listen. He was a true son of a bitch but Kentie was probably right. If anyone knew the truth when it was told, it would be Conwey. Judging from his own circumstances, he might even be ready to join our conspiracy theory club.

We wanted to hop a freight train, but we were between stops and they never slowed enough to even consider jumping into a box car or hooking on to a ladder. I read a book once about a guy who froze to death hanging on to the frame at the end of an ore car out in Nevada. We would walk.

So there we were, walking in the gravel, fog, and mud. I began to whine and complain. I hadn't been sick all winter and I was not in the mood for a sinus infection.

"Good Lord. I've got to get something over my head besides this parka top."

Ever helpful Caleb dog-trotted back twenty yards and picked something out of the ditch.

"Here you go Johnny, this'll go perfect with your Mickey Mouse brain that predicted good weather!"

He brandished an outlandish pink child's bike helmet with Disney decals all over it. In his rapidly deteriorating mood, he meant to poke me, but I was not insulted. I was desperate.

"Give me that."

I had on a wool stocking cap under the ski jacket's hood, which I had pulled so tightly over my head that only my eyes and nose were visible above the tightly pulled drawstrings. I slipped back the hoodie and jammed the child's helmet on over the stocking cap and retied it. I've always been accused of having a small head and for the first time I was glad of it. It fit and it was more insulation. Fuck Caleb. I slipped the hood back up, pulled it as tight as I could, double knotted the drawstring, and marched on. Caleb shook his head, then for the first time in a while, he smiled.

There was some traffic, mostly large trucks, but no passenger cars filled with tourists or summer fishermen. Well soaked after the hike from Edson, we looked beyond disheveled. Our appearance was certainly a contributing factor to our dismal hitchhiking performance. No one bothered to slow down and take an interest in two sopping wet, shabby-looking, down and out bums. We heard a siren howl that quickly increased in volume.

"Drop!" I commanded.

A squad car roared up and over a rise, tires hissing as it sprayed a cold muddy mist into the ditch where we squatted. It was past us before we could react to the cold water. Looking at its red taillights recede, we felt the adrenaline start to course through us again. We had to get out of there. Time for a deus ex machina.

The machina turned out to be a hot shot GMC four wheel drive with its big Lucas fog light panel on. It was what we called a Jimmy back then. As it cruised around a curve and into view, I thought it wasn't slowing. It had a custom deer slayer bumper and a paint job that said macho all over. As it swerved toward us to make sure it splashed through the deepest center of a 10 yard long mud puddle, we could make out two large people on the front bench.

Then it stopped. Backup lights came on as it fishtailed backwards toward us. Hell. Even rednecks have a heart. We ran to meet it. The driver's side door spring open and a big guy jumped out.

"Hi guys! Need a lift?"

I could not make out his features in the mist but he sounded friendly. I wasn't in the mood to judge a good Samaritan by his looks. He walked to the back of the vehicle and opened the tail gate to the enclosed cargo space.

He stepped back and laughed, "Hop in!"

As I put my knee up on the tailgate, I heard Caleb yell "Watch out!" I had a sudden flash of recognition.

"CRACK."

I had another flash—of pain as something whacked the back of my head so hard I saw stars and crumpled like those exploding buildings you see being brought down by demolition experts.

"Shit, you cracked his skull open."

Not exactly.

It was Clint Galle and he had cracked apart my kid's bicycle helmet. I saw stars and swooned. That's when I got the twisted nose I've carried for the rest of my life. On the way down, I bumped the tail gate with my face. Incredible pain washed over me, cleansing me of fear and replacing it with an uncontrollable rage. I cleared my head, and rolled over in time to see the larger brother wrestling Caleb down to the ground. Caleb was strong and wiry but Keaven went three bills and his bulk overwhelmed my furiously struggling partner. Clint hollered.

"Easy. Easy. That's the one they want. If you accidentally kill him before they question him, you and I are going to end up dead—just like his dumbass friend is going to be as soon as we get the hell out of here. Just lay on him, willya?"

He grabbed a roll of black electrician's tape from the back of the Jimmy and wound it around both of Caleb's wrists. I played possum.

Keaven said, "What the hell's the big hurry? We got fucking special agents on our side, right?"

Clint looked up.

"Wrong. We have got to get the hell off of this road. The spooks and the brass are protecting us but Conwey's got a ton of friends and some of his patrol buddies don't believe all this shit about him going rogue. They could be out looking for us because we were the last guys to have a run in with him. It's not likely that one would come along, but what's the odds that we'd just drive along and spot these guys hitching? We gotta get going. Throw the dead one in and then we'll take our boy here to headquarters and get a nice little reward."

They picked me up by my arms and legs and heaved me in like a sack of flour. Caleb followed, landing on top of me with a grunt. They slammed the hatch shut. I felt the big truck settle when the two brothers went around front and climbed in. Left side first, then right as the big springs gave under six hundred pounds of Galle brothers. Caleb flopped around like a shiner in an empty minnow bucket, a poetic analogy since the Galle brothers had scooped us up as if seining minnows. Why, in all of Canada, did our paths have to cross again?

"Hey, you back there. Shut the fuck up before I come back and tape up your damn mouth."

Caleb was screaming and cursing. He was making so much racket, I was afraid that they would actually do that. I pinched him. He gasped, but did not say anything. We made eye contact. I winked.

The truck went silent except for the high speed whine of the big wet all terrain tires. The brothers looked relaxed and seemed to be enjoying the ride. Not for long, I thought.

They turned on the radio. Gordon Lightfoot. I hate him, but he was loud and he distracted our captors. Keaven bellowed out a gross off key mimicry of the beloved Canadian balladeer, "If you could read my mind...if you could read my mind, you'd turn that damn thing off!"

We scanned the back of the cab for weapons. Surprise registered on Caleb's face. I looked where he was looking and saw an old olive drab steel ammunition box about the size of a small cooler. The lid must have popped open during the struggle. Inside were sets of brown packages wrapped like frozen meat from the local locker. There must have been ten of them. Next to the ammo box was a twenty five pound bag of milk replacer for calves. Probably from the local feed mill, judging by the label. One of the small bags in the open box had been torn open, and I could see a white powder partly protected by an inside layer of plastic. Despite a fair amount of recreational drug use in college, it took a moment for things to click.

Drugs were the driving force behind the Galle brothers. The cocaine must have been high grade stuff and they were going to cut it with the Land-O-Lakes Cooperative's finest. I imagined that their continued license to ruin lives depended on their bringing us back to whoever wanted to interrogate Caleb.

The brothers must have recently sniffed. They seemed too cooled out and happy. They should have been on high alert, but of course they thought one of us was dead, one was taped up, and on top of that they were stoned idiots–dangerous stoned idiots.

I made meaningful eye contact with Caleb trying to ascertain if he had given up. He glared back at me, eyes full of silent, willful rage. He'd be OK if I could turn him loose somehow. Keaven and Clint contently drove through the fog, rain, and cigar smoke. They seemed way too happy. I closed my eyes in the hope that my headache would go away. No such luck. I ran a mental inventory of what I had in my pockets. They had not frisked us. In their current mental state it was easy to see why. They were well on their way to inventing short-term memory loss. They were not paying attention.

I had my jack knife. I'd always carried one since fifth grade when my grandfather pronounced I was old enough in front of Mom and Grandma. We had worked out this deal in secret so I'd get to carry the knife for fishing and he would get to take me fishing to prove he was right. It worked out fine. I caught a great large mouth bass and he got the bail of his reel tangled so badly that he used my knife to cut the line free.

I reached into my pocket as quietly as when I used to sneak downstairs at night to raid the refrigerator after my folks had gone to bed. The boys up front were now singing along to Stan Rogers and too busy to notice anything. I reached out and surreptitiously sawed through the Galle's tapework. When I finished, Caleb silently kneaded the feeling back into his hands and gave me a thumbs up.

My nose was killing me. Each bump amplified the sharp pain. Keaven slid the shift lever into fourth gear, then poured the coal to it as we bumped down Highway 17 over the winter frost heaves. The dampness evaporating from our clothes kept fogging up the windows. Keaven turned up the blower on the heater, circulating an unpleasant, humid mix of cigar smoke, grease, sweat and overpowering body odors.

After lighting another zeppelin of a cigar, Clint mused, "They didn't say anything about the other guy did they?"

"Not really. They said bring back the berrypicker and don't hurt him and do whatever it takes."

"Well, what if it took killing his asshole buddy?"

"I s'pose that'd be OK. Why?"

Clint mused as if he were suggesting a stop at Carol's for a cold one before wrapping up for the evening.

"Well that's the sonuvabitch that dumped the beer down my pants. You know what? Payback's a bitch and I'm thinkin' it's time. Pull over when you see a good spot."

We were somewhere on the stretch of deserted highway between Vermillion Bay and Edson. Keaven slowed down and focused both of his brain cells on finding an assassination destination. I was getting ready to move quickly when their radios caught my eye. There were several and they were all on, blinking and flashing, meters indicating static somewhere. A snakepit of wires ran to them from under the dash. I could identify the standard Cobra C.B., and the scanner, but the fourth one had me stumped for a few seconds.

It looked like a police radio. The sharp stainless steel brackets were exact doubles of the ones in Conwey's squad car.

Question: Why would they have a police radio?

Answer: To talk to the police.

Statement: These guys were not police.

Question: Or were they?

There was something here I did not understand.

Chapter 27
"I Forgot"

Highway 17, Ontario, Canada
March 10, 1971

Keaven crossed the double yellow lines and pulled into a driveway.

"Let's park between the drums. There won't be any loggers here tonight as wet as it is."

Keaven was giving the orders.

Drums?

I knew where we were. We were at one of the places where loggers pull in with their trucks and drive between two huge standing culvert style drums which recenter the load of logs. The drums, each mounted vertically, rotate and spring in and out to center the logs sticking out on the truck. We rolled to a stop, scraping wet gravel. Clint belched.

"Let's take Mr. Funnyman with the beer bottle for a little walk. Give him a little of what his buddy did to cousin Lucky."

Keaven took a good pull on his cheap cigar, shut off the engine and pocketed the key. He was having way too much fun. Related to Lucky? Not a good day for us.

They both climbed out and swung their seats forward. Our soggy clothes chilled us as soon as the door opened. They reached in and grabbed, attempting to drag me out of the Jimmy. It was no easy feat. Dead weight is harder to jerk around than a York barbell. Something in the zippered pack built into the back of my coat stuck on the back of the seat. Keaven fixed that. He was persistent, if not gentle. He threw down his cigar and clutched the front of my coat tighter with both hands and heaved. I popped out of the truck like a cork from a bottle of wine. The impact of both of us hitting the slippery mixture of gravel and ice made a splat.

We were both on the ground. To Keaven it was a shock. To me, it was a way out. I got up and got going, wondering what Caleb was up to. I knew when I heard him shout.

"Come here you big son of a bitch! I've had it with you assholes!"

Months of slow healing and frustration were coming out all at once. He would be Clint's personal nightmare if I could just lead Keaven away. I scrambled back past the back of the Jimmy to the trees on the north side of the driveway. Caleb continued to taunt Clint. As I ran by, I saw that he had come up with a wrecking bar and was advancing on Clint like a cat getting ready to spring after twine being pulled under a newspaper. Poor Clint.

Back to the chase. Ordinarily it would have been a good one. Two offensive linemen in a windsprint. But now, after my winter of skiing, chopping wood, and a no fat, wild animal diet, Keaven was no match for me. It got worse for the big guy. After he tripped on one of the basketball-sized boulders marking the driveway border at the base of the drums a Sumo wrestler could have outrun him. I heard his yelps of pain as I moved further into the woods. He must have hurt himself badly because I could hear him yowl and curse. I pictured a dancing bear. Knowing what it felt like to get a good, knife-sharp shot right in the shins, I knew he would need a minute to lick his wounds.

"Let him go. Keaven, get over and help!"

It sounded like Clint was in trouble and scared. I stuck to the woods and paralleled the parking area. I planned to cut back along the marshy edge to be near the front of the Jimmy, but out of the glare of the lights shining through the fog. Caleb and Clint were circling.

"C'mon, kiss my ass, faggot!"

It was Clint daring Caleb to make a stupid move, something he was completely capable of doing. Caleb waved the wrecking bar at Clint, hook end out, ready to swing.

"You're a big man with that bar, aren't you?"

Caleb kept working around him so that his own back was to the glaring fog and headlights with Clint facing them. My windbreaker caught in the brush again, but

I pulled free. The adrenaline was clearing my head. I pushed through the brush. Questions were going through my head as I cleared the last of the scrub hemlock.

How did these guys know that Caleb was involved with Lucky?

How did they know his real name?

What kept getting in the way in my zippered pack?

"The Inspector is going to enjoy that I gave you the same treatment you gave his jailer, ey?"

The title did not make much sense to me then, but I had other problems.

One solution emerged from my internal fog. The lump in the pocket pack was the dynamite with two kinds of caps. Great stuff, but how to use it to best advantage?

Still on the move, I bent low and scurried to the side of the Jimmy and took off the jacket. The stuff was all there but I had no battery or spark. Looking down at my feet, I could see that a spark would not be a problem thanks to the disgusting habits of our hosts. There lay the cheap stogie, still glowing brightly. I checked my trail and heard Keaven crashing off in the boondocks and swamp but saw no sight of him. I knew he would emerge sooner than later. I had to move quickly or we would be back to square one with our friends. They would kill me, retake Caleb, sell their dope and probably reap a cash reward on top of it all. Beautiful.

It was time to do something even if it killed us all. We might not make it, but if that was the case, the Galle brothers were going down, too.

Clang went the bar. I knew the beautiful camo paint job on the Jimmy would need some touch up.

"Hah!, Got you, you son of a bitch!"

Caleb had turned the tables on Clint. As I came around the corner I saw that he had pinned Clint's head on the hood by holding the bar on his neck. I stuffed one of the flame ignition fuse caps deep in the end of the dynamite stick and found the still glowing cigar thrown down by my Galle brother, the one still in the woods. I bit the half inch of soggy tobacco off and spat it out in disgust. Then I sucked the dull coals back into life. Months of hard living had not prepared me for the cheap cigar. I coughed. A bug-eyed Clint looked over in my general direction. Caleb kept applying pressure to his neck by the bar. Caleb looked too.

"John, put down the fucking cigar and help me tie this guy up!"

I looked down at the log chain slung under the gate-crasher bumper and winch. I started wrapping and snugging it around Clint's feet. I was not sure how well the winch cable would bind his hands but it snugged them up tight like the drumsticks on a broasted chicken. I had him bound to the log roller as tight as a rolled rump roast when I heard the concussive report of a heavy caliber pistol. We should have known Keaven would have a gun.

The bullet thunked into the Jimmy's open door, shattering the lock and placing a bulging dimple in the inside steel. I held my ground to finish twisting the wires connecting the blasting cap on each side of the fuse link, and completed my independent science project in the vehicle. Caleb squatted down next to the Jimmy as more shots broke the silence.

"What in the hell are you doing?" he growled.

"Just fixing something. Never mind."

He was about to press the issue when the lost brother scrambled out of the woods.

"There he is. Under the far drum."

Caleb was next to me. We squinted into the fog seeing only the outline of the large barrel mounted on the smaller concrete pillar.

"Keavy! Look out. They're behind the truck!"

Clint did not have much of a voice but it probably was enough to warn Keaven. We were almost out of time.

"How's the pitching arm?" I asked Caleb.

"Pass the stick. I'll hold it. You light it. "

I handed him the prepped dynamite. There was another shot. This one went clean through the windshield. I signaled to the safe side of the Jimmy and we scurried for cover. Another shot ricocheted off the bumper. I sucked on the cigar and tried to light the fuse. The final shot whizzed by my head. It sounded like a bottle rocket as the hot sizzling lead brushed my too long hair. I touched my ear to see if it was still there. I looked up just in time to remember an important detail.

"Caleb! It's LIT! Throw it!"

Caleb's body arched in a fluid pitching motion. He heaved the dynamite up and into the open top of the drum. Through the fog, I could see a sputtering arc going right for the barrel. Just as it went over the edge and out of view there was a flash from the top and a deafening blow. The corrugated metal echoed. Dynamite has great concussive power only if the blast is contained. The log roller was a good container. Something heavy flew past me and clunked off the Jimmy.

"What the hell was that?"

Clint answered.

"It's his foot. You BASTARDS blew my brother to bits!"

Caleb's adrenaline was pumping and he was losing his cool.

166

"Shut up! I don't want to hear from you again unless you know where the rest of that rat bastard is."

He moved in with the bar. Clint flinched and shut up. I thought I saw tears. A hard winter had left me bereft of sympathy.

"No crying allowed big guy." I taunted.

We moved off and wasted five minutes making a wide circle in the brush behind the drum but we could not find Keaven.

"Caleb, dynamite can vaporize stuff. He's gone. Let's get going before…"

I interrupted myself to see what Caleb was pointing at up in a pine tree next to the drum.

"Johnny, I don't think your vaporizer was working 100 percent."

There hung the lower half of the giant logger's torso, dripping unmentionable fluids.

"What about the other guy?" Caleb gestured toward the hapless remaining brother. "He'll get away. He's barely tied."

"Caleb. Listen to me. I'm pulling rank. The cops are coming. They'll be here before he gets loose. In fact if you don't shut up, they'll be here before we get away. We can't drive that wreck. We'll get stopped in a minute, and besides that, we've got a Galle brother tied to the bumper. After me. Now!"

We turned and dog-trotted into the woods and up a fire lane with Caleb grumbling all the way about Clint. We had run about five minutes when he grabbed my arm and stopped in his tracks.

"Caleb! You left the keys in the Jimmy."

"I guess I forgot."

I thought Caleb was going to hit me but before he could, a second tremendous explosion shook the north woods.

Caleb looked at me with narrowed eyes.

"You wired the truck?"

I shrugged.

His eyes widened.

"You didn't tell him?"

"I forgot."

Chapter 28
What Happens to the Eldest
White Stag in the Woods?

Nakotah Rapids, Ontario, Canada
March 11, 1971

I have never liked hospitals. The white tile, cream and tan walls, extra wide doors, antiseptic smells, hushed voices from the rooms along the hall, and pale lights shining from the horizontal fixtures behind each bed give me the creeps and make me queasy.

I had not been in one since I screwed up with my lightweight chainsaw a few years back. I remember flashing sharp steel and blood spewing from the corner of my shoulder to the left nipple on my chest. When I got out, I had an ugly zipper of a scar, a numb spot the size of a dollar bill on my left arm, and a resolve to stay the hell out of hospitals. Now I was back.

Out of the midnight blackness, a lone blue-tinted light glared through a window at the end of the hall. Daylight would be a long time coming. I headed toward the two doors at the end of the hallway and peeked through. Apparently the Nakotah Rapids PD did not take the various manhunt alerts very seriously or maybe back then, it was just a lack of resources. To wit, the Sergeant was guarded by one

Barney Fife type snoozing on a forlorn, padded chair outside a room. His name tag said Stillman. Above him, a black magic marker, "Conwey" was taped on the door. An empty foam coffee cup and a rumpled newspaper lay on the floor.

I heard what sounded like a laugh come from the room. The deputy stirred, pushed open the door and stuck his head in. I heard the booming voice of Sergeant Conwey. The deputy jumped back. His face was red. He looked around nervously and sauntered down the hallway.

Conwey must have been feeling better. I wasn't. My head rung and the dull thudding between my ears increased as I moved down the hall. I was not the guy they were looking for and Caleb was holed up after another cabin break in, but still, I did not want to be stopped.

The hospital smell was starting to get to me. Drugs, urine, alcohol, (the medicinal kind) had overwhelmed me from the time I slipped past the vacated nurses' station until I turned into the room of the Sergeant. That's when things changed. The softly tuned radio played well flavored jazz. Conwey sat somewhat upright, face flushed pleasantly pink and rosy, sipping a chilled Molson, and talking with a blond middle aged nurse. His leg was in the air, hung in a bracket. I could hear the throaty Marilyn Monroe voice of the nurse as I shut the door behind me. I only caught the last part of the conversation.

"I hope you enjoyed the sponge bath as much as I did Wendel."

Her poorly managed frosted blond hair and prominent nose were more than offset by the scenery below her neckline. I saw what Conwey had seen. She was happily well endowed, showed it proudly, and frankly, looked like a hell of a good time. That sly old fox had his ways.

"Your leg is healing nicely. Is the therapy going…"

She saw me and stared at my bloody, dirt streaked jacket and muddy pants. I glanced in the mirror and flinched at the source of her alarm. Coldly appraising the desperate look behind the stubble on my face, she turned back to the sergeant.

"Wendel, you have company," she said with a hint of more than nursing concern.

Her eyes darted nervously as she looked me over and waited for Conwey's response. He looked up and took a sip of beer. The nurse unconsciously smoothed her collar and fiddled with the buttons of her uniform. I suspected that his relaxed demeanor was the only thing preventing a dash for the door or a scream for help.

"It's OK, Doris."

"Hi Sarge, you look better than the last time we met…but how come there are no drips running down that line from this bag of morphine here. You wouldn't have turned it off would you?"

"Well young man, I never was one for drugs so I persuaded Doris here to substitute a six pack of Molson's and a sponge bath for that little plastic tube of poison. See the little plastic clicker wheel there? All she had to do was roll it backwards, shut it off and I'm good to go for God's cure. Want one?"

I moved in closer to the bed where he was strapped, tied, and suspended. It formed a cat's cradle of ropes and plaster with a leg hidden somewhere in the middle of it. On the floor lay photo albums and a note book. Nurse Doris interrupted.

"Wendell, let me take the drip out of your vein. I can't leave the room with it in and unmonitored while you are drinking a beer. Your pain tolerance is off the charts and I'm willing to be disciplined for allowing you a beer or two, but not with an IV still stuck in your arm connected to a morphine bag. I want to take it out."

"Doris, let us visit. I don't think Johnny's here to change the drip volume. Give us ten minutes. We don't have much time. Then you can do your duty. Nobody's going to touch it. If you see our security man, send him out for more beer." Out of the sheets he came up with ten dollars and slipped it to Doris. She gave him a worried look and left.

"I thought you and that skiing partner of yours would be in Florida by now chasing girls and getting a tan."

He was not laughing at his own joke.

"Homework?" I pointed to the photo books laying by his bed.

"Mug shots. I've gone through them two times, trying to see if anybody in Canada has arrested anybody who looks like those American bombers that supposedly crossed over at Niagara Falls last September. For sure, this guy Burt came across. It's funny that a warrant to bring him in was held up just long enough for him to get away in Petersborough and it's suspicious that he managed to get along north of the border for so long with no visible means of support and without getting in any trouble."

It was time to turn serious. We both knew it.

"I need to talk to an honest man. Kentie said you saved each other's lives a long time ago and that he'd trust you with his again."

"It is true. We go back farther than most know. We don't talk about it, ey?"

Conwey was rock rigid and serious. He looked me right in the eyes and said, "I can tell you this. I am the honest man. You can bet your life on it."

I leaned in closer to talk. As I did, I could see that the blood crusted on the edge of my ear caught his bird of prey attention, but his expression did not change.

Every so often you meet someone you instinctively trust. We locked eyes. His steely blues were the guarantee I needed.

"Son, we better talk."

He set down an empty beer bottle and waved his arm to the cooler. There were two beers left, so I tapped them both and passed the first on to him. We both sipped. He set his bottle down and fixed me with a gaze so unwavering that it sent cold chills running up the insides of my arms.

"Where is your friend? Caleb? I need to get some facts straight and fairly soon."

"You know all about Caleb then?"

I felt some relief. I had to believe that Conwey was the honest man. Even in striped pajamas, he was imposing. The hospital closed in on me. The beer lost its tang. I felt like a grade school kid kept after school as the afternoon darkened. All the other kids had gone home and so had my bravado. I needed to tell, and be forgiven, and told that things would be all right.

Conwey took another swig off the bottle and shifted the weight of his cast. The slings and pulleys creaked loudly. After months of talking about nothing with Caleb it was a relief to be given permission to spill my guts. I unzipped my dingy blue ski jacket and began at the beginning. The post card was as logical as any place to start.

"I came up to Canada after my life went to hell and I heard my friend was accused of murder. I got tipped off that the local cops were going to arrest my ass and haul me down to Madison to hand me over to the FBI. I barely escaped. Caleb and I met up after one of the first blizzards and hid out in a camp on the Eagle Lake Chain."

The rest of the story was condensed in a rambling narrative about Cabin #2, the dance, the blizzard, the Galles, and finally, Caleb's nightmare flashbacks to the encounter with LaJeunesse and "Elbie."

"You're telling me that your friend saw Leo Burt on Cache Lake!"

"Sarge, my friend killed Leo Burt on Cache Lake. LaJeunesse too. In self-defense."

"I need to talk to Caleb. Everything is rotten, except for the fact that you scurrilous hippies risked your own necks to save my life." He looked down. "Thank you."

He readjusted himself by pushing some buttons. I could hear the hum and vibration. I did not like being there. The mountain man seemed suddenly older.

He was still King of the Northwoods but his status was changing. In the ancient kingdoms the king never offered thanks. He commended good work, cheered great battles, or ordered off the new hunt. Thanks were left to the women and the priests of the tribe. Conwey was aging before my eyes. I was saddened. My thoughts drifted. What happens to the eldest white stag in the woods when his prime is ended?

"So where is your fugitive buddy exactly?"

Conwey brought me back. He was again in charge. His attitude nearly erased my fears for his well-being. I had to tell the truth. I did not know where Caleb was exactly. He said he was going to tail me to the hospital to see if I was being followed. If it was clear, he would hook up with me when I left.

"I don't know and we don't have much time to talk. When I was a little kid in the fifties, the Mounties would rush in to save the day and the US Cavalry would come to the rescue of the good guys. Now they're after us. How'd we get to be the bad guys? Caleb was attacked for no reason. It's looking like he was attacked by a guy who was sheltering a terrorist. We should be heroes. What's going on?"

"John, settle down. You're not the only innocent party getting hurt. My career is over. My buddies here, like the guy we sent to get more beer, are watching me for now, but the word is out. As soon as they can move me I'm going to headquarters at the direction of Inspector Linley, where I hear I am going to be charged with the manslaughter of LaJeunesse. You boys know that I was never near that scumbag when the trouble happened at Cache Lake."

"Tell me you didn't say Linley."

"I did, John. Inspector Frederick Linley. Why?"

I replied, "That's the guy who beat the hell out of Caleb in jail. Caleb said he was in a mortal sweat to find out about LaJeunesse, and whether Burt was along."

"We might never know for sure, but let's put this together. This mysterious plane, the jail in Nakotah Rapids, and God help us all, Inspector Linley, my boss! He's the one who put me on administrative leave. He's the one floating the rumors that I'm the murderer."

Conwey held up his arm and started ticking off a fact list, raising a finger on his left hand with each bullet point.

"Leo Burt was involved in the Sterling Hall bombing in Madison, Wisconsin.

Shortly after, Leo Burt was stopped, north of Madison, by police near Devil's Lake State Park and let go.

Leo Burt's location in Petersborough, Canada was known but a warrant was held up, allowing him to escape.

Leo Burt then turns up in Quetico Park where your buddy recognizes him when they accidentally meet.

An official plane picked up your buddy and beats him bloody for information.

You find out that some secret branch of the American FBI is after you for information about Caleb."

He was out of fingers and made the final point by clenching and slamming his right fist on the bedside table, knocking off a bedpan. I mulled this over thinking dark thoughts about the governments of men.

"Sarge, you're saying that for some reason, unknown American authorities let Burt go. If that is true, it's possible that they were not flying into the park to catch Burt. They were flying in to help him escape. Or to kill him. Linley is on their side. Why are they doing this? Why are the authorities conspiring to help a terrorist even if it means allowing innocent people to be murdered and an honest police officer to be disgraced?"

"John, I'll try to find out. I've heard enough. You need to get out and get away. Find out a way to contact me through Kentie in a few weeks. I still have more friends and connections than Linley has. Taking me to headquarters will be their undoing. I will find out what is going on even if I do it from jail."

I hesitated before speaking. I had been part of enough of his pain already. But I had to say what was on my mind.

"Sargent, they're killers. What if they have thought about the risk of your turning the tables on them during your imprisonment. Would they kill you?"

"How are they going to do that? I die in jail, nobody's gonna let that rest. My own chiefs have assured me safe transport and I've got my oldest buddy watching over me now."

There was a knock on the door. Stillman had returned. I had never been the religious type, but I grabbed the brave sergeant's hand and said, "God bless, Sarge. We won't let you down."

The hospital hallway was still in the late night. There was an orderly at the front desk but he was busy fiddling with a pack of Chesterfields, with a crossword spread in front of him. As I pushed through the drafty revolving doors, I looked at the melted, muddy, gritty slop on the linoleum floors and thought, "That's what my soul looks like."

Outside the door, the draft had ceased but the biting cold was picking up. As I pulled my coat tightly around my neck, two men in classic tan trench coats got out of a black Lincoln Continental and walked purposely toward the hospital carrying black leather doctors' satchels. They looked important—probably specialists called in for an emergency in ER.

I walked down a street that looked like the background for Edward Hopper's Nighthawks. Caleb stepped out from behind a dumpster in a side alley and matched my strides.

"John. How'd it go?"

"We need to get out of here. The good guys are the bad guys. If you see a cop outside of the locals, they're after us. If you see law enforcement with a stars and stripes patch, they're after us. Let's go."

"All right, I was afraid those two goons would get you."

"What two goons?"

"The two you walked right by. They're spooks. Don't look back! Listen! At the same time they pulled up, I spotted a sharpshooter up on the roof across from the hospital. I think they're some kind of agents. Whatever, they are important enough to merit armed surveillance."

"Caleb. We've got to warn Conwey."

"We are not going back. He'll be OK. He has his man by the door you said."

Caleb was silent while we walked. I knew that silence all too well.

"John, here. You take the key to Burt's locker. They don't want you quite as badly as they want me. Shave your head, shave your beard, dye your hair, catch a bus back across the border, go to Madison and get whatever is in that goddamn locker. Then go to Gerry's dad. I've been thinking. He's an attorney. He's hard core right wing, but kinda like the Sarge, he'll know what to do…Wait. One other thing."

He fished in his pants pocket.

"I've been meaning to give you this, but we've been a little busy. That last night at Cabin #2, I found a topographic map of the Cache lake quadrant. You were sleeping. It'll be more proof."

"So what? Proof of what?"

He opened the map and jammed a cracked, dirty index finger at a smudged x.

"I marked where Burt's body is. The point off the island is distinctive so I'm sure that I've got this marked accurately, at least within 25 yards or so."

"OK, but what are you going to do?"

"I don't think it's safe for me to try and move any distances right now. You get back to the States, get some proof and I'll surface. In the meantime, I'll go back to breaking into backwoods cabins."

"Let's say I get to the locker and take the proof to Gerry's dad and something happens. How are you going to find out?"

"It will be a big scandal and the papers up here will cover it. I'll check the newspapers religiously."

He reached out, took my hand, shook it and jogged off.

I never saw Caleb again.

Chapter 29
"I Found Death"

Nakotah Rapids, Ontario, Canada
March 11, 1971

Caleb decided not to break in anywhere. He took a room for a week in the Audubon Motor Park. Welcome to hell. It stunk of mold, the radiator leaked hot water all over the floor, and the bed sheets appeared to have been donated by Typhoid Mary. It did have a shower. Later that morning he found a Goodwill store and outfitted himself in semi-presentable clothes for a couple of bucks. Clean and reasonably neat, he walked back toward the hospital. When he arrived, he did not recognize the place. The sleepy little public hospital had morphed into a military camp. Armed guards were posted at all entrances. As he watched, he became aware of the faraway thwop-thwop of a helicopter. Shortly, a black Huey with a machine gun mount, landed in the cordoned-off parking lot.

Caleb watched as two American soldiers pushed a gurney covered by an olive drab tarp out the emergency exit. There was a quick transfer and then the chopper was off. What the hell?

He needed to talk to the Sergeant, but nobody was going in or out, least of all a suspected terrorist. It was time to make a rational decision for a change, kill some time, get some sleep and go back in the morning. Easier said than done. He felt a fatigue that went deep into his muscles. It penetrated his bones and went straight to his soul. His forehead was hot and achy, his eyes burned, but he could not settle down. He reached in his pocket to see how much money he had left. Sixty-two dollars American. He passed a package store. Canadian Whiskey—Sale! He bought a bottle, some beef jerky, muttered "thanks" and pushed out through the glass door, jangling the wake-up bells hung above the frame. Thirty seconds later, the bells jangled again and the dispirited clerk looked up to see Caleb re-enter and go over to a ratty post card carrel. Leaning in, he slowly, almost gently, picked up a black and white travelogue card and brought it over to the counter.

The clerk aroused himself from semi-stupor and turned it over to check the price. He read the caption.

"Hmm, Buckhorn Lodge Cabin #2. You came back for this?"

Caleb tossed a nickel on the counter, palmed the card, and stared down the nosey storekeeper.

"It's important to me, OK?"

"No problem mister. Have a good night."

He stayed and hid out, going to small bars and keeping a low profile. Several nights later at the Audubon Motel for the last time, he opened the ratty curtains, allowing the bleak blue-white light from the parking lot to illuminate a block of light on his far wall. He sat on the musty bed and opened his last bottle of Canadian. A glass, wrapped in a cheap paper cover was within arm's reach on the nightstand. He unwrapped it, examined an ancient lipstick smudge on the edge and set it back down. He took a long pull straight from the bottle. Another pull brought back a memory of his great uncle Don.

Great Uncle Don and Great Aunt Fran. They were Catholic. Serious Catholics —said the rosary every night—a fifteen minute operation. Don was getting on, and he might have figured too much praying was cutting into other important diversions. One night he brought a bottle of whiskey to the bedroom and set it beside him as they knelt down to pray. When it was not his turn he took a pull. He enjoyed prayers more than usual that night. It became a habit until Fran brought him up short one night.

"I think it's a sin to drink while you pray."

"Well, Fran, show me the commandment that's been broken there."

She was not to be reasoned with on the matter so he offered a solution.

"What if the priest says it's OK?"

And so it was decided he would go to confession.

The confessional day came. The old man knelt and said, "Father bless me…"

"What have you done my good man?"

"Well, it's not what I did but what I might have done Father. Is it a sin to drink while you pray?"

The priest considered.

"I hate to tell you this, but I believe it is a sin to drink while you pray."

Don sighed and began to rise. Then paused.

"Father?"

"Yes?"

"Would it be a sin to pray while you drink?"

The drinking and praying continued. If it was good enough for great uncle Don it was good enough for Caleb. For the first time in years, he knelt down and prayed.

And drank.

Caleb woke up on the floor. The bottle of Canadian Club was empty, he was on the floor, and his socks were soaked from the leaky radiator. He had a splitting headache. His mouth felt like the Russian army had just marched through barefoot. Rolling on to his hands and knees, he crawled to the edge of the bed and clawed his way up to a sitting position. When he recovered from that, he gingerly stood up and wobbled into the bathroom, threw down four aspirin, staggered back to the bed and passed out.

When he woke up, he was sweating. The radiator was working overtime and an unseasonably clear and bright day was letting in the sun like bad kids burning ants with a magnifying glass, but he felt better. Caleb stood up and fished in his back pockets until he found the severely crinkled Buckhorn Lodge postcard. He moved over to a small desk, took out the postcard of Cabin #2 and thought. An hour passed. Rodin's The Thinker showed more life and movement. There was a ballpoint pen anchored to the scratched-up writing desk by a cheap little chain. He shook his head, ripped off the pen, and wrote on the postcard:

"Boys, it's been good to know you. You may wonder where I went. I went away because I was looking for excitement. I found death. If you look for trouble, you'll find it, just like I did. So stop bitching about the Packers, about whatever your wife was complaining about last night, about your damn taxes, about the DNR. Mick Jagger's right, "You can't always get what you want," but if you're not stupid, "You can get what you need." I wish to hell I was back in the barber shop. If you don't hear from John soon, tell the cops to dredge Cache Lake in Quetico, twenty meters off the end of the big point on the island. You'll find another mixed-up kid down there with a story to tell. —Caleb"

He set the card down, and started to put himself together. Before taking a shower, he decided to check the weather. He opened the door and stepped into a breeze that portended the end of winter. He felt the cool, moist breath of springtime mixed with the sound of running and dripping melt water. He was about to step back inside when a nearby newspaper machine caught his eye. Through the dirty glass door he read a headline that jolted him like 220 volts of electricity. He fished in his pants pocket, found a nickel, plugged it in, ripped out a copy and went back into his room to read. He did not even bother to shut the door to his room but instead sat on the bed as the breeze followed him in and riffled the edges of his newspaper.

Controversial OPP Officer Dead
of Medication Error

Nakotah Rapids authorities and a Nakotah Rapids Hospital spokesperson released a statement today that Sergeant Wendel Conwey was found dead in his room as a result of an apparent medication error. A local nurse, Doris Davens, has been suspended and is believed to be the nurse in charge during the Sergeant's death. The Sergeant, who himself was on administrative leave pending an investigation into his behavior, died of an overdose of morphine. An undisclosed source told this reporter that the Sergeant had an intravenous morphine drip to moderate the pain from severe leg injuries he received when his squad car was struck by a train in Vermillion Bay last week. The medication drip valve was turned completely open, a mistake which has been known to occur, albeit rarely, when health attendants confuse the direction of the wheel on the drip. When asked why the nurse did not notice a deterioration in the Sergeant's vital signs, the source hinted that authorities are looking into the possibility that both she and a guard that were posted at the room, had left their station and were possibly drinking in the staff lounge. Inspector Linley of the OPP released a brief statement. "We are saddened by the Sergeant's death and more saddened by the confusing turn of events, this once respected...

"SON OF A BITCH!"

Bullshit! The morphine drip was turned off and Doris had indicated that he would not be put back on it again until she returned. Someone else turned it on and set up Dorothy for the fall. That fucking Linley. They had him killed. Caleb thought back to the two suits going into the hospital. The timing fit.

He slipped on his clothes, absent-mindedly stuck the postcard in the back pocket of his blue jeans and stormed out of the room, slamming the door so hard it knocked a picture off the wall.

Chapter 30
Timeless Sky

Nakotah Rapids, Ontario, Canada
March 16, 1971

It was not hard to find where Inspector Linley lived. A phone book did the trick. That afternoon, Caleb scouted the place. The Inspector lived in a cabin on the banks of the Seine River, which coursed past the cedar trees on the edge of his yard. Caleb stood behind the cedars and observed his cabin long enough to verify that the Inspector was at home. He watched him pad from room to room. About three o'clock, puffs of smoke, and the smell of burning wood from the chimney indicated that he was cozying up for the rest of the day and night. Caleb wandered off. He would be back.

First, a last meal to kill time before dark. He was not sure what he was going to do but it would be something massive. Cutting back to the highway, he passed a logging camp. The guys were closing up the shop. He heard a powerful diesel chug to a stop and watched a rugged logger in a red and black plaid jacket clamber off a green and yellow ghost of a John Deere log skidder. The logger saw movement in the nearby woods but by the time he focused, Caleb had moved off and was dog-trotting back to a four-corners bar a mile or two back on the road. He went in, sat down and ordered the biggest hamburger they had and a shot of Jack Daniels. Hair of the dog.

He sat there for an hour thinking about two guys lost in the middle of the woods in a blizzard. He thought about a loyal canoe partner, and how he was feeding the fish on the bottom of the Cache River instead of proposing to the love of his life. He remembered a night on top of Sentinel Mountain in Yosemite when he and his partner had been benighted. A vertical mile down the valley floor, car and camp lights shone, but he and his partner might as well have been on Mars, such was the impossible vertical distance in the dark. A gigantic full moon hovered over them as they backed up together for warmth and pulled the ropes over themselves for a little insulation. He wondered about old girlfriends and what it would be like to have children.

A monstrous hillbilly stalked through the landscape of his ravaged memories. He ordered another whiskey as he saw the old man's chest explode into flames, while Leo Burt lay bleeding in the canoe begging for forgiveness for an explosion which had snuffed out the life of a brilliant young researcher. And finally, he saw one who believed, Conwey, smiling at him with a tin can of beer in his giant paw.

The bartender came over.

"You all right? Ey?"

"I'm fine, thanks. I was just thinking about a little logging I got to do and it's gonna be some ugly work."

He stood up to pay. Reaching into his back pocket, he accidentally pulled out the postcard when he grabbed his wallet. The card fell on the floor in a pile of beer and peanut shells. Later that night, a tired barkeeper would sweep it up with the shells and dump it in the trash without a look.

A half hour later, Caleb was back at the logging camp. He walked over in the dark to the John Deere and put his hand out and felt the huge tire chains. He scrambled up between the tires and up to the seat. He brushed off the snow and sat down. It was four-wheel drive and had a cable winch. The wind swirled snow around the tires of the huge machine. He fumbled for a light switch, found it and pulled. Nothing. Of course there were no lights. They were all busted off or burned out. The hell with lights. The moon would do. He felt for the starter control. If it was an industrial version it might have a key switch. Not this one. It was just the good old button. When he pushed it, a few chugging noises joined the wind. He hoped it wasn't a cold blooded rascal that wouldn't fire in the low temperature. He tried again. She started to purr. It had a hand throttle and a foot feed which he tapped to make a little snort. Next the hydraulics. They were in a familiar location. He felt comfortable as the front blade lifted at his command. Caleb put the monster in gear and rumbled off slowly. He was probably unstoppable, but why take a chance on a run-in with a huge boulder or monster tree stump. He kept to what he could make out of the trail, and in about a quarter of a mile he saw the lights of Linley's cabin through the forest.

Linley sat on his four season porch and looked out at the moonlight on the river. It was good to be ten miles out of town, especially at this time of his life. He pulled on an old pipe reflectively, looked up and thoughtfully blew a large ring toward the pine-paneled ceiling. His cousins were dead in some crazy dynamite accident, but he never liked them very much anyway and now there were two less possible sources of leaks to his seamless story. Lucky was dead too and that was also good. The old bear had seemed on the verge of blowing a gasket, and was too unpredictable for comfort, but those FBI fuckers had insisted that plausible deniability demanded a true unaffiliated scoundrel on the point end of smuggling Burt back to the States. Lucky was that. Too bad about the young canoers but they had saved him an unpleasant and dangerous assassination project by killing Lucky and probably themselves in the process. Whatever did happen to those bastards?

All things considered, he was damn lucky to be sitting on his porch. He had taken on enough blame in the Conwey fiasco to cover the higher-ups but not enough to fry his own ass. Too bad about the nurse and cop he'd had to frame. He laughed to himself. Right. Like he gave a damn about some hillbilly cop and that floozy nurse.

It was a messy deal all the way around but it was over. The giant domino theory cover-up made his situation not so precarious. Everybody implicated everybody else and that was as good as he was going to get. And best of all, a significant financial reward was headed his way, postmarked Washington, D.C. It looked like a comfortable early retirement was on the horizon. Life was good.

He looked out at the low clouds scudding against the tops of the trees and felt the wind blow against the house. He tamped out the pipe, pushed up from his rocker and decided on an early bedtime. He wandered into his paneled bedroom, brushed his teeth, and climbed into bed. He fell to sleep immediately as he did always; enjoying the clear conscience that only babies and sociopaths know.

Linley felt and heard his heart pound before he focused on the diesel throb outside of his cabin. The noise seemed as if it were coming from everywhere. His mouth dried up as he realized that his apocalyptic dream was a reality. A huge prehistoric jaw hovered outside of his bedroom window. He grabbed the Brinkman million candlepower spotlight that he kept on his bedstand and shined it out the window. Just before the huge blade smashed through his window and wall, he read the large stylized letters on the side of a diesel logging machine.

"John Deere."

It was the last reading he was to do in this life. With startling quickness the blade angled right and clipped Linley, damaging him mortally, but not killing him. He knew pain and fear as the blade scraped off one of his legs at the knee as if it were an unwanted 6-inch branch from a tree. The log skidder backed out again with the remains of Linley's leg dripping from the blade. Inexpertly, but effectively, Caleb swung the blade three feet and pushed ahead scooping up the free standing LP tank next to the house. Over the blade, Caleb could see Linley screaming in agony as he futilely tried to staunch the bleeding from his severed leg. The sight of his LP tank coming through the wreckage ahead of the blade of the John Deere gave him something to take his mind off the pain.

"NO!"

His screams were lost in the roar of the engine. The LP tank gathered up the rug and an end table as it ground across the floor toward Linley who was desperately trying to crawl away. It pushed into him, smeared him across the floor and compressed him against the wall. The tank ruptured, a spark flashed and the room was engulfed in an explosive WHUMPF of red flame. The log structure went up like kindling, causing the roof to fall in on the skidder.

Sometime later the first of the rural fire department trucks arrived. It took several tankers to extinguish the flames to the point the firefighters could inspect the damage. It would be days before they uncovered the crispy remains of Linley, but the driver of the big log skidder was curiously intact, although blackened and charred beyond recognition.

One of the firefighters shook his head.

"I'll be damned. I been fighting fires for twenty years and I've never seen anything like that, ey. It looks like he's doing it on purpose."

The driver's right arm was burned and stretched so taut by the heat that it was erect, bent at the elbow. One of the digits was still discernible, and it was soldered into the time honored middle finger salute. Water dripped off the driver's extended middle finger and glistened in the moonlight.

"Damn, it almost looks like it's smiling, too."

The firefighter shook his head as he killed the last of the pumps and looked up at the chiaroscuro patterns made by overhead branches against the timeless sky.

Chapter 31
The Best Place to Hide is in a Crowd

Madison, Wisconsin
March 17, 1971

I spent a few days looking for Caleb but I had a feeling I'd never see him again. Caleb haunted me my last night in Canada. I dreamed that he was fighting a policeman. I tried to help him but in my dream my punches were off-target, limp-wristed, powerless slaps. It felt like I was throwing the ineffectual hooks and uppercuts while submerged in a jar of molasses. Caleb looked at me and laughed, grabbed the inspector in a choke hold and stepped backwards, tripping both of them over into a blast furnace. The fire flared and through it I saw two skeletons, one of them grinning. I woke up screaming. It was time to go.

I took a last look at Nakotah Rapids, and then was picked up by a good-natured pulpwood driver at the diner on the outskirts of town. The cold wet snow carried no hint that spring would some day come this far north. The snow was light but biting. I closed the passenger door and rubbed my hands together to alleviate the frosty sting. I told the driver my name was John and looked out the window sensing his concern over my brief introduction. Then the CB crackled with static and he became occupied with news of highway road conditions, various police reports, and run of the mill good buddy greetings all ending with "ey?" I was glad for the warmth as I contemplated my hands. Roughing it with Caleb over the course of the winter had given them a near permanent red color and a tolerance for abuse. It felt good to be in the big cab of the dark green Peterbilt. I shared my side of the cab with a large brown dog named Mickey. Every few minutes or so he migrated back toward Gene the driver for a head rub. I wanted to be an old dog, always one scratch away from contentment.

It was late night on the road, the best time to be a trucker. Gene was a family man, but he told me he enjoyed the route to Thunder Bay. It was short and generally snow clear. He watched the highway and said, "There are some good greasy spoons near the pulp mill as well as an adult entertainment center that some of the drivers talk about. Of course, I don't go for that kind of stuff. My Sarah would not approve. She's a good wife and mother to our seven fine children. Billy is going to tech school in the fall and Holly and the younger ones are still in…"

I fell into a deep sleep in the warm leather seat. The engine rumbled and all the gears were doing what they should. CB or not, I dozed with my left arm wrapped around Mickey, the good brown dog. Figuring a little misdirection could never hurt, I had told Gene I needed to get off at Highway 61 near downtown so I could call friends and flop with them for a couple of days. Before napping, I said I would be heading east to Red Rock, then to Wawa. When we got there, Gene wanted to get on the CB to see if anyone was going that way but I said no. I had plans. Of course they were to get the other way, south of the border, to a small mid-western city, the epicenter of the mess.

I woke up to Mickey licking my ear. Downtown Thunder Bay. There wasn't any thunder but I could see the bay stretch for miles. Gene and Mickey dropped me off at the intersection of Highway 11 and Highway 61. I thanked the grizzled driver, rubbed Mickey's old neck, played with his brown ears, and then gave him a hug and jumped down off the diesel tank.

I didn't want to be downtown but Gene had taken me there because he thought it would be helpful to another brother of the road, and friend of Mickey. I smiled. Never underestimate the power of a good dog to chase away the blues.

Thunder Bay always has a lot of traffic. In mid-spring traffic increases before the thaw as load restrictions go into effect. Trucks have no choice but to haul half loads or no loads. Some truckers just don't drive at all, choosing to drink the winter profits at the local road house or home. And some of those take their frustrations out on spouses or logging buddies. For the local law it is something worse than Halloween in Madison, Wisconsin. It goes on for a month. I would have to be watchful for the bad-natured, over-worked cops trying to keep it all under control.

I found the Canadian equivalent of George Webb's and squandered $1.99 for the burger special, French fries with onion rings, and hot coffee. That left me with $37.25 in my pocket. I reveled in the fullness of my stomach. Later I would drive up Rolaids stock and regret the feast but a traveling man has to eat. The next leg of my journey to the Badger Bus Depot would take me to the Twin Ports.

Thunder Bay to Duluth/Superior really boils down to one road and one rail service. I went out on Highway 61 south, just before daylight and pondered that while drinking coffee at a ratty BP station. It was cold. I had had enough of trains so it was back to hitchhiking. I watched for truckers. Dawn light peeked over the cloud tops as a semi pulled in. Minnesota plates! The driver was a big man wearing a denim and flannel jacket, black cowboy hat, jeans, and boots. He was on his way to a washroom break. It took him a while. I thought about conversation starters.

When he re-emerged, he got some coffee and a box of Little Debbies. I managed to position myself at the counter to ask about bus service to Duluth, just as he arrived. The clerk sighed, and pointed behind her at the bus schedule. Her name tag said, "Cherie." She said, "Read it. Tomorrow afternoon."

"That will be too late. My grandma might not make it more than a day according to Ma. I need to get back there. Is there another bus or some other way to get down there?"

Cherie chewed her gum. I looked down. Then cowboy hat spoke up.

"I'll take him as long as he don't talk too much."

Then to me. "Son, I can get you to Eau Claire. I drop my load at Altoona."

Cherie stopped chewing. "Jack, you sure? Let me share a concern here. He just showed up here an hour ago like he was waiting for a mark."

When he turned to me, I could see part of a tattoo on his neck. It was 'ell's Ang'.

Now I had concerns, but what do you do? I just smiled and chirped up, "Thanks, I'll get my stuff."

Jack checked his rig while I climbed in the cab. Less than a mile down Canadian 61 he said, "I don't mean to pry but I've seen a bunch of you boys. What was it? Low draft number?"

The lie was easy.

"Yeah, I came up with 13, the same as my birthday. It seems it's been my run of luck."

"Don't worry. I was called up for the Berlin crisis and I didn't like it. None of our boys should be in Nam. Lost my son there. The sons of bitches keep looking for excuses to make us think you young folks are commies or something just for doing what Thomas Jefferson said you are supposed to do. When government gets out of hand, you got an obligation to call them out."

A pause while the CB crackled, then he turned back to me. "I ain't as dumb as I look."

He didn't look dumb to me at all. I reassured him, "I get that. More than you know."

"OK. If they stop us at the border, your name is John and I'm your uncle. Got it?"

I nodded, then fell asleep again. The border crossing out of Canada was a wave and a drive through. I woke up when we were out of Canada and just into Minnesota at the welcome sign and guard post.

"Hey Jack, where you going tonight?" The US Border patrol officer asked. "Just the usual. Down to Altoona to drop this timber at the yard like always. Then back to Duluth."

The officer's flashlight swept across the cab.

"You take care. Who's your friend?"

"That's John. My brother's son. Needs a ride to Eau Claire. His granny is in the nursing home. See you next week Jacob."

We were back on the road—61 to 53 and south. The coffee wore off and I dozed again. There was CB radio traffic all night—good buddy stuff as we headed south through good old Wisconsin soil. What to do? I knew a guy in Altoona from my years in Madison but that was a while ago. That wouldn't work. I asked Jack for directions for the biggest truck stop at the freeway so I could hitch a ride south. Jack was on the CB as we came into the north edge of Eau Claire.

"Breaker 19. This is Black Jack. I got a live load to go to Madtown."

CB static broke off to a clear gravel voice. "Black Jack. Go to 15. Irish out."

I saw Jack turn the dial to 15. "I know this trucker, we run together sometimes. Not everybody needs to know our business." Then he spoke to the mike. "Irish, what's your 20?"

"Just at Highway B five miles behind you. I'm going to Portage to trade loads. Is that going to work?"

I nodded and gave a thumbs up to Jack. It was a little out of the way, but very workable.

"Roger that. By the way, this is off the books."

More crackles, then, "Drop the package at Schneller's back lot. I've got a few minutes of business to attend to."

Jack looked at my stocking cap. "Package has a red top and will be inside near the door."

"Roger, I suppose you're still dropping sticks."

"10-4. I have to wait for the fork lift jockeys. See you next time. Out."

"Out."

To me, "He likes one of the waitresses there. Sometimes we have coffee and pie. He has a big beard and you've heard his voice. Just make sure you keep your cap on. You'll know him when you see him."

I walked into the shabby truck stop and sat down at the corner stool, swiveling back and forth on the round top seat. I felt in my pants pocket to touch the locker key. It was still there but time was wasting. Irish finally found me. He was a mountain of a man topped with curly hair. You could not tell where his hair left off and the beard began. The rest was flannel jeans and boots.

"Howdy. I'm Irish. You stay put. I'll soon be back."

Then he was off and gone down the hall. I kept my head low and sipped from my cup. My doughnut was already gone. I was anxious to put more distance and time between myself and anywhere in Canada, not sure I could or would ever go back.

I moved a little so Irish had double wide room when he came back to plant himself on the round red stool to my right. It had taken several minutes for the waitress to just come and take my order but in twenty seconds a cup of black coffee and a large roll with a pat of Wisconsin's finest on the side plate appeared in front of Irish. That was another blow to my ego, which was being freighted on the Titanic of self-concept.

The waitress was back hovering.

"Hello Belle. How are you?" he said.

I saw her blush lightly from the neck. "Fine. The girls will be back home for spring break next week and I'm looking forward to spending time with them. Would you like to come over on your next run? They'd like to see you again."

She was still smiling from when he'd said hello. I put money on the counter and walked over to a stack of newspapers other morning readers had left behind. Belle took my place. Irish looked my way and did a slight head nod. It was fine. Beggars can't be choosers. I wasn't the guy who had driven all night to get the news that he was picking up some shaggy stranger. I grabbed up a crumpled Wisconsin State Journal. There was nothing on the front page that interested me. Inside, Dagwood and Blondie were still having trouble understanding each other. Deep inside on one of the last pages there was something with the dateline Ontario. Suspicious deaths were being investigated. It was possible that they may be tied to other crimes in the Province, no real clues, blah, blah…

No shit.

Belle was on the other side of the counter and Irish was paying. I zipped up my coat, pulled out the stocking cap and walked to the lot out back. I did quick math and realized I could be in Portage in two and a half hours or so. Maybe I'd get a cat nap for most of the time.

I took a guess at the green paint job, gold four leaf clover, and the name O'Shaughnessy's Trucking and headed toward a big old rig in the back of the lot. Irish. Right? I was right because when I looked back, Irish was on his way. The first flakes were falling from a heavy gray sky as we pulled on to I 94. I woke up at the Highway 16 exit. By the time we passed the Sauk-Columbia county line, the snow was five or six inches deep and wet. Irish took a quick look at me.

"I thought I saw you move. We're into some deep stuff here. After I drop the load, I'm going to Stuarts to have them put on the chains. They have several large bays and I've thrown them some business."

I rode with him out to Highway 33 because Irish said he'd take me over to 51 and a pick up return load of plastics. Highway 51 goes into Madison from the east side.

The guy behind the counter told me while Irish was talking to the chain guys, "It'll be easy to get into Madison from there. Black Jack seldom helps out giving rides so there must have been something special about you. You're about the age his son would have been."

He had already called Stuart's from the drop site and that's where we went. They had the chains and jacks out and ready. First the right side, then the left side and we were chained and ready to go through anything. It only took twenty minutes and the job was done. Irish signed the bills as calls started pouring in for tows on I 94 and Highway 51. Blizzards are famous in Wisconsin at state tournament time in March. While they worked on the trucks, the mechanics chatted excitedly about the local team making the tournament.

Whole towns empty and students, parents, and friends board freezing yellow buses which chug through the night to the capital city and the Field House at Camp Randall. Wisconsin in the sixties and seventies was like a family and everyone knew everyone so fans headed in confident that somewhere they would find lodging in a church, a dorm, a campus building or a friendly family with a vague tie to the visiting high school team. It was going to be one of those nights. Weather men were giving expanded reports on the radio. TV coverage had young cub reporters standing outside in the snow with their hair turning white from crystals of snow while snowplows churned in the background.

Inside Irish's cab, the country western station said that the Portage team was already there and buses to see the game were ready with chains on the tires and would be leaving the high school at 4 p.m. with plow escorts to the county line. Dane County plows would meet them near Morrisonville to lead them downtown where the City of Madison crews pledged to help if necessary. Strings had been pulled, deals made. I had just found a way into Madison within blocks of where I needed to go. The bus was scheduled to leave in three hours. The best place to hide is in a crowd. I had Irish let me out when we passed an intersection across from the high school. I was now closer to Madison than I had been in a long time.

I was slept out, so I wandered down to the high school library where a bunch of high school and middle school kids flopped on chairs, donated old couches and the carpeted floors. I looked for a Jack Kerouac book. I should have known it would not have been acceptable in high school, so I settled for Huck Finn and picked a part of the floor where I could keep to myself.

Time passed, and soon I was riding a bus with kids shouting cheers and repeating players' names with more cheering. I asked a cheerleader for a Kleenex and packed my ears. I had not been around this many people in months and they were closing in. If I had been on the adult bus there might have been quiet and a passed flask, but also questions. With my shaggy hair I could play the loner kid come back to see the current team do what they hadn't been able to when I graduated. As the bus dropped us off at Camp Randall I told the driver that I would not be riding back because I was staying with my older brother who was a law student. When he asked my name, I politely grabbed his clipboard and pen and scribbled through my barely legible sign up signature. He asked me something but I was already out the door and headed down the road to the Badger Bus Depot.

Chapter 32
Badger Bus Depot

Madison, Wisconsin
March 19, 1971

The Badger Bus depot was only a couple of blocks off the square in downtown Madison. I looked different than I had when I left Winchester half a year ago. Thirty pounds lighter, but shaggy, I looked like a lumberjack on furlough instead of a gone-to-pot grade school teacher. I had purchased a big sweatshirt emblazoned with a strutting red Bucky Badger to soften the look. I gathered nary a glance as I strolled up to the bank of lockers set back against the bus depot lobby wall. The filthy linoleum floor reminded me of all the other damp, dirty, cold places I had been over the winter. Kind of poetic. Just like my life—damp, dirty and cold. Before opening the metal locker, I thought about where the key had been, including Caleb's digestive tract. I shook my head. Caleb would be laughing.

The locker clicked open. Inside was a gray canvas gym bag with red handles. I grabbed it, checked once to see if there was anything else, and walked until I reached Tramini's—a working-class Italian bar on the south side. Twenty-five cents bought me an ice cold tap of Hamm's beer. I took it to a booth and sipped, then slid the gym bag off the bench seat and rested it on the table in front of me. A couple of heads at the bar turned at the sound of unzipping, then went back to the sounds of hushed bar conversation. Brother Otis was on the juke box. I wondered

195

what he had been making out of his life as his little plane nose dived into Lake Monona, taking away one of our R&B greats. I hoped he died in peace. As I nervously tapped my glass on the tabletop, I hummed, "…and this loneliness won't leave me alone." I pulled out a reel-to-reel tape from the gym bag. I held it up, puzzled. That attracted too many stares so I put it away and reached for a manila folder. I opened it and read from a piece of expensive rag paper embossed with the seal of the FBI:

June 16, 1970

Dear Leo,

I don't like what you are doing any better than you do but "Searchlight" insists. I especially do not like being in the middle of this. I love my country, but if this goes south, if someone gets hurt, I want proof that I was only following the orders. I am sending it to you because I don't trust them. They would be a group that no one knows exists. They are part of the department, but outside of it at the same time. They run a covert operation outside of official channels and answer only to "Searchlight"—if they answer to anyone at all. I am sure they raided and examined my apartment yesterday. They follow me everywhere but this isn't my first rodeo. I made sure I was alone before I wrote this and I am dumping it in the mail to you before they become my second skin. Enclosed is a tape of "Searchlight" telling me exactly what he wants done and why he is going to do it. How do I have it? It's a little-known fact to some of us on the inside that he tapes his conversations. We call them the "Oval Office Tapes." It's going to bring him down one of these days. You would not believe the dirty tricks he's up to. (One of these days, the word Watergate is going to mean something very special to the world.) It's new taping technology and his secretary, Rosemary, is always erasing or losing the tapes, which is why I dared to steal this for thirty minutes to duplicate it. If someone saw it was missing, they'd probably blame Rosemary. But no one was paying attention and I made this copy. They'll kill you if they know you have it. Use it only if you or I are accused of being directly involved in terrorist acts. Hopefully, this letter is never seen by anyone. If it is, we'll go to jail. But at least we won't be assassinated if it becomes public, which is why I am taking such a chance in mailing it in the first place. Good luck out there in Madison. I know you believe in what you are doing and that there are financial and career rewards if you succeed but double check all the information they give you before you do anything. That fertilizer and fuel oil bomb they taught you about? You have no idea how powerful it is. We do not want anyone to get hurt. Your cover has been superb and no one should be able to figure out you were working for us but know that if someone does, you are expendable.

CYA.

—Kelly

I sipped my beer again. Who was "Searchlight"?

What's an oval office?

Kelly? Is this from Billy the cop's FBI dad? And if it is, were we all pawns in a dark and murderous plot to bomb a public university?

.

Chapter 33
Alone Again

Mazomanie, Wisconsin
March 19, 1971

Gerry's father's office was on Main Street in Mazomanie. Despite a squeaky clean reputation, windows appeared unwashed and there was a dark pallor within. I saw cobwebs on the sill as I sat at the small round table, awaiting Mr. Roper. A pert, young secretary saw me looking and said, "He just hasn't shown much interest in keeping the place up since his son passed. He never had a janitor but now he shows no interest in doing the cleaning that he used to do. Things are getting a little shabby. Sorry."

"I understand."

An oak door off to the side of her desk opened. Mr. Roper stepped through.

"John? Step in please."

We shook hands. I reminded him that he had met me once at Gerry's graduation. He seemed not to remember but brightened when I added, "I was a close friend of Caleb's."

"So John, my secretary tells me that this has something to do with my son's death. Did you two have some shared land holdings up north or something?'

"Mr. Roper, we shared a trust—Caleb, Gerry, and I. Now only I am left. I am not strong enough to carry it alone."

He blanched, then sat down with a dazed look on his face. When he had composed himself, he asked, "Do you want some coffee?"

"Sure."

"Sally, bring a cup of coffee for John, please, and then hold my calls."

While I waited for the coffee, I examined the wall. Instead of the usual degrees and diplomas, there were sports pictures. Pictures of Gerry kicking off the pitcher's box as he delivered a 90 mph high school fastball, Gerry shooting an old fashioned running one-hander in some Wisconsin school gym right out of Hoosiers and Gerry sinking a ten foot putt while Dad held the flag.

The father's eyes were moist.

"What happened? No bullshit."

"Mr. Roper, before I begin, I need you to give me your word. Whatever you hear, whether you believe it or not, we never talked. I walk out of here and you do not report me, you do not call the cops. Whatever you do, you do it on your own and leave me out of it."

"Son, do I look like the kind of guy who makes deals about my boy?"

He didn't.

"You tell me what you know. I'll do what I think is right. That's your deal."

I thought about it. I could probably bolt. After a winter of hard knocks, I knew the old man couldn't stop me even if he was definitely scary looking. What were my options? Slim and none. More convincingly, I knew from Gerry and Caleb that he had a reputation as a man with whom one did not trifle. I had been a pretty rational guy for most of my life, and look what it had done. That rational thinking got me a fantasy life built around booze and a crappy marriage. For the past six months, I had screwed the rules and the rationality and gone with my gut. I was still alive and not just physically. Even though I was miserable, I was existentially alive too.

So I went on and told him. All of it. Then I showed him the papers. He read them and looked up.

"Give me the tape."

To the intercom he said, "Sally, bring in the reel-to-reel player please."

In a matter of minutes we were listening to several voices discussing how the anti-war movement was gaining enough momentum that it might ruin the re-election chances of the sitting president. A throaty voice that we knew from the evening news sound bites said, "And you really think you can trust these bastards to break into the Watergate Hotel once the Dems get set up there, without it connecting to the Committee to Re-elect the President?"

What the hell was the Watergate Hotel? The voice went on.

"All right. You do what you want on that one as long as I get complete and plausible deniability. I'm more interested in what's going on at the University of Wisconsin. They have not had classes there for weeks. Hard-working blue collar steel workers and farmers are starting to wonder if these hippies might not have a point. It's a house of cards falling down around us. I can't keep the lid on what we're doing in Cambodia much longer. They're commies, but they're smart and if we don't do something to discredit the Madison peace movement, I think the wheels are going to fall off."

Then we listened, mouths agape, as other voices described how they had placed moles in the anti-war ranks.

"We've got one guy, boss, you would love. Catholic, square jawed, a jock, smart. He got disillusioned with the crew team and it made him blow a gasket. It threw him for such a loop that it didn't just turn him against sports, he generalized it to the whole UW establishment. He's flipped out and he believes the only way to save UW from the right wing crazies that he thinks ruin everything from the science labs to the weight room, is to bring down the power structure. He's not a killer, but we've sounded him out on organizing a bombing that can be traced back to the anti-war movement and levered against the soft UW administration that let that campus get out of hand in the first place. He's even recruited some dupes to do the dirty work. These guys are so stupid they'll be caught in a matter of days. We'll give our boy cover, get him to Canada and watch for the reaction. If we time this right and if the Watergate thing works out, I think we're good as gold for the re-election."

I did not know what Watergate was, I barely knew where Cambodia was located, but I knew all too well the deep gruff voice that closed the conversation. I visualized the blue six o'clock shadow on the jowly cheeks, the widow's peak, and the remarkable nose that went with the voice.

"Gentleman, fifty years from now, people will study this terrible decision and know that it saved the country. Do it."

When the tape ran out, Mr. Roper did not move. He stared out the window through the dusty venetian blinds which had not been cleaned since Gerry disappeared. One might have thought that he was examining the customers going in and out of the bank next door but I knew he was lost deep in thought.

I cleared my throat and got up. He blinked, looked at me and said, "Come back here tomorrow at four o'clock."

I put my hand on the doorknob. He spoke one more time.

"It's nothing personal. I need time to think. I need to be alone. Do you have a place to stay?"

"Not really," I said.

"Like I said, John, it's not personal. You need to get away from me for awhile but I don't want you to be picked up by the cops or something worse. I'll have my secretary call the Best Western two blocks down. Stay there tonight. We'll see you tomorrow."

My hand was about played out but I might as well go all in, push the rest of my chips on the table and see what the hole cards were. I knew if somehow I survived all this, I was going to have to get a better perspective on life. Lately I had been sinking back into my old habits of too many solitary conversations with my old friends the Christian Brothers, not to mention Jack and Jim. That being said, I wandered over to the local grocery store and bought the cheapest beer I could find. Edelweiss. "A case of good judgment" it bragged on the label. Why did they ever stop making slogans like that? I picked up a pizza and went to the motel room, reserved in my name and paid for, exactly as promised. I ate the pizza, drank the beer, watched an episode of the Hogan's Heroes and went to bed.

The next morning after a shower, I walked over to the Blue Willow diner. While I was sipping coffee, waiting for my eggs, I asked the guy on my right if I could borrow his paper when he was done with it. He slid over the front page and the sports section. I picked up the State Journal's unique "peach sheet," a special colored section that grabbed sports lovers' attention. The Badgers were mediocre again. Big deal. I was not in the mood for international news but I flipped over the front page anyhow.

What I saw took away my appetite.

American Suspected of
Suicide-Homicide In Ontario

A respected RCMP Inspector was killed Tuesday night in his home outside of Nakotah Rapids, Canada, in a gruesome attack apparently perpetrated by American Caleb Pratt. Pratt has been the subject of a month-long manhunt and is also suspected of killing a local guide, Lucky LaJeunesse. Sources report that Pratt stole a log skidder from a nearby logging camp and drove it to Inspector Linley's house where he pushed an LP tank through the front wall, causing an explosion that destroyed the house and killed both men. Police are unusually secretive about the details of this case so far and are not providing any possible motives.

I put down the paper. I was alone.

DAN WOLL and JOHN W. LYON

Chapter 34
"All Stand"

Maryland, USA
March 20, 1971

Did you ever wonder what the Ice Age was like? Check out a March afternoon in Wisconsin. Four o'clock finally rolled around and I headed up toward Roper's office. The sidewalks were gritty with sand and salt that had been spread in a futile attempt to keep them slip free. My mood was as dark as Caleb's eyes had once been. I entered the office and scraped off my shoes the best I could on a rough brown hemp foot mat. Mr. Roper sat at his desk fiddling with a manila envelope.

"John, your story makes sense. I called up the Federal Justice Building and got an agent I know on the phone. I told him what I had. He told me that they would come out to see me in an hour. Just like that. They were not suggesting. I did not like the sounds of that. They changed their attitude very quickly when I informed them that I had made multiple copies of all documents and tapes and sent them to twelve independent sources who could be trusted to keep the material confidential unless something untoward were to happen to you or me. In that case, the sources pledged to release the material to media outlets independent of the FBI. I think they were going to kill me, John. I spoke frankly with them, told them what I suspected. All pretenses were dropped. They told me that they believed me, that they would not hurt me, but they had to call my bluff and see proof. Shortly after that the first helicopter ever to visit Mazomanie landed in the local park, and unloaded two agents and a complement of heavily armed guards. I showed them a copy of the papers and we listened to the tape. They asked what I wanted. I said the heads of whoever was responsible for Gerry's death and I would accept no compromises."

He flipped the same newspaper I had seen earlier in the day up on the desk. We agreed that the Canadian end of the murders had been addressed with a vengeance by Caleb. Mr. Roper frowned and went on.

"I told them that was not enough. I needed to go a step higher and see who was at the top, who was in charge of putting this all together. They said that on the Canadian side it was Linley and that would have to be good enough. I picked up the phone and started to dial one of my associates who would trigger the release of the material. FBI agents begging is a pathetic sight, let me tell you. I gave them an ultimatum—tell me who was responsible or I would go public. The agent told me that we were in a game of what he called mutually assured destruction. They acknowledged that if I went public, I would topple their house of cards and bring down some very powerful people. On the other hand, if I did that I was assured that you and I would be killed as payback. I have no doubt they meant it. They want to cut a deal. I have no stomach for it. They want you to go. Here is an airplane ticket to Washington D. C. You should go. I scared them, but honestly, I'm caved in. I'm done. I've got the triggers set to end it all for both sides, but after a night to sleep on it, I'm not doing it. It's up to you. Caleb killed the guy who murdered Gerry and the corrupt official who started it. It goes higher. I'll leave it up to you from here. Even if it gets us both killed, maybe it's worth it."

I considered.

"Mr. Roper, at this point, it's not that I really give a shit anymore about my life but what is to guarantee that they are not just taking me someplace to execute me."

"John, they won't. Mutually assured destruction. They can NOT have these documents public and the documents will go nationwide if you are harmed. I want you to go there and see what you can work out to set this right and exact some final justice … and yes, revenge. I am having a cab sent out from Madison to pick you up. It will be here in twenty minutes. Be ready."

"A cab ride to Madison!"

"John, expenses are not the issue in this matter."

He flipped the ticket on the desk, got up abruptly, wiped his eyes and walked out, slamming the door behind him. I never saw him again.

The cabbie hustled but I was still cutting it close when I arrived at the Madison airport. I found that I had been booked on a direct flight to Philadelphia with a connection to D.C. When I walked down the airplane stairs in D.C. I was immediately met by two stocky men with official-looking US seals on the breast pockets of their blue blazers.

"John, come with us."

I followed. Instead of going into the airport, we walked on the tarmac around the corner of the terminal. There sat a large midnight blue chopper with a USAF star and stripe on it. It wasn't quite a shove but they kept nudging and guiding me toward it and up the ladder. I was too tired not to comply. On board, flight helmets were passed out. Mine was different. The visor was blackened.

"John we're not going to hurt you. Some of the boys in here don't want to be a part of this any more than you do and we would just as soon not have you remembering too many faces or name tags."

With the helmet visor blacked out, I started to fall into a sensory deprivation swoon until I felt the powerful helicopter lift, and then sensed a downward deflection of the nose, forward movement and a sensation of speed. Wherever we were going, we were going there as fast as the helicopter would go.

At one point, I asked, "Do I get to know where I am going?"

A wise guy answered, "Sure. You're going to camp."

I felt anger start to surge through my shoulders and a loss of control come over me until the voice identified with blue blazer touched me and said, "It's OK. Actually, you are going to a camp. The most special camp in the world. Relax. Please."

Finally, I felt the ship's forward motion stop. We were hovering and then slowly descending until there was a bump and a final sag as the wheel shocks compressed on the ground. Strong hands lifted the helmet off my head and pointed me to the door in a manner that ensured I could not look back at the flight crew. I stepped down the portable stairway onto a grassy landing pad that was covered with dead pine needles from the surrounding forest. Clouds scudded overhead in a light breeze coming from the low mountains on the horizon. I could see small cabins through the trees. All this for a Boy Scout camp?

"Where the hell are we?" I asked.

"If you can't figure it out, they wasted their time bringing you here."

My question led to a much rougher shove in the direction of the largest cabin at the end of a path leading away from the helicopter landing pad. As we drew near,

Marines stood at parade rest in front of an American flag. The guards obscured a plaque that became visible as I moved closer.

CAMP DAVID

Behind the plaque was my destination—a large cabin, and possibly the final answers at the end of an odyssey that had cost me all of my friends and my life as I knew it. We entered a large pine-paneled room with rough-hewn board floors and a large stone fireplace on the far wall. I made a small judgment at that point that I had seen enough pine paneling to last me for the rest of my life. That vow was made a long time ago, and I've lived a lot of places since, but never in a room with pine-paneled walls.

A full colonel walked in and stood in front of me. If he expected me to stand up and salute, he was mistaken. Years later an author named Least Heat Moon would talk about passing from the "I can't take it anymore," to "I don't give a damn" stage. I was at the "I don't give a damn" stage, an army of one with no allegiance to anyone. The colonel gathered himself.

"First son, we need to get clear on…"

"No sir, let me correct you. YOU need to get clear on some things. I'm done. I'm burned out. All my friends are dead. I'm here for one thing. A pound of flesh and I'm the one giving the orders and demands. I'm not dealing. The worst you can do is kill me. You have been trying to do that to me all winter. If I leave here with anything less than what I want, or if I do not go back at all because you make me disappear, everything I know is locked and loaded to go out immediately to ABC, NBC, CBS, the New York Times, TIME magazine … for starters. You want to hear the rest? Don't even start with me. Just tell me who I am going to see."

A guard put his hand on my shoulder and I started to speak. I jumped up, and he put me in a brutal hammerlock, but not before I could scream, "Fine, KILL ME, do it! Do it!"

The Colonel spoke. "Let him go!"

He addressed me, "You are going to see the man in charge. We know what you can do. I think you know what we can do. Time out. Listen. Then you can choose if you want to work with us. If not, everyone involved dies because that will be our only recourse to try and save this mess."

I sat down in a heavy log chair at a long wooden meeting table.

The colonel said to the sergeant, "We're ready."

The sergeant left, returned in a minute, braced himself at attention and hollered, "Attention. All stand!"

I didn't.

The sergeant headed for me purposefully. The colonel interrupted.

"Sergeant. At ease."

"But sir…"

"I said, Sergeant, STAND DOWN"

I turned away from the door, put my feet up on the chair next to me, crossed my hands behind my head and looked out the window. From behind me, I heard a voice I recognized from the tapes and TV newscasts say, "Hello John."

I turned and could not help myself. Involuntarily, I stood up and said, "Mr. President."

Chapter 35
The Inevitable?

Maryland, USA
March 20, 1971

The president turned to the Colonel. "We need to be alone. Exactly as we discussed."

"Are you sure, sir?"

"Exactly as we discussed!"

The colonel stepped forward. "May I inform the detainee of the constraints of the conversation?"

I interrupted, "I am not your fucking detainee!" The president rubbed his brow and sighed audibly. "Colonel, I need you to leave. I will explain later."

The officer and the guards turned to leave. I saw one of them roll his eyes. Asshole. The door shut. We were alone.

The president looked at me. He was somber and sad.

"John, there are things I cannot control. You've probably figured out that they are watching us on closed circuit TV. There is no sound. I was able to maintain that. However, if they see any gesture from you that looks threatening, they will come in and shoot to kill. My life has fallen apart at the moment of my greatest triumph—the presidency. I'm not sure I would try to resist if you did assault me. I would deserve it. This is just the way the game is being played out."

I sat back and relaxed a little bit.

"John, the wheels have come off. You may not believe me, but I do not support the continuation of this insane war. I am losing my conservative base because privately I am arguing for a more conciliatory stance in the Paris peace talks. We would not even have been in this position if it were not for those soft-headed Kennedys and good old LBJ who stuck us in the big muddy over in Asia. I am trying to extract us with dignity, but there is a political reality. No one is more aware of the loss of lives in Vietnam than I. However, as I said, I am a realist. We have enemies who will do great harm if they perceive too great a weakness in our national fabric. In order to withdraw and start over fresh, we need to do it from a position of strength. We were obtaining that position of strength until the war protests escalated. I was desperate. If that sounds like an excuse, my closest advisors on staff convinced me, that as long as there was not a loss of human life, we had to manufacture something dramatic and horrifying and blame it on the anti-war movement. It would allow us to finish our secret operations in Cambodia and Laos compelling the North to come to the peace table for a final reconciliation and agreement. I was promised that there would be no one in Sterling Hall. I should have known better. These are people who believe torture is all right, they lie about the weapons our enemies have in order to divert more and more resources to their control of the military. They are willing to do almost anything to scare the public into divesting itself of its constitutional right to oversight but I never thought they would stoop to murder. Maybe they didn't mean to take a life, but keeping people safe certainly wasn't one of their top priorities and it should have been. Then it started to snowball and you and your friends came along and forced a reckoning. We can get out of this war. I will set the peace process in motion. But not if you and your attorney friend go public. That would set off a firestorm that could threaten the integrity of our country."

"So you're saying I should just forget about it."

"No, I'm making you a deal and a promise. I will be out of office shortly after the next election, which I'm going to win. I need to win to get the peace process going in Paris. Then I will resign to an honorable man who will continue the peace process."

I shook my head. Outside I could see pine boughs moving in a slight breeze.

"You are probably wondering how I could be so stupid as to allow all of this to be taped. The fact of the matter is, I installed that tape recording system to set in motion the mechanism of my own political self-destruction. What I did not know is that my eager beaver staff enabled it prior to when I wanted to be recorded. Part of the successful re-election strategy which will succeed involves a break-in at the Democratic National Headquarters, once it is up and running, to access private information. As that particular dirty trick ramps up, I'll make sure it is recorded. Then I'll see to it that the tapes fall into the hands of the media, and blame it on my poor secretary Rosemary's incompetence. Unless you derail things. The resulting firestorm will compel my resignation—small contrition for what else I have done—but I need to win re-election to stay in office long enough to get the peace machinery rolling.

But all that is changed now. The taping worked perfectly—too soon. You now have proof that I was complicit in a murder. Here's what I ask. Hold off. No one is going to touch you. Watch what happens. If I don't follow through, if the war doesn't end in the next presidential term, go ahead and release everything. I'll understand. You've lost your friends. You want revenge. Is that revenge worth destroying any chance of peace in Vietnam?"

I pressed the issue by softly asking him, "Do you understand, Mr. President, that my material goes public no matter what you promise, if anything happens to me?"

"I'm aware you have a vengeful, experienced, connected attorney on your side that has distributed multiple copies of all the information and buried them behind layers of anonymous connections. That said, there are men on the other side of the wall, prepared, and yes, eager to come in and shoot you. It may not end there. They might act outside of my directions and go out in a paroxysm of rage, attempting to pull back all the information through murder and terror starting with your friend's father. Nobody wins in that scenario. You'll be killed. Your friend's father will be killed. I'll be disgraced further, but most of all there will be no peace as the country fractures over whether the violence is the act of true patriots or reactionary fascists. It's possible you and I are debating whether to allow a civil war."

I considered. I was bargaining with the President of the United States. Caleb used to talk about how no one would ever see the best thing you ever did. I cleared my throat.

"OK. Here's the deal. You are to be out of office before the end of the next term. The war is over within that term—ended either by you or your successor. If all that comes to pass, the tapes will stay buried until Mr. Roper and I die of natural deaths. Neither of us are stupid enough to think that your "staff" are not capable of arranging for us to die of natural causes. Induced heart attacks, car accidents, stuff like that. They better ask themselves if they feel lucky. Mr. Roper told me that our deaths will trigger public autopsies and investigations that will put the Warren Commission to shame. Call your boys off. In ten or twenty years, no one will care."

"I hope so, John. You will need to keep your safeguards in place for a long time. The key operatives in the Sterling bombing are very young and very determined. The mutually assured destruction system must stay armed. Keep your safety net until forty years or so have passed—maybe an election year? I've given my life to the political service of this country. I came from nothing. I suffered disgrace in the fifties. I fought back. Finally I realized my dream to become the President of the United States. But I never thought it would come to this end. Now that I've got many more yesterdays than tomorrows, I see things that I did not see before that will help this country. If you allow me to continue for a year or two, not only will I extract us from that mess in Vietnam, but I'll set in motion the mechanism for disarmament and rapprochement with the Soviet Union. I've also had secret conversations which will allow us to coexist with what will be the most powerful country in the world in the next century—China."

The president stood up and shambled in that signature hunchback posture over to a window. He stared out, rubbed his hand through his widow's peak and returned. I reached across the table, shook his hand, and said, "Deal."

The president made a motion that was picked up by a closed circuit camera somewhere. The guards immediately re-entered. Within ten minutes, I was back on the helicopter, and not long after that, boarding a plane back to Madison.

I went back to Winchester. Strings were pulled from above. They gave me my teaching job back. The things that the president foretold did come to pass, exactly as he said. Shocking tapes showed the president to be a participant in talks to raid the Watergate Hotel. He resigned in disgrace, but not before withdrawal was underway in Vietnam, détente and an anti-ballistic missile treaty was initiated with the Soviet Union and a groundbreaking visit to the People's Republic of China had occurred.

I did not live happily ever after. I was teaching and coaching, but it was never the same. In my prime years, I drifted through a series of meaningless relationships. I was incapable of connecting. I felt unlikeable and unworthy. Caleb and Gerry would have laughed but the only solace I found was in the pursuit of the extreme. I became an accomplished skier, took up mountaineering and ultramarathoning. Five years ago, I had a heart attack that ended all of that. I kept fit, took long walks in the woods, but without that ability to get out on the edge, I felt more worthless than ever. I was starting to understand what Caleb meant when he used to say, "If you're not on the edge, you're taking up too much space." I was taking up too much space.

Recent political news, however, has given me a renewed sense of direction. I've been dreaming about Caleb, and Linley and Gerry again. I see that burning log skidder and Caleb's grinning skeleton, charred middle finger raised in an eternal salute to those who would impinge on his freedom. I think about current important political figures and in researching them, I find they were around in the inner circle of the President who made peace with me years ago.

I see a brave young president who promises change and peace and equity under attack, torpedoed by lies and half truths in order to sow a field of rage which will grow in abundance if nothing is done. Where will the next Sterling Hall be? Is it inevitable? Is there a way to stop it?

Chapter 36
The Summit of El Capitan

Yosemite Park, California
The Future

The top of El Capitan in winter is one of the loneliest places on earth.

Almost a mile above the canyon floor, a lone skier gingerly sidestepped his way toward the precipice. When he was close enough to see the Merced River thousands of feet below, he stopped. Five, ten, fifteen minutes, he stood motionless in the chapel of alpine peace. He took a deep breath, carefully turned and herringboned back up the sloping summit to the climbers' tree 100 yards back from the lip of the greatest climbing wall in North America.

He had been to this tree a long time ago, when climbing El Cap was still a big deal. At that time, only a handful of climbers, the best in the world, had found their way up that vertical desert. He had followed the hikers' trail ten miles up the rugged backside slopes and forests to wait at the top and see if his friend, Caleb, would join the ranks of the few who had conquered El Capitan's fearsome Salathe Wall.

Caleb had been on the wall for almost seven days when John reached the top. He remembered standing at the top alone, waiting and thinking about how he had advised his friend to bring more than four days of water. That was a long time ago.

217

He looked at the old pine tree, draped with dozens of ruined climbing shoes. It was a tradition that at the top, triumphant climbers would take off their shoes, ruined by the razor sharp crystal granite of El Cap and tie them in the tree. Caleb had done that when there were only a few shoes in the tree. He wondered if they were still up there.

He retrieved his pack and took a thick leather notebook out. His mittens hampered him. He carefully removed them, opened the notebook to the back pages and took out a pen. Standing in the pink alpenglow of early winter afternoon, he painstakingly added a few sentences.

> It's happening all over again. They fixed an election to get in power in 2000 then went right back to Searchlight's playbook. They took advantage of a terrorist attack on US soil. Thousands died, the towers fell, but they got their way. With 9/11 as gasoline on the flames, they went to war against a country that held no mass weapons of destruction but plenty of oil. It worked. Just as the Sterling Hall bombing galvanized anger against the peace movement, 9/11 and disinformation energized a suicidal economic policy developed to drive a vengeful senseless war. It cost them the 2008 election but they managed to sow a field of rage across the country against the peace movement which is coming due again—unless someone does something to stop them.

> I can.

> Here in this pack is proof of how we murdered our own in 1970 to advance a war. This tape and document leads the way to names and places that answer once and for all what happened that stormy August night in Madison forty years ago. How does this help now? Read the names again. The best and the brightest are not dead—they are in their sixties and political prime, buried inside the charred soul of the Pentagon, the White House and the Congress. It's time for a reckoning. The release of this information will implicate some of the most powerful, respected leaders of the new millennium as those complicit in the bombing of an American university. They're doing it again. Someone will find this. It will be a climber, in which case it will be a person who will take any risk to seek freedom from the stultifying rules of the powers that be. Gerry's dad passed away a few years ago and I'm going where no one will ever hurt me again. Take this tape, and play it. Take these coordinates that mark Leo Burt's resting place and send it to every major paper in America.

I'm old, and lonely and willing to go, as long as it is on my terms. Do me justice.

God Bless America,

John

He looked up, tears streaking his cheek and closed the book. He reached in the pack again and produced a small waterproof filing box and a heavy duty garbage bag. He wrapped the manuscript and what looked like a small doughnut carefully in the garbage bag, put it in the waterproof box, sealed it, and locked it with a small padlock. As he looked up the canyon at magnificent Half Dome, he took a climber's sling off his shoulder, and tossed it over the lowest branch on the ancient pine. He reached into his pocket and pulled out a forty-year-old carabiner that had held Caleb forty years ago and secured the filing box to the sling. He stepped back and watched his work slowly rock back and forth in the fading sunlight.

He turned and oriented himself in the tracks he had made coming and going to the lip. And then he poled. Slowly at first, but inexorably, gravity did its work and accelerated him toward the edge. Thousands of miles of mountain skiing experience overrode any hesitation he might have felt. He stood straight and relaxed as he rocketed toward the abyss. When he reached the edge, he bent his knees and exploded outward into the crimson sunset and arctic air, 4,000 feet above the Merced Valley.

ABOUT THE AUTHORS

John Lyon was a farm kid, then former teacher and principal, river boat captain on the Wisconsin River at the Dells and an employee in the fraud department of a regional cellular company. He is a part-time instructor at Madison College's two northern campuses. He enjoys trains and riding them and is a member of the Mid Continent Railway Museum located at North Freedom, Wisconsin. Other activities include fishing in Ontario, Canada and on Pelican Lake, Wisconsin with friends.

John Lyon passed away shortly after he wrote this brief summary of his life, but that was like John. He was not one to talk about himself and he is greatly missed.

Dan Woll is a former public school teacher, principal and superintendent. His educational philosophy is informed by two years in an inner city public school on the East Coast as a member of the American Teacher Corps and years in his beloved small town Wisconsin. He has extensive technical rock climbing experience including ascents of Devil's Tower, Half Dome, and El Capitan. His climbing days appear to be behind him but he continues to be a competitive cyclist. He lives in River Falls, Wisconsin with his wife, Beth. They have three grown daughters.

CPSIA information can be obtained at www.ICGtesting.com
Printed in the USA
LVOW06s0515301115

464636LV00001BA/76/P